CURSED BY DEATH

MELISSA MARR

To Charles Marr (1945-2015)
I hope the whisky is all single malt, and this book appears by your desk in the land of the dead.
Save a glass for when I get to the other side.

AND

To Sera Lewis,
This is your fault.

PARTIAL BOOK LIST

Signed Copies:

To order signed copies of my books (with ebook included in many cases), go to MelissaMarrBooks.com

Recent Adult Fantasy :

The Wicked & The Dead (2020)

Cold Iron Heart (2020)

Upcoming Adult Thriller (An Audible Original):

Pretty Broken Things (2020)

Upcoming Adult Urban Fantasy:

The Kiss & The Killer (March 2021)

Backlist of Interest:

Adult Fantasy for HarperCollins/Wm Morrow

Graveminder (2011)

The Arrivals (2012)

PAST Collections:

Tales of Folk & Fey (2019)

Dark Court Faery Tales (2019)

This Fond Madness (2017)

Young Adult Novels with HarperTeen

Wicked Lovely (2007)

Ink Exchange (2008)

Fragile Eternity (2009)

Radiant Shadows (2010)

Darkest Mercy (2011)

Wicked Lovely: Desert Tales (2012)

Carnival of Secrets (2012)

Made For You (2013)

Seven Black Diamonds (2015)

One Blood Ruby (2016)

Faery Tales & Nightmares (short story collection)

I
BYRON MONTGOMERY

Opening the tunnel to the land of the dead hadn't become any more appealing with time. If Byron Montgomery had his way, they'd seal the damn thing. He wasn't fool enough to think he'd be getting his way any time soon, though. The contract he'd signed was binding until death, and knowing for certain what death actually *held* cured him of any urge to run full out toward it.

Or maybe the cure was that, because of the curse, his longtime on-and-off-again girlfriend, lover, one-that-almost-got-away was now tied to him, as he was to her, in a way that was more committed than matrimony.

Curses were forever; no divorce could dissolve them.

So, Byron had been back and forth between the lands of the living and the dead far too often. He hoped that they'd soon reach a calm pace, a normal life in Claysville, but they weren't there yet. Honestly, he wasn't sure that normal was still an option for him.

At the least, he hoped for fewer trips to the land of the dead; the thought of being there all the time made him want to be sure he took every possible vitamin, exercised in excess, anything to keep healthy and avoid dying. Of course, he also wanted to do those things so he was strong enough to protect Rebekkah from the dead things that woke in the living world. Protecting Bek had always been a part of his life. It was an irresistible impulse.

"You stay at my side," he told Rebekkah. "No matter what you see or hear, you stay beside me."

Rebekkah nodded, but she was already too far gone to hear him. Her eyes slid to silver, and her focus was on the dead who waited beyond the door. He suspected she'd stay among them if she could.

"Bek?" he urged.

She made an agreeing sound, but when the dead called to her, he was forgotten. He was a tether, but sometimes he wasn't sure he was enough.

Byron slid his hand along the side of the faded cabinet that held the unused bottles of embalming supplies. It hid the doorway. Byron had the dubious honor of being the only one in the world who could travel through it at will. Rebekkah could go, but only at his side. Anyone but the Graveminder and Undertaker who crossed would stay there.

With a *snick*, the cabinet swung to the side. In front of him was a tunnel. The length of it varied depending on the whims of the bastard who ran the land of the dead. Far too much of Byron's life seemed to hinge on said bastard's whims.

"I'm sorry," Rebekkah said.

She stood beside him now, clutching his arm too tightly. The way she gazed into the tunnel was in direct opposition to his reaction. While he hated the tunnel, the land of the dead, and Death himself, Rebekkah was thoroughly enamored.

Byron entwined his fingers with hers. "I know."

"If I could go by myself—"

"I'd still go with you." He didn't think a time would come when the fear of losing Rebekkah would fade.

In both worlds, she was a target, vulnerable to the dead and somehow unable to stay angry with them despite their monstrosity. He didn't have that problem—either of them really. He had anger aplenty, and he could only be killed in *this* world. Over there, he could get shot repeatedly without dying. Even Death himself couldn't kill Byron, but Rebekkah's death there—or here—would mean Byron died as well.

With his free hand, he patted the gun at his hip, the bullets in his pocket, and the small parcel in his inside jacket pocket. Assured that he had everything, he reached out and took the torch from the wall of the tunnel.

To him, it appeared almost medieval. His tendency toward logic rebelled as the rag-wrapped wood flared to life in his hand. He wanted to believe there was science behind this and so many of the things that had no answer beyond magic. The laws that had made sense to him for all his life were the laws of man, not the laws that governed the life of the Undertaker. There was magic to it, and no amount of questioning made that change.

Together, he and Rebekkah stepped into the tunnel. Winds lashed at him almost instantly, ripping away any warmth and making him grit his teeth. He glanced at the woman holding his hand. Her eyes glowed silver in the dim light of the tunnel, and her face was tilted as if the cutting wind was pleasurable.

Maybe to her it was.

"It's been too long," she whispered, but he wasn't sure if she spoke to him or the lost souls in the tunnel.

She'd had no luck figuring out how to help the lost ones to move over to the land of the dead, but she had told them of her intentions.

As if sharing her with the corporeal dead isn't bad enough, I need to deal with ghosts, too.

He didn't agree with her plan, but understanding the dead wasn't his job.

2

REBEKKAH BARROW

REBEKKAH WATCHED THE FLICKERS OF THE DEAD AS THEY TRIED TO curl closer, drawing her warmth like the chill of being caught between lands could be reduced by stealing her heat. And she wanted to give it to them, share whatever she could. Aside from her cat, Cherub, Rebekkah had never been responsible for another being—yet now, she was the caretaker of the Hungry Dead, those lost ones who weren't properly tethered to the earth.

"Graveminder," *he* whispered, voice like a rising wind ricocheting around the tunnel.

Rebekkah could tell the speaker was a man. That was new. One of the lost dead had grown stronger with each trip. It was him that she considered as she walked, his ability to connect to her so clearly. There was an anger there inside him, a rage, but she suspected it wasn't at her specifically. Who knew how long they'd been caught between worlds like moths crashing into windows on all sides? Rebekkah would be angry, too.

The voices of the trapped dead rose, twisting into whispers and screams until Rebekkah was unable to move.

"Take me.

"Free me."

"*Save* me."

"I'm trying," she swore to each and all of the spirits that lingered there.

"Keep moving," Byron urged, pulling her forward.

"I need you, Graveminder." It was *him* that she heard clearly. The man, the dead soul lost in the tunnel, responded more and more each passing. This time she could see the shape of a man, growing clearer each time she crossed.

Maybe she wasn't strictly required to go to the land of the dead as often as she did, but she had a theory. If they drew strength from her, if that heat they pulled from her was nourishing to them, perhaps she could lead them to safety. One by one, she'd rescue them.

Rebekkah knew she ought to share her plan with Byron, but she also knew he wouldn't approve. The heat she shared with the dead left her weakened. Their hunger stole her energy. As a result, lately, the crossing left her more tired than it ought to.

When she felt the touch, felt a man's hand brush her hair back, she tensed. The more they were near her, the more they strengthened.

She had to tell Byron. She should've already warned him. "Byron?"

"Right here, Bek." He was at her side, hand in hers.

Rebekkah glanced over and saw that he held a gun in the other hand. *Not him.* She swallowed. A dead man was touching her. She'd made progress. It was as if she'd lured a wild creature to her. She didn't want to spook him.

"They're stronger," she whispered.

"Great." Byron's voice said what he didn't, that the idea of stronger spirits reaching out wasn't one he relished.

"I can *hear* him. One voice. Clearer than the rest." She leaned into the spirits, feeling the usual fleeting touches, but then one was different. "I can save him."

The voices grew louder.

Rebekkah concentrated on him, trying to see him. Her vision

shifted—or maybe he did. Either way, she saw a hand. A clear, defined hand as solid as her own body reaching out. The forearm appeared, muscular, scarred. The edge of a blue sleeve came clearer.

She reached out, brushed fingertips. She was pulling away from Byron in the process. She needed to grab him, the lost soul.

"So close," a man whispered. "Save me, Graveminder."

"I'm here," she promised.

Byron glanced over. "What the fuck?"

Abruptly, Byron tugged her away, pulling her hand away from the spirit and spinning her to his opposite side. His gun was raised. His body was in front of her like a shield.

Within moments, he was all but shoving her through the gate on the other side of the tunnel and into the land of the dead--where she tumbled into Charles' arms.

Mr. D, Death himself, held her readily, as if he'd been poised there waiting. He wore the guise of a 1930s era gangster, dapper and dangerous. "Hello, my dear."

Rebekkah was held against his chest with the sort of affection that bordered on inappropriate.

"Charlie," Byron said, as he stepped out of the tunnel. "Release her."

Rebekkah said nothing. Every time she arrived, even after a couple months of coming here, she had to pause to take it in.

She knew that Byron saw a world that was only in shades of gray. To him, the world was washed out, lacking vibrance, but she saw this world as the dead would—vibrant and rich, richer than the living world. Death called to her in every form. The land. The spirits in the tunnel.

The *man*. It was a result of what she was, the Graveminder.

And Byron resented the dead for the way they lured her in. Most of all, he resented the man who currently looked like Rebekkah was his every dream come true.

"I wasn't expecting you again so soon," Mr. D said, holding her lightly so she could move away but not withdrawing despite Byron's terse words. "I trust that you are well, Rebekkah?"

"I am." Rebekkah stepped out of reach, barely glancing at the ruler of this odd world. Then she looked at Byron. "*He* might not be."

Charles grinned. "Trouble?"

"Stay out of it," Rebekkah snapped.

Death held his hands up and took a step back from her.

"You. What was *that*?" she asked Byron. "He was so close and—"

"And who was he, Bek? What do you know about him? They're angry." Byron's voice grew louder by the moment. "They're dead. They're hungry. They've starved for God knows how long."

"So?"

"*So*?" Byron stepped closer. "Holding hands with things that want to eat your face seems more dangerous than wise, so I stopped you. That's my *job*, Bek, I keep you alive. Protect you from"—he gestured out at the city that looked like an old mining town here—"*them*."

"They're lost," she said quietly. "The spirits in there are just the dead who slipped away in the passage. I have to help them. I had his hand. Maybe I could've brought him here. Maybe he has answers on how to help them all. Maybe--"

"And maybe he'd have killed you," Byron said.

They stood there, staring at each other. Tears slid down her cheeks. After a moment, she said, "Go see Alicia or something. I need to talk to Charles about this."

Then Rebekkah Barrow looked at Death and said, "Would you answer a few questions?"

He shrugged. "Why not?"

"Truthfully, Charles." Rebekkah smiled at him as if the being that had cursed them all was nothing more than the sweet, well-dressed man he pretended to be. He wasn't, not a man and not sweet. Mr. D was capricious and deadly. He was cruel and patient. He was, in a word, Death.

⸙ 3 ⸙

BYRON MONTGOMERY

GUARDS SURROUNDED REBEKKAH, AND DESPITE EVERY OUNCE OF dislike that Byron felt for Charlie, he knew that no person—*being*—in either world would try as hard to keep her safe as Charlie would. As much as they didn't like one another, Byron and Mr. D had this one thing and only this one thing in common: Rebekkah's safety was everything.

Byron tucked his pistol back in its holster and headed deeper into the peculiar town that resided at the entrance to the land of the dead. It wasn't always the same, seeming to flex and shift as if it were a living organism. It was, like the magic that made the dead walk here and allowed Byron and Rebekkah to visit, unsettling to him. Towns ought to stay the way you left them, but the land of the dead was not like that.

He walked, waiting for one of the few constants here. The center of the town was bisected by a space where the emptiness stretched into the distance in both directions.

Byron checked his watch, pausing along with various strangers.

One man was obviously new. He started to cross the invisible track, just as a train tore through the intersection. It was absolutely soundless; no tracks or rail lined the street; and in moments, it was just a speck in the distance.

The man was gone. His body carried off by the train. Byron had no idea where it went or began, but the trains that raced over it moved faster even than the high-speed trains of the living world.

All he knew was that the trains were as like as not to splatter bodies on their paths. Sometimes he thought the conductor sped or slowed in order to increase the odds of hitting bodies.

In the distance, past the part of the town where Byron typically stayed, was a tall city that jutted into the grey sky. Several towering sky-scrapers speared the sky, and a cloud of pollution lingered mid-way up around them. Lights flicked on and off as the inhabitants of that part of the world went about their un-lives.

To the left, currently, was a sea. On the sea, the masts of ships rolled off either to or from shores that might not exist. Despite the reasons he was here, the fact that he was bound to Rebekkah's mission, the fleeting urge to board a ship—to take her and set to sea —came over him sometimes. Where would they go if they boarded such vessels? What strange things lived in that water? And was there, like old maps, a place where the sea simply spilled off the edge?

"Undertaker," a woman in a fox stole—complete with fox head still attached—greeted as Byron crossed into Charlie's preferred part of town.

It looked like a Depression era city. Less poverty than the real depression, but the suits, cars, and clubs were the stuff of the early 1900s. That did not, of course, mean these residents were of the 1900s. The land of the death formed neighborhoods for residents, but they were more Disneyland or studio sets than real. It was as if the world here was made up of fantasy versions of time periods, and the dead could choose to reside wherever it was familiar *or* in the region modeled on an era they'd dreamed of in life.

There was a strange charm in it.

As he walked, Byron wondered if the land stretched forever and somewhere out there his parents were waiting. He wondered if Bek's stepsister, Ella, had found a place here.

"If you're out there," he whispered, "I hope you found peace."

He watched for Ella, but he hadn't seen her or his parents here. Ever. The Graveminder couldn't see *her* dead, but he wasn't sure if he was limited, too. Charlie hadn't answered. All Byron knew was that he hadn't seen any of his loved ones, and that Bek couldn't see her ancestors.

A woman with a Tommy gun slipped out of the door of a modern car, something sleek and curved.

When the car slid up beside him with the armed woman, Byron's hand went to his gun.

"*Psh*. Not aiming for you, Undertaker." The short-haired, flapper-dress-wearing woman grinned. "Watch this."

She aimed at a building. As the double doors opened, she called out, "Hey, Henry!"

A man in a sharp suit looked up. "Now, Jules . . ."

When she started laughing, Byron took cover.

"Julie! I said she was just a f--" The man's words ended as Julie mowed him, his friends, and the woman friend all gyrated like marionettes from Julie's rain of bullets.

Once they were all down, Julie nodded. "Just a friend, my ass," she muttered. "I'm not spending eternity as second fiddle."

Byron said nothing as she walked out and collected all the men's guns—as well as the woman's ring and shoes. "Taking my man, and my ring! I ought to shoot you daily."

Once they were disarmed, Julie sashayed back to her car and tossed her loot in the passenger seat. He couldn't blame her. Once they all got up, they wouldn't hesitate to shoot back. Life in the land of the dead was prone to shoot-first kind of mentality.

"You ought to look up Alicia Barrow, miss," Byron told her. "She's always looking for a good gun."

Julie laughed. "Oh, I only shoot Henry, his fool friends and his trollops."

Byron shook his head and left. When he reached the part of the land of the dead that he visited most often, he relaxed a bit, finding a familiar comfort at the shift to the 1800s. The world became a black and white Western town: wooden buildings, plank walkways, dancing girls, and worn cowboys.

He made his way to Alicia's base of operations: General Goods. No one thought it was a store just for bolts of cloth or new boots, though. If they did, they weren't paying attention to the group of gun-toting men who lingered outside the door.

Frankie Lee, one of Alicia's most trusted, nodded. "Undertaker."

"The boss is in a mood," Milt added quietly. It wasn't a judgment on Alicia. None of her men would judge her. To them, the former Graveminder had hung the moon, and at her word, they'd go to a permanent second death at her whim. No task was too far for them, not when it came to Alicia.

And Byron understood. He felt the pull to protect her, too. Something about a Graveminder—living or dead—pulled at him. The same was true of the dead.

"Alicia?" he called, standing to the left of the door.

She was a shoot first, talk eventually kind of woman. "Undertaker."

"Don't shoot me," he added, opening the door.

Her answering laugh eased his worry a little.

The sight of her never failed to make him appreciate her strength. She was a fierce-looking woman in snug jeans and a half-buttoned man's shirt. Today, she wore a vest over it. As usual, a gun holster hung around her lean hips, and a knife long enough to be a sword was strapped to her thigh. Being dead meant she didn't look like she had over two hundred years of experience, but most of it came after her untimely death.

She smiled at him and said, "Come on in, Undertaker. I have things to tell you."

And he knew well enough that something was wrong. Her voice was far kinder than normal. Friendly even. That didn't bode well.

4
AMITY BLUE

CLAYSVILLE WAS TYPICALLY RELAXED, AND TODAY, GALLAGHER'S bar was quiet and dim, just the way Amity Blue wanted. It wasn't open yet, and technically, she didn't need to be there. There was nowhere else she'd rather be, though. Quiet and calm, dark and alone, it was the mood she sought.

"Home sweet home," Amity muttered, closing the door behind her and throwing the lock. "Boss?"

Silence was her only answer—and with these damned headaches, she was extra happy for the quiet. Daniel Greeley, her boss and owner of Gallagher's, was a good guy, more or less old enough to be her dad. He was hard to beat throwing darts, and his sense of humor floated between "dad jokes" and dry wit.

Grateful for the solitude, Amity walked behind the bar. The place seemed eerie when it was closed. Chairs up, and stools stacked. More than once after a long shift, she'd mistaken the thin frame of chairs or stools for people.

She tossed her coat and bag onto a steel cooler behind the bar.

Then she poured herself a glass of plain soda with a bunch of fruit. Sweet, cold, and refreshing, it was her bartender's special. More than a few patrons had thought they had vodka soda but ended up with her non-alcoholic drink because hydration matters when drinking excessively.

And Claysville residents drank. There were more bars than churches and synagogues, and that was saying something here. This was a town that ran on prayer and liquor.

The bar was her home, more than her actual home—especially the last few weeks since her sister, Bonnie Jean, had died. Her lover, Byron, had left her. Her best friend, Bek, was now dating the man who had been in Amity's bed.

Despite her mood, she shook her head. "I'm living a damn country song."

Admittedly, Amity hadn't been *in love* with Byron Montgomery, but it still stung to be left. And he'd been in her bed long enough that she'd missed talking to him. Of course, he was the sort of man she wouldn't have looked twice at if she was outside Claysville, but leaving wasn't an option.

No one born here left, not for good. A few left for a while, but everyone born here died here.

And although Amity hadn't been super-close with Bonnie Jean, *her* death was hard. Her sister was the responsible one, the civic-minded, devoted to the town kind of person. Her skirts were pressed, and her smiles were tight. They were likely only friends because they shared blood, but they were *sisters*.

Everything had changed.

But Amity still spent her evenings gathering stray bottles, emptying ashtrays, and swishing crumbs onto the floor. She didn't change, but everything felt different now. She felt like she knew things that didn't match what used to make sense. It wasn't in a what-am-I-doing-with-my-life way. Amity *liked* being a bartender, and until now, she'd really liked the fact that in her entire life, she'd never once met anyone who was an alcoholic.

Amity went through the motions of setting up the bar. She filled the garnish trays with olives, cocktail onions, cherries, lemon and lime wedges, and a few twists. Cutting and organizing was the sort of rote activity that she could handle fine.

Why didn't people get sick?

Or leave?

She felt like red-hot coals poured into the space behind her eyes. Her stomach started threatening to throw up last week's meals, and Amity Blue dropped to her knees.

Whimpering, she crawled over to the humming beer cooler and pressed her face to the cold steel.

"Please please please," she prayed.

The stabbing sensation in her head didn't let up.

"Fuck," she whispered, vaguely aware that she was sliding down the cooler to the floor.

Then her eyes stopped focusing and she lost consciousness.

WHEN SHE OPENED HER EYES, DANIEL WAS THERE. HER BOSS WAS crouched down at her side. "Amity!"

She blinked up at him. "Hey."

"What are you doing?"

"Napping?" A forced smile was the best she could do.

Her boss scooped her up, lifting her and carrying her to a table. He lowered her to a chair and asked, "Do you need me to call someone? The doctor or Byron or . . ."

"Hmmm. Ex or maybe my dead sister or dead friend? Hard call, right?" Amity stared at her boss. Her attitude ought to get her a lecture, but Daniel sighed.

"I'm not your enemy." He looked at her head, feeling carefully for a bump. "What happened?"

"Another headache." She shrugged and then pointed. "Purse."

Her boss grabbed her oversized satchel and carried it like it might explode or bite. Amity rolled her eyes, only to discover that it hurt too much to do *that* again. She dug around in the bag, pulling out a small handgun, just a .22, and a tube of lipstick. A few tampons, a bag of tissues, and a bright green rabbit's foot joined the rest on the table.

"A-ha!" She held up a bottle of pills, honestly she probably had enough in her system, but the headaches weren't getting any better. She shook out another pill, dry swallowed it, and asked, "Drink?"

Her boss poured a glass of house white. "Here."

Amity raised her brows at that, but she'd try that, too.

"No better then?"

"Not really," she hedged. The headaches were starting to become so nonstop that she was beginning to think she ought to be alarmed. What if it was an aneurism or something? *No one* in Claysville had any diseases. There was no liver failure, no cancer, no heart disease, or even rare diseases. People in Claysville never got sick with anything that could kill them. In Claysville, people either died of old age, accidents, or from the random mountain lion attacks that plagued the town from time to time.

Amity had never thought about how fucking weird that was until right around when the mountain lion attacks stopped. Shouldn't someone notice that there were no sick people in Claysville? It wasn't like folks were health conscious. People ate fatty foods, smoked, and drank a lot. There ought to be consequences. There were elsewhere.

"You should've told me," Daniel accused.

Amity said nothing. She wasn't missing work, and he was her boss not her bestie. Why should she tell him? She'd been at work one night about three weeks prior and collapsed with the worst migraine of her life. The doctor claimed that she was fine, and really everyone in Claysville got bad migraines, so it wasn't a big deal. That was the only health issue they all had, fierce headaches.

His advice was dismissive at best: "A day off, a good long bubble bath, maybe a night out with friends, and you'll be right as rain."

The problem was that since that night she'd developed all of these crazy memories-that-weren't. Things she knew that made absolutely perfect sense had been replaced with mental "home movie clips" of things that were impossible.

A man levitating just off the ground, passing through town with Maylene Barrow.

Troy attacking Amity, trying to bite *her. Rebekkah Barrow arriving afterwards.*

A teen girl in ratty jeans and a black hoodie vanishing like smoke.

Rebekkah and Byron leading Troy into the funeral home.

Bonnie Jean's dead body as Mayor Whittaker talked about "killing the monster that did this."

Amity wiped her hand over the table, drumming her fingers absently.

The constant detail at the center of so many of her memories—if that's what they really were—was that the Barrow family and the undertaker, Byron, were involved in the odd things in her mind.

"Amity? Did you hear me?"

She looked up at the sound of the voice. "What?"

Daniel stood beside her. She'd been half-out-of-it a lot since her monster migraine.

"I said, 'Do you need me to walk you home?'" Daniel repeated.

"I'm good," she lied. "I could still work—"

"No." He looked at her for a moment, studying her with the same intensity her physician had, and Amity thought—not for the first time—that it was a shame he was old enough to be her father. Daniel was one of the kindest men she'd met in her twenty-four years. He didn't judge her for the skeleton's hand barrettes in her hair, her slogan covered tee-shirts, or the wide range of music she played in the hours when the bar was quiet.

If he wasn't so old, he'd be irresistible.

Bonnie Jean had a thing for older men.

Used *to have a thing for them*, she corrected herself.

Thinking of her sister in the past tense seemed wrong, but Bonnie Jean was dead. She was killed by a mountain lion. Even as Amity thought it, she knew something was off about that explanation.

"I'm good, boss. Right as rain." She met his gaze. "But if you're not going to let me work—"

"I'm not," he injected.

"Then I'm going home," she continued. "Maybe I just need more sleep."

Amity knew that wasn't it, and she was fairly sure he did, too. She had a theory forming, though, and telling her boss that she thought there was a conspiracy seemed like a bad idea. Of course, she was also suspecting that he was in on it, along with her former friend, her ex, and who knows how many other people.

But how could they all be in on it? And why did it make her head ache?

5

MICHAEL

On the outskirts of Claysville, Michael opened his eyes in confusion. He wasn't entirely sure how much time had passed since he'd last woken up. He was in the exact same spot, alone, and unable to remember much of anything. Maybe it was from the drugs or maybe the booze or maybe he'd hit his head when he blacked out; whatever it was, he felt like there were a lot more things he knew *before*.

The garage wasn't always a ruined building. He had a vague sense of that detail, of the thought that before the fire it was a business. The charred remains had been condemned. That was why he had started coming here with his friends . . . or why they came here.

Were they here first?

He rubbed his temples as if he could find the answers by applying pressure.

"Hello?" A flashlight beam accompanied the voice.

Michael tried to remember which girl the voice belonged to as he watched the light come closer, the beam illuminating charred shelves and thick dust. She was his friend, probably, but he wasn't as sure they were friends as he had been when he woke up the first time. He realized he must be still drunk or high—or both.

The girl, Courtney, rounded the corner and saw him. Her mouth dropped open for a moment, and then she shut it with a snap. Her eyes widened. Obviously, she wasn't looking for him after all. She was staring at him with a strange sort of intensity.

"Hi." He tried a friendly smile.

"Michael? I thought . . . I mean . . . " She shined the beam over him. "*Holy fuck.* We thought you were dead."

"Because I blacked out?"

She shook her head. "No. . . because you didn't have a pulse."

He laughed. "You were high."

"True." Courtney wrapped her arms around his neck and crushed herself again him in a big hug. He didn't object. He wasn't entirely sure, but he had a hazy notion that this was just her way. He wouldn't call it a memory, just a feeling.

"I'm right here," he told her, holding her tightly. She smelled good. She smelled like sex and warmth wrapped in smoke.

One of her hands twined into his hair. "Do you have anything?"

"Any . . . You weren't looking for *me*, were you?"

"Don't be like that. You know I like you." She pressed against him. The hand that she didn't have in his hair slid over his ass.

This he remembered: the times she'd done this very same thing. At first, he'd thought it was affection. Then he'd realized that she was stealing whatever he had on him, money or drugs. She considered it something else, pre-payments. Courtney always paid in trade for the things she stole.

And I was loser enough to accept it.

"I'd have come looking for you if I knew you were still here. You know that!" Courtney's hand slid around to his front pockets since he had nothing to steal in his back ones. "Everyone knows I like you best."

Lies.

"Do you have anything?" she whined. "It's been weeks since you took care of me."

"Weeks?" Michael echoed. "It was last night."

"I haven't seen you in over a month. No one has. Then Jilly vanished. Dave was mad at first, and then he was worried when we didn't hear from her. Oh, is she here too?" She stepped back. Now that she had determined that his pockets were empty, he wasn't as interesting to her.

He had a suspicion that he wasn't interesting to anyone, not really.

"Jilly . . ." Michael remembered her, and at the mention of her, he had the vague sense that he had seen her, too. His brain felt fuzzy, though.

Courtney was looking around now. She'd picked up a jacket, possibly his jacket, and was rifling through the pockets. "Dave was supposed to meet me last week, but he didn't show so I thought maybe he came here."

"Oh." Michael had the niggling sense that Dave *had* come here, that he had seen Jilly, that Courtney was telling the truth about how long it had been. He turned and walked away from her, a growing suspicion creeping over him as vague memories started to come together.

The more he remembered, the faster he went.

They came. They stayed.

Courtney followed, her flashlight wavering wildly as she tried to keep up. "Michael! Wait for me, damn it!" She bumped into the back of him. Her arms slid around him then, and she laughed. "Nice, jackass! You could've told me they were back here."

The beam of light fell on Dave and Jilly. They were all tangled together.

Courtney giggled, but then she stepped forward and her giggles stopped. "Jilly? Dave?"

"They stayed," he told her, calm filling him at the admission. They stayed. They *cared* for him.

Courtney couldn't stop staring at them, but she didn't take another step toward them. Her voice grew thinner and softer. "Guys?"

Michael grabbed her wrist.

"What are they doing?"

"Nothing."

"Why aren't they *moving* or answering me?" Courtney whispered and then, as his grip tightened, she immediately yelled, "Dave!"

"I gave you everything you ever wanted." Michael turned her so that her back was to the half-eaten bodies. "Didn't I?"

"You're scaring me."

"I forget so much. I try. They helped. I even know your name. That's new. Every time I eat, I remember more." Michael rubbed his face against her hair. "Will you help me? I always helped you."

She looked over her shoulder. "Ohmygod, they're dead. They're *dead.*" She tugged away from him. "I won't tell. Just let me—"

"You can help me, too." And then Michael sank his teeth into her skin.

Courtney helped, but he knew he had to find someone else, not her. There was *someone* calling to him, but Michael had no idea how to find her.

Maybe it would make sense after he ate more.

6

AMITY BLUE

AMITY WAS AT THE LIBRARY, A QUAINT OLD BUILDING THAT ALWAYS smelled vaguely of peppermint gum. The carpet was a worn green layer, too bright to be mistaken for grass and too dark to be thought of as clean. The air was chilly, and the library—as usual—was hopping. Honestly, it was as busy as a bar, but a lot brighter.

Amity had spent a few hours looking at the old newspapers on microfiche at the library. Somehow, Claysville was historically a hot spot for death-by-puma, yet the national statistics on such deaths didn't ever include their town.

"Amity?"

She lifted her gaze from the article and realized that her boss was there watching her. Her boss was in the library.

"Are you *sure* you're okay?"

"Sure." She stared at him. "Why are you in the library?"

"Leigh called," he said. "Told me you were here, and I just wanted to see how you were."

The librarian called her boss—but Daniel looked at her like it was perfectly normal. It wasn't. Why was she the only one who could see that?

"Between Bonnie Jean and Troy and the migraines"—Amity caught hold of Daniel's gaze—"I'm probably a little tired, but I'm fine."

Daniel's brow wrinkled. "You're allowed to grieve, you know. Do you need some time off?"

"No." Amity Blue was not the sort of person to weep or wail, and if she did, it would be in the privacy of her achingly empty apartment where no one else saw. Daniel should know better than to think she would crumple.

He's trying to help, she reminded herself in a mental voice that sounded like her sister's. Amity suspected it was a coping mechanism of sorts, imagining the lectures she'd never hear again. . . or it was further proof that she'd lost her mind.

Amity turned her back to Daniel, ostensibly to gather up her books. "We need to get the bar ready. Unless no one was in last night, I'll need another bottle of Jack from the storage room."

As she shoved her stuff into the canvas grocery sack she'd brought, she realized that Daniel was looking at the essay she'd printed. "Mountain lions, huh?"

"Mmm." She wasn't going to explain herself, and not just because none of this shit made any sense.

Some people might not think Amity was very smart because she chose bartending as a career, but she liked it. Being a bartender made Amity feel connected, like she was a part of something larger than herself. Plus, a town this size only had so many doctors or dentists. No one got sick; no one ever left. And most shops were family run. You ended up doing what your parents did. That was how it worked here.

Daniel walked closer, so they were side-by-side. Then he said, "You know you can tell me anything, don't you. Maybe when you're ready, we could talk about you joining the town coun—"

"No." She backed away from him. "I'm not my sister, and I'm not going to become Miss Civic Duty just because she got killed by . . ."

"By?"

"A mountain lion," Amity answered quietly. She nodded at the pages. "It happens, right?"

Daniel nodded once. "Byron put it down, though. Claysville's safe again."

Hiding her scoff of disbelief, Amity nodded. That was the right reaction. Smile and nod. The simple truth was that mountain lion kills weren't common anywhere in the state, except Claysville. In fact, they weren't *common* anywhere in the country. Amity had looked up statistics: there was less than one death annually for the whole of the United States as far back as 1991, and the majority of those seemed to be in California.

"I'll walk you to the bar. Do you need anything else?" Daniel gestured at the library in general.

"No."

He was halfway across the room before Amity gave in to the impulse and said, "I didn't know Byron even hunted. Not that we spent a lot of our time talking, but it seems like that would've been something he'd have mentioned. A mountain lion is pretty serious game for someone who doesn't hunt at all. Why was *he* the one to go after it?"

Daniel glanced back as he said, "Think about the council, Amity. I could tell Mayor Liz that you want your sister's seat."

Either she was getting more paranoid or the council was in on it. That was why he was trying to send her there. Was it worth it to talk to them? Better than talking to her friend and ex-lover?

Tomorrow, she decided. *Tomorrow I'm going to confront Bek and Byron.*

If that didn't work, she'd see the mayor—because no one seemed to even be trying to hide the fact that they had a secret.

❧ 7 ❧

ALICIA BARROW

Byron hadn't even closed the door to the General Goods store in the land of the dead before Alicia was behind the counter pacing.

"The old bastard's in trouble." Alicia knew she sounded angrier than she ought to in front of anyone other than her boys, but she felt a fondness for the Undertaker that made her guard slip more and more often. He was good people, the sort she wouldn't hesitate to recruit if he were dead.

"What is it?" Byron asked.

She forced herself to straighten up. It didn't do anyone—*especially me*—a bit of good to be maudlin. She put one hand, palm-flat, on the edge of the glass counter. With the other, she retrieved the notebook from where it was hidden under the register. "Charlie's in trouble."

Byron met her gaze. "I thought that was a good thing."

"Maybe. Maybe not." She slapped her notebook on the counter. "If he's replaced ..." Unwelcome fear washed over her. The old bastard had been a source of anger and stress since when Alicia was still a live woman.

Back then, she'd been his Graveminder, living her life in service to the dead and the man who ran the land of the dead; she'd kept the dead in their graves as best she could, and she'd hunted down the ones that didn't stay dead. All of that she could handle well enough. It was what she was born to do, what her mother had done before her. She didn't love her lot in life, but she was at peace with it, until her baby died. Nothing mattered then, not her husband Conner, not the consequences of failing at her vocation. All that she wanted was her baby back—so she let him wake.

And Charlie killed her and Conner both for it.

"I hate Charlie," she whispered, as much to remind herself as to assure Byron. She'd spent every day since her death here working to thwart Charlie. Her husband, *her* Undertaker, wasn't here, but Alicia hadn't followed him to another place, wherever that was. She'd stayed, dedicating herself to protecting the dead here, determined to stand in opposition to the monster she'd once trusted.

The hate Alicia felt for Charlie outweighed everything. She held Byron's gaze, daring him to question her, but Rebekkah's Undertaker was a smart man: he kept his obvious doubts to himself.

"I hate him," she repeated louder, "but he's kept order here. He's fair often enough, and if he's under attack, I don't know . . . I don't even know *what* could attack him."

"Right. Devil you know." Byron tapped the cover of her notebook. "Tell me."

Mutely, Alicia opened the cover and spun the notebook around so it was readable to him.

Byron read her scribbled notes, the lists of anomalies, the changed route of the train, the buildings that had collapsed, the missing fields on the far edge of the 1950s.

"Fields?" Byron lifted his gaze from the page. "I'll never get used to this place, will I?"

"I haven't." She offered a tentative smile. It wasn't but a couple centuries ago that she'd first stepped into this strange world and tried to make sense of the impossible. Unlike Byron and Rebekkah, she'd had the advantage of growing up aware of the role she was to fulfill. It was still overwhelming.

"You're doing well," she assured him. "And I'm not even sure this is our business to meddle in, but I'm not sure how it'll affect things on the other side ... or if it will or ... anything."

She reminded herself that the land of the living wasn't her responsibility. Whatever—if anything—changed there wasn't her problem.

"Things are starting to settle down," Byron said.

Alicia stepped out from behind the counter and walked to the windows at the front of the store. In the street outside, she saw two of her boys standing guard. Milt and Frankie Lee had moved so they were on opposite ends of the block. They made no pretense of stealth. Milt could blend into the background if he chose.

Frankie Lee, on the other hand, was bold as brass. Young when he died, handsome then and now. Raised a criminal. Frankie Lee was fearless on his worst day, and his loyalty was such that on his best days he was the sort of soldier who'd walk into a fire with every imaginable weapon aimed at him if she said it was necessary. She shook her head. Boys like him were a special challenge. He'd question her if he had doubts—and they had the time for discussion—but if she said it wasn't open for negotiation, he'd wade in where even lunatics feared to tread.

"The devil I know is the devil I can manage," she admitted to Byron. "He's been lord of this place since it existed, but someone or something is causing trouble. People are noticing. Doubt isn't something the dead handle well. We like our routine, our order, and part of that order is that the old bastard is omnipotent."

Byron came up beside her. He didn't touch her with affection, and she knew he wouldn't but she had that awkward moment of wishing he would not because of *him* but because he was alive or maybe simply because he was an Undertaker.

"What do you need me to do?"

"That's the hell of it: I don't know." She watched Frankie Lee, saw the moment he realized she was at the window. He glanced her way.

She shook her head once, and he went back to his studious observation of the area around her block of shops. The people who lived and worked in her block counted on her to guide them and keep them safe.

Well, safe as one could be in the land of the dead working for the woman who headed the only true criminal enterprise in the land of the dead.

"Alicia." Byron put a hand on her shoulder, half-turning her toward him. "We're family," he said. "Granted, most people don't talk to their dead relatives but—"

"If we were family, you *couldn't* talk to me." Alicia smiled wryly.

"I see you because I'm the Undertaker, Alicia," Byron said with a sigh. "I know the rules. We're *family*, but I get the exemption to see you, because you're a Graveminder."

She shrugged.

"Hell, in my book, what we both are is more reason to call us family. This curse binds all of us in a way that not even blood does. You have my gun, Alicia, same as Bek does," he continued, keeping his voice casual like it wasn't any big thing what he was saying to her, like offering *that* kind of loyalty to her was commonplace.

"Rebekkah's lucky. Maylene was, too."

Byron met Alicia's eyes and said, "We'll sort this out—as a family"

"Maybe." She stepped away and folded her arms. "I don't know what to do, but I thought you and Rebekkah ought to know that something's wrong. Tell her. Maybe Charlie will talk to her. Maybe it's nothing. Maybe it won't affect your world, so it's not your problem."

Byron was obstinate in the way of generations of Undertakers before him. He pulled her to him in a quick embrace. "If it's *your* problem, I'll still want to help."

Alicia jerked away, almost stumbling in the process. "Are you trying to get shot again?"

Byron grinned. "I'll talk to Bek, and we'll see what we can figure out."

"Thanks," she said.

Frankie Lee came slamming in the door.

"Boss?"

"It's fine, Frankie Lee." She motioned to the door. "The Undertaker was just leaving."

Byron's expression was once more guarded as he looked at Frankie Lee, and she realized with a start that he relaxed around her, but not as much them. His lot was strange, being between the living and the dead, and while she wasn't able to cross over as she had when she was a live Graveminder, she understood what he and Rebekkah were experiencing better than anyone else they knew.

"Undertaker?"

He looked at her, but he angled to keep Frankie Lee in sight, too.

"If she has questions, and trusts you enough to have you ask them of me, I'd answer a few things for her."

Shock briefly fluttered over Frankie Lee's expression, but Byron didn't blink. He stared at her for a long moment, before admitting, "I can't figure you out. Is this a bargain or . . ."

She turned her back to him. "No strings."

The silence behind her was thick enough that she almost wondered if they'd left, but she knew Frankie Lee better than that—plus the door didn't open or close quietly enough to allow anyone to surprise her that way. There was a reason she didn't oil the hinges.

Alicia didn't turn back to face them as she added, "Doesn't change *our* business, Undertaker, but I like the two of you so . . . what the hell."

The door opened and closed then, but she still stayed facing away from the windows.

Absently, she spun her wedding band, and then lowered her head as Frankie Lee's too astute gaze caught her.

"He's dead."

"So am I," she snapped.

Frankie Lee said quietly. "He's gone, 'licia."

"It's my fault."

"Maybe, but you've spent a century here paying penance. He's long since forgiven you, or—"

She started to interrupt, but Frankie Lee spoke over her, "*Or* he wasn't worthy of you. Charles's forgiven you too. The only one holding on to old guilt is you."

Alicia was stunned silent. Charlie was the only one who ever dared bring up the past. Of course, aside from him, Frankie Lee was the only one who knew. One late night with too many drinks, and she'd told him everything.

Big mistake, that was.

"When you're ready to forgive yourself, you'll need to decide whether to stay here or move on. If you want to stay, I'm happy to be. . ."

His words faded, and she asked, "Be what?"

He grinned then, and she realized he'd baited her—and it had worked. "Guess we'll figure that out if you decide you want to know."

Her mouth opened, but no words came out. She closed it and shook her head. Byron hugging her. Frankie Lee flirting with her. The fucking world wasn't making sense.

8
CHARLES

Charles walked through his kingdom with Rebekkah. It was a moment of true peace when he had one of his Graveminders at his side. A part of him would always love them. Every last one held a sliver of his heart in her hand. He mourned their eventual deaths, and he cherished the gift of their presence.

His current Graveminder was lost in thoughts she wasn't sharing, and he tried to keep his focus on her. His mind slid away to the weird flux in the land of the dead. Someone was figuring out how to bend things, and Charles wasn't quite sure how they'd begun to do so.

Or how to stop them.

"Charles?" Rebekkah squeezed his forearm. Her hand was there when they walked. He might have started his existence as something less corporeal, but he was a man-shaped being now. He had manners.

A gentleman's manners.

Abigail had taught him that, made him more human with her love.

"Charles!" Abig—no, *Rebekkah* said.

"Yes, dear?"

She motioned to the steps of his home and said, "Marie."

One of his trusted servants, Marie, was dead on the marble step outside Charles' home. Admittedly, being dead wasn't unusual here: Everyone but the Graveminder and her Undertaker was dead. Yet, even here, there was dead, and then there was *dead*. Marie was in that final state, a removal from this world and from Charles' command.

And I didn't do it.

Charles wasn't entirely sure where those who were fallen to a second death went, and he didn't have resources to consult on such esoteric matters. It was possible that they went to another land of the dead, a place ruled by another despot; it was equally possible that they simply ceased being.

The only thing Charles had known for certain was that a second death—a permanent removal from his domain—was something only he could cause. His role as ruler over the unruly dead allowed him to do what no one else here could do—except he had not, would not, have killed Marie.

"Charles?" A light touch on his arm drew his attention to the woman by his side. "What happened?"

He shook his head. He didn't want to lie to her, but he didn't know what had happened—and saying that seemed problematic in another way. How could he promise to keep her safe if he didn't know what had happened?

"I'm not sure. Yet." Charles motioned to his guards, who surrounded them like a wall. The Graveminders were each beloved to him, since Abigail, the first of his Graveminders, had created a breach in the veil between the living and the dead.

Charles took Rebekkah's hand in his and silently led her past Marie's empty shell.

The door to his home opened as they approached it. The guards' faces made it clear that they were unaware of Marie's true state. If they'd known, they'd have moved her shell.

"Marie is gone. Have her taken to her chambers for the time." Charles didn't pause to watch them do so.

A thread of fear, unlike most anything he'd felt in his millennia of existence, rippled through him.

First dilemma first.

Silently, Charles led his living, very vulnerable Graveminder up the massive staircase to the second floor of the house.

"Charles?" Her voice was less calm this time.

"Not yet, my dear." He walked to the end of the hallway and opened the door to his conservatory. Plants, a few that ought not co-exist, tables, and fountains filled the space. It was a room he didn't open to any but his most trusted. Despite the plants, there were no windows. It was secure. In the land of the dead, the things that appeared alive grew on their own, by his whim and will.

"What's going on?" Rebekkah asked as soon as the door closed behind them.

"Marie is dead. *Truly* dead." Charles walked directly to the decanter and glasses on his sideboard and poured them each a generous measure of whiskey.

"Right, but everyone here is dead."

"No. Dead to *here*. She won't wake as they typically do." Charles held out her glass.

"I don't understand. I thought only you could do that?"

Charles threw back his whiskey. "Until this is solved, you must stay on that side. You cannot come here again until I say otherwise."

"But—"

"No." He cut her off.

"And if someone wakes?"

"The Undertaker will escort you home." Charles said, ignoring that question entirely.

At the sound of the door knob turning, Charles raised a gun and shoved her behind him.

Ward appeared as the door opened. "I'm here, sir."

Charles lowered his gun. "Marie is gone."

"Yes."

Charles gestured to Rebekkah. "You will protect Miss Barrow. No one enters. No one other than Miss Barrow or the Undertaker. If anyone else--"

"I shall shoot them, sir."

"Repeatedly," Charles added.

"Of course, sir," Ward said mildly. "I would enjoy spending time speaking to the current Miss Barrow." He paused, met Charles' eyes, and added, "Shall I presume you are going to see the *unpleasant* Miss Barrow?"

"Keep Rebekkah safe," Charles said, rather than admit what Ward already knew. "I trust no one else to do this."

And then he left Rebekkah alone in the opulent room with Ward.

9
ALICIA BARROW

ALICIA WAS CALMING HERSELF BY MAKING BULLETS WHEN THE door opened to reveal the old bastard himself. In all the years she'd been here in the shop, she could count the number of times that he'd crossed her threshold.

She was so startled by his presence here that she reverted to her living attitude toward him. Her voice sounded friendly, almost affectionate as she said, "Charlie?"

And instead of calling her out on it, the old bastard went one worse on her. He looked at her with all the softness that had led to her second worst mistake in her living years.

"And that's why I'm here, why I forgive the madness you cause me, Miss Barrow," he said far-too-kindly. "I remember the way you were. Before Conner. Before things changed."

Alicia's next words weren't ones she'd ever say in public: "That was fling, and it was over two hundred years ago, Charlie. You can't think I still feel anything for you."

"You do, or you would've moved on," he said baldly. Apparently, they were both feeling uncharacteristically honest. "When I told you that Conner was in the next world—"

"When you *told* me that?" she interrupted. There was an evasiveness, a way that he handled difficult truths, but she'd believed better of him. On this, at least, she'd thought she could trust him. "Where is my husband, Charlie?"

The dapper embodiment of death sighed. "Could we quarrel later, my dear?"

At that moment, Alicia realized that he was afraid, and Alicia wasn't interested in facing whatever had sparked his worry enough to bring him to her door like an average man. Death was not to feel fear. He was not to tremble. He was not to look behind him warily.

"What's going on?" she asked, setting aside her questions about her dead husband for the moment. They would be answered. She was sure of it, but perhaps not right this moment.

"Someone has *killed* Marie." Charlie spoke with such inflections that she knew he did not mean the sort of deaths they all indulged in. Most death here was temporary, inconvenient. It used to unsettle her, but a couple of centuries changed things.

"Only you can—"

"And yet she is dead," he said with an unfamiliar edge.

Alicia had a complicated mix of emotions. On one hand, this was rightly alarming. On the other, it confirmed her belief that something had changed. And in a trickle of feelings that she ought not have, she felt excited. After two centuries with no threat at all, that rush that she'd once known as the Graveminder came surging to the surface—and under that, in a forbidden part of her mind, was the excitement that he'd come to her.

Does he think I was somehow responsible?

She refused to look at him as she started to gather weapons. They'd need to get the Graveminder and Undertaker out of here. They were always far too vulnerable, but this? This was untenable.

Without lifting her gaze from the bullets, guns, knives, and a few —*milder*—homemade grenades, Alicia asked, "Why are you *here*?"

Charlie made a noise of frustration, being stepping closer to the counter. At a thought, he removed her counter. It appeared in another spot in the shop, so nothing separated the two of them but their clothes. No barrier. Nothing to keep their distance. He'd not done that since she met her husband. Once, longer ago than she would admit to remembering, she'd enjoyed his power of the world around them. She'd marveled at it then.

Now, Death reached out and cupped her face in his hands. "Because, in all of eternity, I've lain with one living woman. I loved Abigail, but she went to her marriage bed a virgin. Only you, Alicia. No other living woman. No other virgin."

Every crude or insulting words she'd thrown at him like bombs these last two hundred years seemed out of reach as Charlie stared at her. Mentally, Alicia added *this* to her list of the things Death was not to do, but it was futile. Nothing she could think of, tell herself, or say would change the fact that he had not lied when he'd told her he'd cared. Whatever else he was, Charlie was a man in that moment, and by the way he looked at her, she was afraid he might not have been lying all those years ago when he said he'd loved her.

Alicia stared at him. Her mouth opened in an attempt to say something awful, anything to make him stop looking at her that way. Her day of surprises was officially at the point of having one too many shocks.

And whether by accident or not, Charlie chose to read the parting of her lips as an invitation to kiss her. His lips were as teasing as she remembered. If anything, his kiss was sweeter after the years of quarrels and machinations. He pulled her closer, somehow his hand had found its way to the low of her back and slid lower still. Palm cupping the curve of her ass, Charlie held her with the familiarity of the lover that he'd once been.

She remembered this, that feeling that everything in her was *home*, that no other place or person would leave her feeling this complete. And for a moment, she relaxed into his kiss. She closed her eyes and let herself be the woman she'd been then, innocent and so-very-tempted by being Death's lover.

"Alicia?" Byron's voice broke the moment.

Undertaker.

Like my husband.

Alicia stepped out of Charlie's arms and turned her gaze to Byron. "We need to go, Undertaker. Time for you to go home."

Charlie and Byron both watched her for a too-long moment, but then, Charlie looked again like the vaguely amused man he so often resembled. He said, "Rebekkah is safe. Guarded. You must take her to your world. I was here to find you and Miss Ba—"

"You clearly found her," Byron said venomously.

And Charlie rattled her mind again as he smoothly lied: "I forced a kiss on her." He glanced at Alicia, bowed briefly, and said, "My worry caused a leave of my senses. Will you forgive me, Miss Barrow?"

"For that kiss? Yes," she said. Old habits were too hard to break. Being careful with her words with Charlie was a habit she couldn't ignore.

She glanced at Byron and said, "Gather the boys. Someone else is bending the world."

"Is Rebekkah—"

"Safe," Charlie said firmly. "I made sure of it before I came to find you and Miss Barrow."

When Byron stepped outside, Alicia took a steadying breath and told Charlie: "I'm sorry I doubted you back then."

He bowed his head and said, "I forgive you for *that*, my dear."

And despite herself, Alicia grinned at him. "Let's go hunting."

"After we see them home," he modified.

They left to collect the living Graveminder, Alicia's descendent, and see her back to the land of living.

As they walked, Byron glared at Charlie and pronounced, "I doubt any of us like you."

At that, Charlie sighed. "I gift you with the most amazing woman living today, and you still hate me. Every Undertaker."

"We hate you because of how you look at them," Byron pointed out.

Several bullets went zinging by, and Alicia's boys all took up their arms. A flurry of shots on both sides resulted in one of their group taking a shot to the gut and several others on the dusty ground. No warning. No reason. Sometimes that just happened.

Just as suddenly as it had happened, the skirmish ended.

They turned the corner, Charlie's place in sight, when Charlie stood beside him again. He sounded wrong as he muttered, "What you hate, Undertaker, is the way *they* look at *me*."

"Alicia!" Byron yelled.

She turned to see them. Death had at least three bleeding wounds. Bullets always caused him pain, but they didn't do through his form. They didn't spurt blood or make Death waver on his feet.

Charlie looked down and said, "Well, that's new, isn't it?"

Seeing him crumple sent shards of terror ricocheting throughout Alicia's body. He was impervious. She'd shot him herself more than a few times over the years. Hell, the first few years after her death, she'd shot him every time he tried to speak to her.

To say she hadn't dealt with the death of her child well was the politest way to explain the hardest experience in her life or death. Alicia grieved like she loved, and she filled her duties with that same intensity.

"Help him up," she barked. "Frankie—"

"Eyes on every street, boss. We got it." Frankie Lee knew what she needed in a crisis. In this, he was remarkable. "No guns."

"Undertaker, you stay close." Alicia suddenly felt every thrill of terror, of danger, that had once been the thing that powered her through exhaustion. She did her duty to anchor the dead when she was living, but at that time, folks too often ended up in shallow graves. And when she didn't know, she couldn't tend them to keep them dead. Back then, being a Graveminder was as much hunting as it was caring.

Alicia watched as two of her boys scooped Charlie up and carried him up the stairs to his palatial home. They didn't question her, not even now. From the look on Frankie Lee's face, there would be questions from him later, though. For now, they went inside, and she directed to them to the safest room in the house.

His guards waited there with guns raised.

"Open the fucking door." Alicia glared at them. If she had to, she'd gun them all down. Whatever that need was that she'd been born with, that pressing insistence to care for the dead, it was raring up like a monster caught just under her flesh. She would protect Death himself.

"As Miss B'row says," Charlie murmured weakly. "Can't let *him* near her."

"Who?" Alicia asked. "Let *who* near me? Who shot you?"

Charlie closed his eyes.

The guards opened the door, and they all trooped inside—only to find Ward there. Presumably, Rebekkah was there, too. Alicia couldn't see her former Graveminders, though. Byron went over, and for a moment, he blinked out of sight.

Embracing her.

"Let's go, Undertaker. Grab her. You both need to go home," Alicia ordered.

Ward was already settling Charlie on the floor, tore his shirt, and in that always-prepared way of his, had a pair of forceps in hand to retrieve the bullets that had lodged in Charlie's previously impervious flesh.

Then in a moment that shocked her as much as—based on his expression--it shocked Ward, she said, "You keep him safe, Ward. I'll get them out, but . . . no one comes in here."

Strange respect in his eyes, Ward said, "Indeed, Miss Barrow."

Alicia couldn't see or hear Rebekkah Barrow, but by the way Byron reached out into what appeared empty air and was now holding his arms as if there was a body in them, Alicia assumed the living Graveminder was upset.

"We need to go," Byron said.

"Need Graveminders safe." Charlie looked like he was in shock, perhaps from the pain or injury. Such a thing was unprecedented. He'd walked through a rain of bullets before, protected her with his body. It had hurt; he'd told her that afterwards. He hadn't been *injured*, though.

And he certainly hadn't looked like he might die.

Can Death die?

"Alicia is going to take us to the gate," Byron said. He paused and then met Alicia's eyes. With a strange tightness of voice, he added, "Charlie was 'panicking over your safety' Bek says. He came to get you after Marie died."

Ward removed another slug from Charlie's stomach.

Charlie turned his head to stared at the empty air, closed his eyes, and after a moment, he began coughing. "Stay over there. Stay in Claysville."

Byron glared. "And if the dead wake what are we to do?"

"Cecilia trapped them before. It is not"—he winced as Ward dug deeper into his wound in search of a bullet fragment—"ideal, but neither is risking her death."

10
REBEKKAH BARROW

Rebekkah stepped back into the Montgomery Family Funeral Home—they'd changed the name after Byron took over—and released Byron's hand. Too many questions and too much worry pressed on her. Charles was the embodiment of death. That meant he was a force, as well as a being. There were other embodiments of death, though. Was Charles at risk? He'd bled. Death shouldn't bleed.

"He'll be okay," Byron said. "Alicia and Ward and all of Alicia's people—"

"He's *Death.* Who can injure Death?" Rebekkah asked.

Byron shook his head. "He said it could change something over here. Maybe his vulnerability filters to here? I don't know."

"Patrols?" she asked.

"After you do your rounds." Byron frowned. "I'll go see the council. Talk to Liz."

As much as Rebekkah wanted to be a better person, she was grateful that he was dealing with the council. She didn't hold any real grudge against her cousin, Liz Barrow, but they'd never been close. And well, she *did* hold grudges against the council. They'd been less than stellar at filling the vacant seats left by the deaths of Bonnie Jean Blue and abrupt resignation of Mayor Whittaker. Liz was appointed mayor, and she stepped up a few weeks ago.

The sheriff was not willing to join, and they weren't willing to force him. That left a new mayor, a pub owner, and three religious leaders to handle matters. It wasn't enough.

"Rounds at the graves, a patrol, and then . . . maybe talk to the new McInney . . . or Ev?" Rebekkah said. "The sheriff's wife or cousin ought to be on the council if he refuses."

"Bek, Chris and Ev have a house full of kids," Byron started, sounding more than a little overprotective. "And Colton just moved home and—"

"Because you and I had so much warning?" Rebekkah closed her eyes, counting to get beyond her panic. He was dealing with it by feeling protective, and she was dealing with it by wanting more people aware of the risks. As calmly as she could, Rebekkah said, "If things are off, we need all the council seats filled."

Byron wrapped his arms around her. "We'll get through it if it happens, but"—he kissed her gently—"I'll explain what I can to them. I can't force them to join."

And Rebekkah sighed. He was the voice of reason that she needed sometimes. More cautious than she'd like other times, but the truth was that she was scared of failing the Hungry Dead, of failing Byron, of losing more lives—and tonight, she was scared for Charles.

LATE THE NEXT MORNING, REBEKKAH STOOD AT GREEN GROVE Cemetery waiting for services to end so she could start her job. The mourners, for their part, noticed her no more than they noticed the gravestones or the trees, but that was a result of being the Graveminder. The majority of the residents of Claysville couldn't remember that the dead sometimes walked.

Not everyone forgets.

Rebekkah didn't. The Undertaker didn't. And the members of the town council were able to remember. They were the ones charged with making the day-to-day decisions of Claysville. One of those council members, Reverend McLendon, stood at the graveside now. Hopefully, Byron was talking to the others.

Her voice lifted as she recited, "Those who have done good will rise to live, and those who have done evil will rise to be condemned."

The answering silence was only broken by muffled sobs and soft sniffles. Like many of the graveside mourners, Rebekkah kept her gaze downcast. Her reason, however, was not grief. She'd seen what happened after a person died. The reverend had too. It wasn't only the good who were prone to rising—at least not in Claysville.

Even though the reverend knew the dead could rise, she, like most every other person in Rebekkah's life, was able to cling to the beautiful truths of an afterlife of peace and contentment for the righteous. Maybe there even was such a place, but it wasn't the one Rebekkah visited.

As the rain poured down on her, Rebekkah thought about the distance between the truth and the words the reverend spoke. Every generation had an Undertaker and a Graveminder. She'd inherited this duty from her grandmother, Maylene, just as Byron had inherited his duty from his father. There was no refusing it, no ignoring it.

And one day the dead will kill me or I'll pass this curse on to a child of my own.

Rebekkah struggled against the sense that she was trapped. She'd tried to run. She'd tried to resist her feelings for Byron. It was pointless. They were, quite literally, partners. He fit her gaps in a way that no other living person could. The only other man who had truly tempted her was . . . not a man. Death himself caught her eye.

The nature of the job.

She suspected Mr. D caught every Graveminder's eye, whether or not they admitted it. Both Death and the land of the dead were alluring—and nothing like any of the holy books made it sound. The place was a strange, twisted blend of eras all co-existing under the rule of the enigmatic Mr. D.

Charles kept her safe, as he had ever other Graveminder before her. How could he not be tempting?

It's not personal.

She was still worrying about him today. There was no way to get messages from there to here or here to there. She had no idea how he was after the unprecedented shooting.

Reverend McLendon had to raise her voice slightly to be heard over a roll of thunder. "As we commit this body to the earth, we commit this spirit into your keeping."

The reverend glanced briefly at Rebekkah.

She nodded and bowed her head. Ignoring her duty would result in Hungry Dead, murderers that would prey on the town. Rebekkah would not fail the deceased—or the living—if at all possible.

Since Rebekkah wasn't family to the deceased, she stood outside the tent that stretched over the assembled mourners. It was her personal tradition, respecting their distance. Today, it was a very cold, wet tradition.

"We pray that you'll be merciful with each of us, until we too shall come to our final resting place. Amen," the Reverend said.

As the final words of the service were uttered, Rebekkah lifted her head—and found that the Reverend's gaze was fastened on her. The no-nonsense woman wouldn't stop and talk; none of the religious leaders liked to speak too much to the Graveminder. They accepted the inevitable necessity of her job, but Rebekkah reminded them too much of the gulf between their faith and reality. Being the breathing reminder of ugly truths simply didn't inspire a lot of camaraderie.

Rebekkah waited until the reverend and the mourners left, and then she went to the fresh grave to begin her work.

She opened the same rose-etched flask that had been carried by generations of Barrow women flask, took a sip, and then tilted it over the grave once. As she poured whiskey and Holy Water on the soil, she said, "He's been well loved."

She took a second sip and then lifted the flask in a toast to the sky. "From my lips to your ears, you old bastard."

Then she tilted it over the grave a second time, vaguely amused today that she was calling Charles unpleasant names even as she worried over him. Such was the tradition though. The words were ritual.

"Sleep well, Joseph. Stay where I put you, you hear?" She took a third sip and then poured the flask's contents onto the earth a third time.

After she'd started the business of anchoring Joseph to death, Rebekkah made her way through the rest of the cemetery, stopping to clear debris from stones, pour a bit of drink onto soil, and say her words. The simple concoction of whiskey and water was always in her pocket, carried in the flask that her grandmother had carried until a few months ago.

Like her grandmother, Rebekkah spoke the same words to the dead that the women in her family had for centuries, reminding them that they were to stay at rest, promising that they would be remembered; she followed the rules just as her grandmother and almost a dozen women before her had. And like those women, Rebekkah felt a kinship with the dead that the living—all save one—could no longer offer.

An hour passed, and the soft rain that had been falling all day continued to soak her, but she barely noticed it now. Once she was about her business, not much distracted her any more. Outside the graveyard, the world seemed so intrusive. Here, Rebekkah knew peace.

"Sleep well," she whispered for the fourteenth time that day. This grave was always the last on her rounds. She visited every recent grave in Claysville for the year after they died, but some were harder than others.

Carefully, Rebekkah brushed her hand across the stone. She wasn't sure if the gestures or the way she talked to them mattered, but it made her feel better—especially now that she kneeled at the grave of Bonnie Jean Blue.

Gently, she added, "You stay where I put you, you hear?"

Bonnie Jean had been killed when several of the dead had risen. That was before Rebekkah knew about the contract, before she knew any of this. Even though those attacks weren't Rebekkah's fault, she *felt* responsible, more so perhaps because she'd it was her own aunt, Cissy, who'd set the dead free.

Rebekkah forced those thoughts away and concentrated on the grave in front of her. It was the last stop of the day, one she saved till the end of her rounds specifically so she could linger longer.

Across from her, Rebekkah's childhood friend waited. Rebekkah carefully did not lift her gaze to watch Amity, and Amity made no move to approach her. Amity Blue was the one person Rebekkah had stayed in touch with after she left, the one friend who's been there through loss and love. And now, she was standing in the rain as if they were strangers.

Hopefully only temporarily.

They'd both had a lot of losses lately, though: Rebekkah's grandmother, Maylene; Amity's sister, Bonnie Jean; their friend, Troy; and more than a half dozen others had all died because of the Hungry Dead.

"Amity seems to be coping better," Rebekkah whispered to Bonnie Jean's grave. "I wish I could tell her what really happened, but she wouldn't remember. I don't know how you handled this part. Keeping these sorts of secrets makes me crazy."

In her mind Rebekkah imagined Bonnie Jean's face, her voice, the words that she'd say. It was a game Rebekkah played to make these conversations seem a little less one-sided. Talking to the dead wasn't always easy.

Rebekkah kneeled in front of Bonnie Jean's gravestone for another few moments, and then she touched the stone as if it were the hand of a friend. "I'm looking out for her as best I can. She's been distant since Byron and I became . . . whatever we are, but I'm not giving up on Amity."

Then, Rebekkah walked out of the cemetery and toward the old farmhouse that she'd inherited along with the responsibility for the town's dead. For all of her dreams of a different life, she'd found a surprising amount of happiness here in Claysville tending the graves, finding her routines, and a getting to know the man who'd made her stomach knot up since they were teenagers.

II
AMITY BLUE

Amity felt better simply at seeing Rebekkah—which she added to her growing list of what-the-fuck. It wasn't an emotional kind of better. She *physically* felt better; her headaches vanished little-by-little around Rebekkah. It made no sense. People didn't heal by their very presence, but Amity had a growing pressure inside that made her want to see Rebekkah, check on Rebekkah. It was new and different.

Amity thought about possible reasons at work that night. Could her headache be cured by her belief that Rebekkah made her feel better? Was it psychosomatic? She thought back over those memories:

A man levitating just off the ground, passing through town with Maylene Barrow.

Troy attacking Amity, trying to bite *her. Rebekkah Barrow arriving afterwards.*

A teen girl in ratty jeans and a black hoodie vanishing like smoke.

Rebekkah and Byron leading Troy into the funeral home.

Bonnie Jean's dead body as Mayor Whittaker talked about "killing the monster that did this."

Maybe they were real memories. Maybe because they were tied to Rebekkah it helped her head hurt less. . .? Amity snorted. That was ludicrous. Nothing made sense. It hadn't since around the time her sister died and Troy vanished.

She was still thinking about it when she watched the last of the customers leave Gallagher's. One was a stranger, a girl who'd come to town while she was on a cross-country bike trip. The thought of that, of seeing all of that expanse of the nation, left Amity feeling angry.

I ought to do it. Just leave.

For the first time in her life it seemed possible. Maybe she could leave ... ? It wasn't like she'd never considered it before, of course, but the urge was usually followed by a weighty feeling as if all the air in her chest was being squeezed out. Thoughts of moving had always made her choke—sometimes literally.

Maybe knowing that there were two versions of reality made something shift.

After she locked the door behind them and started to clean the bar, she was alone with her thoughts.

"We are born and die here, and in between those two moments, we try to make the best of the lot we drew." That was one of those saying that her sister used to repeat. It was the mayor's words, Mayor Nicolas Whittaker. Once upon a time, Bonnie Jean thought she was going to end up Mrs. Mayor Whittaker.

A rattle at the door had Amity dropping bottles—and pulling her dead sister's gun out of the under-the-bar shelf where Amity had been storing it when she was at work. After Troy, and Bonnie, and the rest, Amity wasn't going to go unarmed again.

Even if it is mountain lions.

Of course, mountain lions don't slap their hands against the glass like this person was doing. Large hands. A man. That was all she could say for sure.

"Troy?" she called shakily.

Silence.

"Damn it, if that's you, Troy, I'm going to kill you." Amity felt foolish, but maybe she was being haunted. It made about as much sense as anything else. Gun steady in her hand, she called out, "And if you're not Troy, I'm still liable to shoot you!"

No one answered.

A logical voice reminded her that Troy was probably dead. No one left Claysville, and no one had seen Troy. That meant he was probably dead.

And dead men don't knock on windows.

Minutes passed and the hand thunked against the back door. It was like someone was too drunk to grab the handle, or too high, or just fucking with her. Whatever it was, it didn't make Amity feel like leaving the bar.

There weren't a lot of choices, though. She could sleep here, hope whoever it was wasn't going to break in, or she could leave. Leaving meant hoping she was fast enough with a gun—and that whatever was out there was going to be stopped by a bullet. Neither option sounded great.

Amity grabbed her phone and dialed the sheriff's number.

"McInney," he answered.

"Someone's outside the bar," Amity said. "Gallagher's. Trying to get in."

"Stay on the line," he ordered. "Christopher is out on the other side of town, but I'm five minutes away. Stay inside. I'm on the way."

Amity paused at that. "I thought you said McInney?"

The man on the other end of the line sounded like he was grinning as he answered, "Darlin, do you know how many McInneys there are?"

The lightness of his voice did as much to ease Amity's nerves as the knowledge that she wasn't going to be alone. "A few," she admitted. "I didn't know that there were any others in the sheriff's office, though."

"I just moved home," the man said. "We caused enough trouble as kids that Chris says McInney adults ought to be legally bound to keep order around here."

Amity started to smile, but then the window on the front door cracked as the hand slammed into it again.

Amity let out a sound. Not a scream, but louder than a gasp. It embarrassed her. She wasn't some fainting damsel. She'd tossed grown men out, waded into barfights. Some jerk trying to scare her wasn't going to win.

"What's going on?"

She took a calming breath before saying, "Fucker's going to get shot if he comes through the door." Louder, she called, "You hear me, asshole? I *will* shoot."

"Pulling in," the McInney on the phone said. "Stay inside."

Amity heard him cut off the engine. The car door was silent opening, but she heard it slam shut. Then she heard nothing else. Her hand tightened on the gun.

She braced for the sounds of violence, fists meeting flesh. There was nothing. No yells. It was only silence and the soft noises of a man, an unnamed McInney, breathing.

Then, he half-whispered, "What in the hell?"

A moment passed.

"Are you okay?" she whispered.

"I'm checking the perimeter," McInney said.

Inside the bar, Amity waited, staring at the familiar tables and chairs rather than the spiderweb of cracks in the glass. Someone wanted in—or just wanted to terrify her. Memories of Troy flashed back.

Rebekkah and Byron leading Troy.

Troy biting her.

Troy. Is. Dead. That's what she wrote in her notebook. She used to use it to try to remember things. Maylene Barrow had helped her, taught her tricks to help remember. It wasn't the same as remembering, but it helped.

If Troy really was dead, how did he attack me?

Are there other dead people walking around?

Dead folk didn't walk into funeral homes. Was he alive? Had he come back? But it didn't seem right that he'd be hitting the doors and trying to scare her.

Amity clutched the phone as she thought, listening, hoping that there were answers and—at the same time—that there was no one there.

"Is that you, McInney?" she whispered, staring at the shadow outside the door. Her other hand still held her sister's pistol. She didn't raise it. Accidentally shooting the deputy wasn't on her plans for the night.

"Yeah." His voice sounded tight, not quite as rattled as she felt but still off. "Don't shoot."

"Front door?"

"Yeah. Can you let me in?"

Hesitantly, Amity put down the gun. It was either that or the phone, and in that moment, she wanted to be able to hear Deputy McInney's voice.

"It's me. Alone. At the front door," he reassured her.

Amity walked over, and despite what he'd just said, she felt her adrenaline spike as she unlocked the door. There, standing with the street lights behind him was a man who was undeniably one of the McInney men. Like Christopher, the sheriff, he was the kind of broad-shouldered, towering man that would be handy in a brawl.

"Miz Blue," he said, ducking his head slightly as if he were bowing.

"A McInney to the bone," she said. Amity scrolled through what she knew of the sheriff's family. Christopher had a couple brothers and a lot of sisters, but there were a bunch of McInney cousins. This had to be a cousin. "Are you all so polite?"

Deputy McInney grinned. "My mama would find out if I wasn't." He shook his head. "Well, she would've if she were still with us . . . but there's Evelyn. Cousin Chris married a woman that makes both our mamas seem meek."

"Colton?"

He nodded and stepped further into the room. "Good guess.

Most folks can't decide if I'm me or if I'm Taylor."

Amity reached past him and shoved the door closed. After a brief flicker of hesitation, she threw the lock, too. Whatever or whoever was out there wasn't someone she wanted to see.

"Drink?" Amity gestured back at the bar.

Colton glanced at his watch. "Told Chris I'd cover things for another fifteen minutes."

Amity went around behind the bar where she felt secure. Colton wasn't a threat. He was a good guy, easy to look at and easy to trust. If she were the sort to like law, she'd find him attractive. She did find him attractive. Truthfully, she had a type: strong, a little bit dangerous, and smart assed. Troy was more of a smart ass than Byron, and Byron was more dangerous. He hadn't let that temper out, but she knew it was in there. Colton was tense, as if he'd need to use the gun at his hip.

"Anything out there?"

"I didn't see anyone, but windows don't crack on their own." He glanced at the door. "Anyone giving you trouble lately?"

That was a complicated question. Her ex, Troy, bit her. Amity was also fairly sure he was dead when he did so. That seemed wrong to say. Some part of her whispered that these were not things to discuss. She pulled open a cooler and grabbed a beer. "Guinness?"

Colton gave a curt nod.

She opened it and slid it to him.

Then she grabbed the top-shelf whiskey and a glass for herself. "I'm off the clock," she said with a glance at him.

Colton held up both hands. "No judgment."

"Good." She poured a generous serving. Then Amity hopped up onto the bar, swung her legs over, and jumped down. She pulled out a stool beside Colton.

Colton held his beer, but he didn't drink.

"You're not going to get drunk on that, especially in the next ten minutes," Amity pointed out. Her gaze strayed again to the cracked glass.

"You need to call the boss about that?" He glanced toward the window, attention straying briefly to the pistol on one of the tables.

Amity shook her head, sipped her drink, and tried to let her body relax. The drink would help. Being in Colton's company seemed to be doing the same.

"I'll cover it up tonight," she said. "If I call before we fix it, he'll freak out. Then he'll be here, and we'll be stuck. I don't need to deal with people worrying over nothing."

Colton leveled a stare at her. "Someone causing trouble is worth worrying. Are you here alone often?"

"If I wanted nagging, I'd have called Daniel, not the sheriff's office," Amity added. "He worries. They *all* seem to worry lately."

"I'm sorry about Bonnie." Colton met her gaze. "It was just the two of you, right?"

Amity nodded and took another—longer—swallow of her drink.

"No wonder you were spooked when someone came around here," he added.

Without meaning to, she added, "Plus, Maylene—"

"Miz Barrow?"

She nodded. "We were friends. Then she died. Troy left or died or both. Then Bonnie Jean." Amity's hand shook slightly. "Seems like everyone I cared about was dying or leaving me."

For a moment, Colton said nothing, but after a long pause, he asked, "Leaving?"

Amity shrugged. "Byron. Tossed me out the door so fast my panties weren't on." She finished her drink. "Classic story, you know? Ex-girlfriend comes back. New girl is old news."

After another look at his watch, Colton lifted his drink and drained a third of the bottle. "Darlin, Montgomery was always going to marry Rebekkah. You knew that as well as anyone else that saw them together."

Amity sighed and changed the topic: "Did you see anyone outside? A car leaving? Or . . . anything?"

Colton took another swig of his drink. "Thought I did, but . . ."

Thoughts of all the things that didn't make sense swirled together in Amity's mind, and she was afraid of what he'd say next. She'd seen plenty of weird things, had memories that made no sense, but this was something else. It *had* to be because her weirdness meter was maxed out lately.

"Whoever it was must have already left." Colton met her gaze. "You know how you see things because you expect to . . .?"

"Mmm."

"When I reached out to grab him, there was nothing there. Just smoke or fog or something," he explained. "I imagined seeing someone."

Something in her mind clicked. Memories of Troy. Questions she had for Maylene. Amity glanced at Colton. "Least it wasn't a mountain lion."

He didn't laugh like she expected. Instead he leveled a look at her. Colton McInney suddenly looked a whole lot more interesting as some sort of small-town or sheriff's office or maybe just McInney genes switched on. He seemed like a knight in a pair of well-fit trousers, and she was certain that whatever "steed" he had was likely four-wheel-drive. He was still there to rescue her, and right now, she wasn't objecting.

"How about I drive you home when you're ready?" he said.

Despite her silly thoughts of knights and rescues, Amity just nodded and admitted, "I'd like that."

She stared at the man. Unlike most everyone here, Colton wasn't born and raised in Claysville. He'd visited, but his mama had been one of the rare souls who wandered through town. Colton had traveled, and Amity envied it.

But he was here now, and he was setting down roots harder and faster than a strong weed—and tonight she was mighty grateful for it. Something about him made her feel safe, and she wasn't foolish enough to think it was his badge or gun. Plenty of men with badges weren't to be trusted, but Colton was one of the good guys.

Amity was sure of that.

12
COLTON MCINNEY

THEY FOUND A BUNCH OF CARDBOARD AND DUCT TAPE AND covered the cracked window. The break wasn't enough to crawl through, and unless someone had inhumanly long arms, they weren't going to reach the deadbolt even if they did push through the cracked window. He still felt like he was missing some details—and Amity was tense in that way that any police officer knew meant she was holding back.

Colton watched Amity with the same kind of wariness he'd watched copperheads when he came upon them. Both were beautiful creatures, but deadlier than he was wanting to tangle with if he angered one accidentally. The difference, of course, was that venomous snakes weren't the sort of thing to leave him feeling like he wanted to toss himself in front of predators or beg to touch them.

Typically, neither were women. He liked them well enough, but not in a sort of lingering around hoping for a second date way. Colton liked his freedom. He liked not sharing a dresser. He liked not sharing a house. He liked the sense that he could move on. He mama had been a wanderer. She'd stopped in Claysville long enough to end up pregnant, but she was long gone when she gave birth to Colton and hadn't turned back afterwards. She sent a letter or call to his father, and then every year or so, she sent Colton.

He'd mostly spent summers here, but until she'd passed away, he'd never thought much of coming back. That changed a few weeks back. The urge hit him suddenly. In a matter of weeks, he'd packed up and gone back to the house that he once shared with his father in childhood. The "itch" he'd always had to move vanished, and damned if he knew why.

Now he was having a different sort of urge—one that seemed as sensible as snuggling up to feral things.

Colton stared at Amity, half because he needed to hear himself say such a ridiculous thing and the other half because he genuinely meant it when he admitted, "I'd feel better if I could be sure you were home safe."

Amity stared at him. She looked delicate, ethereal with white-blond hair. There was something angelic about her—not in the fiery wrath of God way, but in the holiday-movie way where angels were sweet and reminiscent of icy days. Amity had that, an icy hue to her skin and hair, as if she were a Christmas tree topper or black-and-white movie femme fatale.

She was fit, too, and looked like she could command control in a situation. Her clothes weren't subtle. She had a skirt that was slit up to her hip, and when she moved the skirt flashed glimpses of toned, bare legs. He knew from visits home that she tended toward slogan-covered shirts, but tonight, she was wearing a plain blue top. Bracelets jingled on her wrists, and her earrings seemed to chime when she moved. The necklace she had on dropped into her cleavage so all he knew was that it vanished where his gaze couldn't follow.

Amity grabbed her bag, a giant satchel that looked like she could carry her groceries and a change of clothes. "You're staring, deputy."

"You're pretty." He felt like a fool as soon as he said it. He regularly charmed women, but not with high school clumsiness like that.

Amity laughed and reached out to touch his arm. "You are, too, deputy."

"I don't think so." He shook his head. He wasn't the sort of man who'd ever been called pretty. "Trouble" maybe. He'd heard "cowboy" a few times and "bouncer." He wasn't a clod, but he was far from the kind of guy who could wear guy-liner like his nephew Elias did. The only black marks that had ever been on Colton's face were bruises.

"Do you doubt my judgment?" she teased.

"Pretty, huh?" he asked Amity. Maybe it was just her bartender habits, or maybe it was the weird night, but he'd take it. "I'll accept it if that's the best you have. . ."

"I bought you a drink, didn't I?"

"That you did." Colton looked her over again. It had been a while since he'd met anyone who caught his eye like Amity was. Lightly, he added, "Next one's on me."

She flashed him a smile as she walked over to the bar with the remains of a roll of duct tape and a pair of scissors.

Looking at the patched window, Colton shook his head. The threat wasn't the broken glass. It was in the fact that someone wanted in badly enough to try to batter down the door. "Did you toss anyone out earlier? Angry drunk come back and—"

"No," Amity said. "Not all this week, in fact." She gave him a wry smile. "Daniel's not the only one treating me like I might break because Bonnie died."

She sounded like she was trying to act like it was no big deal, but her voice cracked slightly on the last few words.

Then, Amity grabbed the revolver she'd left on one of the wooden tables near the door, checked the safety, and flipped her skirt to the side. She shoved the gun into a holster that she had on her leg.

When she noticed him watching, she pulled the skirt further to the side, so he could see that she kept a gun there. "I'm not defenseless."

"I wasn't looking at the gun," he said levelly. "No man with working eyes would be right now."

"Oh?"

"Legs like that . . ." He shook his head. "I may need to come around after work more often."

"I close at two most nights. Out the door by three. No work on Mondays or Tuesdays. Those are my weekend," she said.

Colton felt a twinge of regret as she dropped the edge of her skirt and hid her legs again. "Any chance I could give you a ride home if I got here at closing?"

"One drink and you're inviting me to your home?" she teased. "Slow down, deputy. I like to take my time."

His earlier thoughts that Amity was anything like angelic fled. That tone in her voice was far from innocent, and he was suddenly extra grateful that he was the one who replied to her call.

"Did I make you uncomfortable, deputy?" Amity asked after a moment.

"My name is not 'deputy' when I'm off the clock," he said. "It's Colton."

"Colton," she repeated.

"I'm trying to be a gentleman here," he said as her hand trailed over his arm, as if it was an absent gesture. Logic reminded him that her job was to make a man want to linger, but he didn't think he was fool enough to fall for empty flirtations. "I know your job means flirting, so I'm not going to—"

"So, you're backing out on me?"

"What?"

She turned the bolt and glanced back at him. "I thought you were taking me home, Colton ..."

And he wished he hadn't told her to call him by his name. He already wanted to hear her say it in other circumstances. There was something *good* about hearing his name on her lips.

"I'm not like this," he announced as he walked over and stepped into the grey hours of the day, not quite morning but enough on the far side of night that morning was thinking about arriving.

Amity pulled the door, locked it, and turned to face him.

Colton resisted the urge to hold her to his side. Admittedly, he was raised to treat a woman with respect, but whatever he felt toward her seemed more intense, more instant, and he wasn't that sort of man. He was a fairly steady guy, not much rattled him, and no woman had ever caught his eye.

But he wanted to protect Amity, to find a way to be near her, and that was unusual.

She was pretty, more than pretty. He had a lifetime of fleeting encounters, so it wasn't that the idea of taking Amity Blue home was out of character. It was the idea that he wanted to take her home and keep her there. In his bed. In his life. They had crossed paths over the years, but it wasn't like he could recall even speaking with her one-on-one before tonight.

As they walked toward his truck, he scanned the area, just in case the joker who spooked her was out there waiting. He was fairly sure it was not a significant danger, but he wasn't fully certain. Better to be vigilant. She wouldn't be the first bartender to pick up a stalker. A pretty woman alone was often a target, and a pretty flirtatious one was doubly so.

At the truck, he opened her door and held out a hand.

"You really are chivalrous," she said with a light laugh.

"I want to keep you safe." He matched his tone to hers, but the words weren't light to him. He meant it.

She stared at him for a moment before saying, "I feel safer with you here than I think I ever have in my life." She paused, hand out to keep him from closing the door. "That's weird, right?"

Colton nodded. "It is."

Then he closed the door and went around to his side of the truck.

Once he slid into the vehicle and started it, he scanned the area again. Whatever had threatened her was out there, and he couldn't imagine leaving her unprotected. "Do you get hassled a lot here?"

"Are you implying that this was *my fault,* deputy?"

"No!" Colton turned to face her. "It's never a woman's fault when men stalk or harass them."

She settled, like a bird whose feathers had been ruffled.

He backed out and started to drive. Several moments slipped away in silence before he had to say, "I don't know why, but I don't want to leave you somewhere where I can't reach you if you need me."

Her hand reached across the space between them and landed on his leg. "I get it."

He turned the corner to head out of town, and her hand tightened on his leg.

"I get it," she repeated. She directed him to a little house not even a mile from the bar. "There. The purple one."

"I could sleep on the sofa," he offered once he parked.

Amity shook her head. "Not quite what I was thinking."

"We both feel strong feelings for no reason," he started. He didn't know how to say that he was a one-night-stand man, but he tried. "I don't get emotional about people I—"

"Same. . . well, Byron but that was more *friends* maybe?"

"I don't want to be your friend, Amity Blue." He caught her hand and waited until she was looking at him before he added, "And that ought to scare me a lot more than it does, so . . . I'll take the sofa for tonight because I'm not in the mind to mess up whatever this spark is by acting too fast." He leaned a little closer. "But, no mistake, I'd like to get to know you in a more Biblical way."

She cracked a smile. "There's nothing particularly religious in the thoughts I was having, Colton."

"Then, clearly Montgomery didn't do right by you. Most women I've known in a more naked way start singing halleluiah and speaking in what might very well be tongues." Colton shrugged. "But not all men can deliver. Sad to hear about poor Montgomery's lack of skills."

He walked around the truck to her door and opened it. "I bet you could sing praises that would be downright inspiring."

Amity laughed and accepted his outstretched hand. She got out of the truck. "Another night I will expect you to back up that cockiness, Deputy."

"Yes, ma'am." He dipped his head. "I already look forward to that."

Then she sighed. "But I guess you'll stay in the guest room . . .?"

Colton knew damn well that she was leaving an offer on the table, and a part of him—a rather loud voice that was far from logic—thought he was being a fool. What harm was there in just a little bit of loving?

But as he followed her, Colton realized he was watching her the way that wasn't simple hunger. He'd laughed at friends who were smitten, but that was what he felt. It didn't make a lick of sense, but he felt like God Himself had tossed an arrow Cupid had left lying around. And the resulting mix of lust and affection made everything about Amity Blue seem precarious.

And Colton wasn't one for arguing with the Lord's design, but he also wasn't one for bedding down with a woman who made his heart seem like it was debating a heart attack. He wasn't afraid, necessarily, but he wasn't sure he was looking to set down deep roots in Claysville. A job for a bit working for his cousin was a lot different than settling in with a woman who made him feel complicated things.

13

CHRISTOPHER MCINNEY

Sheriff McInney didn't think of himself as a terribly complicated man. He liked things to be in order, watching football in the fall and baseball in the spring, steaks on the grill, and sex with his wife. Though if pressed, he would admit to liking her company and her cooking as much as the sex. A long time ago, he'd liked the sex more, but he was pushing forty and starting to think he had fallen further in love with his wife than he'd meant to do.

"Chris?"

"In here, Ev." He was cleaning the upholstery of the 1970 Chevelle that his father had once owned. He didn't get to take the car out as much with four kids at home, but he enjoyed keeping it tidy for when the rare chance presented itself.

Evelyn stood at the garage door. Dawn light behind her and coffee mug in hand, she still made him grateful she'd been fool enough to pick him. Lord knew he'd been reckless when they were young. Their eldest came along not long after the wedding.

"Colton called last night," she said. "Trouble out at Gallagher's."

"Bar brawl?"

She shook her head. "Someone was trying to get in. Poor bartender was there all alone, too."

"Dan call it into the office yet?" Christopher wasn't going to bother much with it if Dan hadn't called. Unlike his cousin Colton, Christopher knew that sometimes weird things just happened in town, and the ones that were particular oddities were not the purview of the sheriff's department. Those were handled by the Barrow woman.

"He did not," Ev confirmed. "Just Colton. He's thorough."

Christopher nodded, thinking over his options. When he was on the clock, he could drive over and check with Dan. Greeley was on the council, so if he said it was nothing, it was nothing.

Still. . . Christopher felt like he ought to also tell the Barrow woman and Byron, too. Weird happenings meant that the Barrow woman needed to know, and of course, that Christopher needed to be careful not to ask questions. His daddy taught him that one. Being sheriff was a McInney tradition, and one reason they succeed at it as a family is that they were all raised not to ask too many questions when something peculiar happened.

Christopher made a note to talk to Colton about that detail. He'd made his cousin a deputy, hoping that the stability of it would help Colton realize he needed to settle back in Claysville. No good came to those who left.

And Christopher privately thought that knowing *why* was probably worse than the headaches. Those were just from screwing up and knowing things that were above his pay grade. Avoiding certain topics meant avoiding pain.

He'd almost forgotten Evelyn was still there, but then she spoke up. "That mountain lion was caught, right? The one that killed Miss Maylene?"

"Yes ma'am." Christopher nodded his head. "Montgomery put it down. Just like his father did when we were kids. If it's not Montgomery, it's the Barrow woman. They do a lot of service to our community."

Ev came further into the garage. "If you want to join the council, it's ok—"

"No, ma'am." He stood and took her hands. "You made me swear no secrets. I won't break my word."

"I meant about regular life and you know"—his wife glanced at the house as if one of the kids might be sprinting toward them and overhear, and then she whispered—"sex."

"No secrets there." Christopher kissed her, thinking briefly that he was blessed. "I like it. And you. And having it with you." He paused and grinned at her. "And I tolerate those kids that happen sometimes because of the sex."

Ev laughed. "You tolerate them, huh?"

"Yes, ma'am." He nodded, trying and failing to stifle another grin. If he was an insecure man, he might thing Evelyn married him on account of the lack of restrictions on McInney men. Most families had to apply to have kids on account of no one born there leaving, but *some* of the families had exemptions. McInney's always had a houseful of kids if they wanted.

"Things have been odd lately," Ev said, voice soft enough that he knew she was about to skirt the conversations that they ought not have. "So many people died, and since you're the sheriff and—"

"No." Christopher pulled her closer. "No secrets. . . being on their council isn't what I need or want. Sometimes when I think I might remember things, well, I'm pretty damn sure that I don't *really* want to know."

She relaxed into him. "Cousin Colton?"

Christopher nodded. "Might be for the best if someone knew the things that they all know. There's always a seat for the Sheriff's Department. Mayor, a few merchants, preacher types, undertaker, and the Barrow woman."

"Don't you think it's odd that there's a spot specifically for that one family?" Ev asked, voice muffled against his chest.

Christopher pushed her away and stared into her face. "No, and neither do you."

She winced at the edge of the headache she would have if she kept asking questions. Then she nodded, "Of course. Come on in the house; I'll fix us breakfast."

At that, Christopher mock-flinched. "There are children in there, ma'am."

Evelyn laughed. "I blame you for it. No other family multiplies like a McInney."

"It's because we always win the hands of the prettiest, most irresistible"—he smacked her ass—"brides."

"Mm-hmm." She took his hand in hers though as they walked across their yard toward the house.

He was blessed with a great wife, healthy kids, and a job he liked. Life in Claysville was pretty near perfect.

14
AMITY BLUE

AMITY WOKE, STILL ALONE IN HER BED AND FEELING REFRESHED. Somehow, six hours sleep had left her feeling more energized that she had felt in weeks. In those scant hours, Amity had slept like nothing was wrong in all of the world—and as much as it pained her to admit, she knew it was because Colton was there, too. It made no sense whatsoever, but knowing that there was deputy made her rest deeply.

Much like her headaches were better around Rebekkah, her peace of mind was better with the deputy there in her home.

No, if she was going to be honest, she was going to be *all the way* honest: it was Colton, the man, who made her feel safe. Not "the deputy." *Him*. The man who'd looked at her with lust in his eyes—and then slept in her guest bed. No other person would make her feel so secure. She knew it in her bones. Something was different about him.

It was weird, but at least this wasn't another case of monsters or migraines.

The door to the guest room was open, so she glanced inside. Colton was sprawled out face-down in the small bed, covers twisted so much that she could see that he was sleeping in nothing but his shorts. Lean legs. Torso that was muscular enough to say that he was active, but not bulky like he spent all his free time in a gym. A tattoo of some sort snaked along his back and vanished under the sheet.

"I can move over if you want to come in and take a look closer," a sleep-roughened voice said.

"Maybe later." She lifted her gaze to meet his. "Just checking you out for now."

"Good. I'd hate to be the only one thinking along those lines," Colton said, eyes skimming over the oversized shirt she threw on before wandering out of her room. When he reached her eyes, he asked, "Boyfriend or girlfriend or anything I ought to know, Miz Blue?"

"No." Amity stayed in the doorway as Colton rolled over, twisting the sheet around him in the process. She swallowed. "My bed's been empty since Byron. Before him Troy. I'm a serial monogamist, I guess. And you?"

He looked to the side. "I've been a bit less monogamous."

"I see," she said. Amity wasn't the sort to question what other folks did in the privacy of their bedrooms or motels or whatever, but she wasn't the kind of woman who shared well. "That's too bad."

She turned and started toward the kitchen when Colton called out, "But people change. With the right incentive. And you look a lot like incentive to me."

Amity sighed and looked back at him. "I've heard some bad lines before, Deputy, but that—"

"Colton," he interrupted. He sat up, giving her an unimpeded view of a strong chest and tight abs. "And you know as well as I do that for some reason, I don't mean it as a line."

"Which is reason enough to keep me in the doorway," she admitted, voice low like she was praying or embarrassed. "I'm going to fix coffee, so my mouth stops letting words out before my brain catches up."

"Let me get dressed, Miz Blue, and I'll join you for some of that coffee."

He nodded, and she went to fix the coffee—and try to come up with any logical reason to explain these feelings, or vanishing people, or mountain lions in Claysville. Nothing made any damn sense the last few weeks.

By the time she was finishing her coffee, Colton came to the kitchen, wearing jeans and forgetting his shirt. She paused, cup lifted and took in the sight. A fine specimen of manhood, barefoot, shirtless, and still drowsy-eyed shouldn't have her feeling like her skin was too tight.

From the way Colton looked at her, she was fairly certain that he felt it, too.

"Dressed is a relative concept, I see." Amity motioned to the coffee pot.

He gestured to her bare legs.

"My house," she said with a half-shrug.

"I like the house rules." He fixed his coffee, pouring enough sugar and powdered creamer into it that she had to shudder.

"You're wasting the taste with all that mess you're dumping into it." She pointed at the bag. "Imported. My number one indulgence lately. Doesn't need all of"—she waved at the creamer and sugar and canned whipped cream he'd found in her fridge—"stuff."

"Why do you have it then?"

"Powdered creamer is ... from having guests," she muttered.

Colton held up the whipped cream and shook it. "And this? Planning to fix pie?"

Honestly, she had it for coffee drinks with a dose of liqueur, but instead of admitting that, she licked her lips and eyed his bare chest. "No."

Colton closed his eyes. She could see that he was saying something to himself, quietly mouthing words.

"Colton . . .?"

"Reciting baseball stats," he said, opening one eye. "Or possibly gaming stats."

She giggled. Goodness help her, she *giggled.*

"You're a witch or something, Miz Blue. Succubus? Devil?"

"Just a girl," Amity said softly. "Born, raised, and likely to die here in Claysville. Bartender. Nothing special . . ."

"Lies." He carried his coffee to the table, took a sip, and asked, "Siren?"

"Not as I'm aware. Never even seen the ocean . . ."

Amity hadn't ever been outside the limits of Claysville. She'd been born, lived, and expected to die in the small town where her family had lived for as many generations as the town had existed. That didn't mean she was *content* with her lot in life, but it was what it was. She'd never walked along far away city streets or nearby-but-still-out-of-reach beaches. Her entire life began and ended in the boundaries of the town where she'd been born, where she'd lived, and where she'd expected to die.

Most every one of the thousand residents stayed where they'd been born. Her parents still lived in the house where Amity and her sister Bonnie Jean had grown up. Most people didn't leave Claysville. They stayed, hoped there were no new mountain lion attacks and made do with what they had.

Until Bonnie Jean's death, Amity did the same.

Now, Amity remembered the recent past altogether differently than everyone else. She also remembered when her ex, Troy, had attacked her—with his teeth.

"He wasn't right. I know that. I saw him before ... and I wrote notes to myself. Sometimes notes help me remember things. Usually." Amity reached into her jacket pocket and withdrew a small black notebook. "Here. This is what I know."

Byron took it and flipped it open.

"The end. I saw him earlier, and I wrote it down." Amity stared at Byron as he turned the pages.

When he reached the very last page, he turned the notebook toward Amity and Rebekkah.

Amity saw the words she'd written in heavy block print: "TROY. IS. DEAD. TELL BEK." The words were underlined several times.

"Amity?" Byron said. "Talk to me."

Amity still had her head tucked between her upraised knees. Her voice was muffled. "He bit me. Earlier, I saw him, and I ran. Maylene said to tell you if anything weird ever happened and she's gone." Amity turned her head to the side and looked directly at Rebekkah. "What does it mean? Is he a vampire?"

"No. It just means I need to stop him from hurting anyone," Rebekkah said. "I will, Amity. I promise."

"And me? Will I get . . . sick?" Amity didn't look away. "I feel queasy just trying to force myself to keep it in my head . . . or maybe because I'm missing a chunk of skin."

"Or both." Rebekkah put her hand on the side of Amity's head and smoothed back her hair. "Some things are easier to let yourself forget."

"I don't like forgetting. It's why I keep the journal." Amity laughed, but it sounded more like a sob.

Byron tucked Amity's journal in his pocket. "Here comes Chris."

The sheriff pulled up, a team of EMTs right behind him. Christopher got out of his car and stepped onto the sidewalk.

"What happened?"

Byron didn't hesitate. "A dog or something got her. We heard her scream, and we found her like this."

Amity blinked up at him, her head had started to hurt, but she pushed against it. Not a dog. Why is he lying? *She opened her mouth to speak, but Rebekkah and Byron were already leaving.*

"Joe?" the sheriff yelled. "Another damn dog bite."

Although Amity had never lived anywhere but Claysville, she knew enough to tell a dog from her ex-boyfriend.

"Amity?" Colton asked.

"Sorry. I was thinking." She gave him a smile, and as weird as it was, she wanted to tell him. Everything. She wanted to tell him everything.

Thank God for coffee, she thought as she forced herself to walk over to the counter and pour another, properly black, cup of coffee.

The night before, Amity hadn't made it to bed until almost 3am. Colton being here let her sleep, but she still needed a few more hours. Admittedly it wasn't unusual to be awake that late on a weekend, but weeknights were usually earlier. There were a few heavy drinkers last night and by the time she closed the bar, finished cleanup, and reconciled the register, she was exhausted.

And then *someone tried to break in.*

"I need to head out soon," Colton said, voice low and careful.

"Same."

He seemed surprised, but he didn't ask where or why—and she didn't feel like telling him that she had an appointment to watch her former friend stand at her sister's grave. It was the first thing she hadn't admitted, or at least wanted to.

Rebekkah would be at the cemetery by mid-day. She always was. Amity poured another coffee down her throat while Colton got dressed.

"I wasn't joking," Colton said when he walked into the kitchen, fully dressed now. He lifted his mug of coffee. "Earlier."

"About your lack of monogamy? Not my bus—"

"Not that. I mean, yes, that was true, but I want it to be your business." He rubbed his hand over his face like he could wipe away his agitation. "I want you. And not just for a night. I want to get to know you."

Amity shook her head. "I'm not looking for anyone." She exhaled, watching him tense as she sighed. "I don't know you, and whatever last night was . . . maybe it was an adrenaline high of something. After the . . ."

"Ghost attacked?"

She pressed her lips together. "There was someone there."

He nodded. "There was. And I'm going over there to check it out this morning."

"Okay." Amity shrugged and sipped her coffee. Then she stood up and started to walk away.

Colton grabbed her and pulled her into his lap. She settled there like it was normal, natural.

"This okay?"

She wrapped an arm around his neck. "Yes."

"I went to the same school as you. Three years ahead of you." He lowered his arm, so it was wrapped around her low back. "You used to study in the library at lunch."

"So, you know a couple things about me. It's a small town." Without thinking of how odd it might seem, she sniffed him.

"You swam better than most of the swim team," he added, tilting his head so his throat was exposed.

"You know a *few* things," she amended. "That's not reason enough—"

"To agree to get to know me?" He reached up with his other hand and trailed it softly over her hair. "Really? I can't even get *that* much of a concession."

He turned his head toward her like her might kiss her.

"You're telling me that—before *you*—Troy was always a monogamous guy? Or that Byron was?" Colton's voice dropped deeper. "Because I sowed a few oats, I'm disqualified from getting to know you?"

"I'm not looking for anything, but if I was . . ."

"I'm listening," he said.

"If I *was*—and I'm not—I'm not interesting in being with someone who has his boots under a whole row of beds, you know?"

"I can give you my word that my boots will not be anywhere else . . . that I'll be *celibate* while I get to know you. Would that be enough to convince you to get to know me?"

"Why?" she breathed the question.

He shook his head. "I have no idea, but it makes sense. Just . . . let me get to know you."

"You don't think this is crazy?" Amity pressed. "This draw."

Colton gave her a wry grin. "We live in a crazy town. You know that."

Then Amity gave into the impulse she'd had since she caught him staring while she holstered her pistol the night before. She pressed her lips to his, her whole body to his, and she kissed him.

Colton's arms held her steady as her mouth slanted over his. He let her have control for a moment, and then he met her tentative kiss with one that was far surer.

And for all that Amity had good intention, cautious ones, she felt like he'd dropped a match in dry kindling. Her body reminded her that it had been a minute since anyone kissed her, since anyone set her blood on fire. Her gentle kiss turned into the kind of kiss that sent dishes clattering to the floor.

Somehow she ended up straddling him. Her legs wrapped around his hips, and arms twined around his neck. A wicked voice whispered that there was no reason they couldn't do this. She could reach down, unfasten his jeans, and—

Amity pulled back. "No."

Colton leaned his head back, and she scrambled off his. Her legs were shaky, but she was on her own feet.

"Whatever hormones or grief or whatever this is," she started, "I'm not going to fuck you in my kitchen the day after we met."

"High school," he muttered. "Met you years ago."

"Whatever." Amity paced away from him and folded her arms over her chest. "I'm grieving or something, and I'm not going to use you."

Colton sighed. "You wouldn't be using me."

Amity looked at him and softly said, "I know most people in Claysville can't think about the weird shit that happens here, but lately I can." She stepped closer and took his hand. "You seem like a good man, but this"—she gestured between hem—"this is on the list of weird shit."

Seeming reluctant, Colton nodded. "Fair enough."

For a long moment they stood there in silence until Amity said, "*Fine*, I'd like to get to know you. Maybe it's weird or my grief . . . or . . . I don't even know, but I still would like to talk to you again."

Colton smiled widely. "I'll see you at work tonight. I'd feel better if I knew you had a safe ride home."

"Weird," Amity pointed out. "That's weird."

"Maybe." He shrugged. "I'll still be there to drive you home."

"Fine. I'll see you tonight," she agreed.

Then she shooed him out of her house and got dressed to wait for Rebekkah. She was the one woman—other than the council—who might have answers, and Amity had a growing list of questions.

15

LIZ BARROW

LIZ WASN'T BUILT FOR PATIENCE, AND NOW THAT SHE'D FOUND HER temper, it was very obvious. She'd discovered the hard way that what she thought was patience was simply overlooking bullshit to avoid conflict. She'd tolerated her late mother's mad plans, tried waiting for an opening to undo it, and now, she was done with avoiding conflict. Too little, too late perhaps—her sister was dead—but it was better than continuing to be a doormat.

Unlike her relatives, Liz would serve this town as mayor.

The Barrow family—which was now just Rebekkah and Liz—was born specifically to serve Claysville. Their grandmother, Maylene Barrow, had been the last Graveminder, and Liz's late mother had thought that there was *power* in that role.

Minding dead folks and risking death in myriad ways hadn't much appealed to Liz, but her mother didn't care. And back then, Liz let herself avoid saying what she really thought. No more. That Liz was over. Now, she spoke up.

As she sat in her new office, Liz thought not for the first or twenty-first time that there was a lot to be said for minding the town itself—not that she thought the lot would fall to her. Claysville natives lived very long lives, and Nicolas Whittaker—the last mayor—had squatted in the mayoral role for almost all of Liz's life.

"Mayor Liz?" her assistant, Chelly, asked. She was old enough to be Liz's mother, but a lot less mean. Chelly stood in the now-open door, a vision in a pencil skirt and blouse. Whittaker called her a secretary, but Liz was damned if she'd call a woman who knew her job better than she did a "secretary." They might be in Claysville, but no law said they had to pretend it was the 1950s.

"Chelly?" Liz willed herself not to sound too eager. Settling into the job was like starting a race at the end of a lap. She knew there would be another lap sooner or later, but right now, she felt like a figurehead.

"Mr. Greeley is in the waiting room," Chelly said. "I told him I'd see if you're free, and that we had to go over your schedule adjustments."

Her grin made clear that she was well-aware of Liz's general restlessness and the lack of schedule adjustments. Liz's job was high on smiling, but she was looking forward to, well, anything other than appearances.

"I'm bored, so obviously I'll see him, but if he wants me to appear and smile somewhere, I may need an alibi."

"Fair enough," Chelly said.

Liz looked around the office. "And I kind of hate how much this place screams Whittaker men."

Chelly snorted in laughter. "The bar or the desk or . . ."

"I like the wood and leather, but I'll pass on the liquor." Liz decided in a rush that if she was going to do this, she was going to claim it. "Can we get a tea and coffee bar instead? Maybe some curtains that don't make me feel like I'm stuck in the land of hangovers? And plants? I want . . . I don't know a tree or something."

At that, Chelly smiled widely. "I can do that. Meeting adjourned?"

"Show Mr. Greeley in, please." Liz tried to find a comfortable position in the desk chair. It felt too vast for her body, too used to another person's shape; she made a note to change that too.

Daniel Greeley came in with the ease of someone who was used to any setting. He was a bar owner, perpetually single, and on the council for as long as Liz knew there was a council. She couldn't guess his age, though. Old enough to be her father, but not by much.

"Miss Barrow," he started.

"Mayor Liz, please. My cousin is the current Miss Barrow," Liz corrected.

Daniel smiled approvingly. "Yes, ma'am, Miss Liz. I wanted to let you know that we'll be needing to do an informal census. See who all's missing."

Liz folded her hands together, a part of her worried that she'd be a suspect. Her mother, after all, had been the last person to start raising the dead. Another part of her thought Daniel was a bit too sure of himself.

"Was there a body?" she asked.

"Not yet. Well, probably, this is, but not that we found yet," Daniel said, as calm as if he was talking about fallen tree branches.

"So . . . why?"

"Amity had a visitor," he said. "At work. Colton was there, but. . . there were no live visitors there. Someone woke."

Liz stared at him, wondering if she'd get that calm one day. "How do you—"

"Critter cams," he said. "Last mayor had us install them at a few places. You'd be surprised what all you see."

At that thought, Liz shuddered. She had enough secrets for a lifetime already. "And my cousin?"

"Will know today," Daniel said.

"She should already know," Liz reprimanded.

Daniel nodded once. "Our sheriff likely ought to be replaced once Colton's up to speed too, Mayor. Nicolas was fine with letting him avoid the council, but too many lax choices led to . . ."

"My mother raising the dead, murdering people, and leaving the town with a Graveminder who had to learn mid-disaster?" Liz finished. "Trust me, Mr. Greeley, I am well aware of just why casual adherence to policy is untenable. My sister is dead, and so is grandmother. My predecessor was relaxed, but you will find that I'm very keen on rules."

Daniel stood and nodded his head. "Glad to hear it, Miss Liz."

When he excused himself to leave, Liz sad, "Mr. Greeley?"

He met her eyes.

"I understand that your I'm-an-easygoing-guy thing works on a lot of people," she began, voice far too like her mother's voice, "but I am the mayor of this town. I may be young, but I am also a Barrow. That means I've known the secrets since I learned my letters."

"Ma'am."

"So don't think that you can aw-shucks your way around me," Liz said, still channeling her mother's "stern voice." Liz stood and stepped from behind her desk. "You are a merchant representative on the council, but at the end of the day, you are one voice. I am the mayor and a Barrow woman, so think very carefully the next time you speak to me as if I'm wet behind the ears."

Daniel Greeley smiled, widely and genuinely this time. "Good to know, Mayor Liz."

16

COLTON MCINNEY

COLTON LEFT AMITY'S PLACE WITH A SMILE AND THE MEMORY OF A kiss that had him wanting to glare at any man who so much as glanced at her. A part of his mind whispered that he wasn't a jealous man, but a louder voice said that she was a once-in-a-lifetime woman.

He drove out to Gallagher's, questions at the ready.

When he arrived, he found Dan Greeley there with a table saw and lumber. He was, like most of the town, healthier than anyone would expect in a dead-end town filled with people who existed on a diet of excess booze and fried food.

"Colton!" Dan paused when he saw him walk up. "Your cousin said you were back. Finally back for good?"

Colton shrugged. "Over in Myrtle Beach, and I felt a pressing need to be here. Figure there must be a reason, especially as I was always ready to shake the Claysville dust off my heels."

Dan paused. "Home for good, then?"

"Accepted the damn job," he said. "Thinking about it. Can't bring myself to want to go."

A look of curiosity flittered over the older man's face before he hoisted the wood and walked away to fit it into the window frame. "Well, there's a seat or two on the council opened up . . ."

"Not really one for politics," Colton said, debating how much to push since Dan was hiding something and not even pretending not to be.

"Hold this?"

Colton went over and held the plywood in place. "We patched it last night."

"Heard you were here with Amity. How are her headaches today?" Dan didn't look at him as he positioned the nail gun.

"She seemed fine this morn . . ." Colton's words died as Dan grinned and met his eyes, ad Colton realized what he'd admitted. He added, "I slept in her guest room."

"How was her headache?" Dan asked again.

"Didn't have one." Colton shrugged. "Not last night or today. We were spooked by someone. Trick of light and someone quick enough to get away while we were chasing lights." He laughed. "If I believed in ghosts . . ."

A few minutes passed in silence as they covered the window, and then Dan asked, "Do you?"

"Do I what?"

"Believe in ghosts." Dan looked serious.

Colton paused at it. He didn't want to mock superstitions. Claysville was a small town, and small towns were a breeding ground for foolish notions. Cautiously, he said, "Not usually."

After a few moments, Dan excused himself to clean up the tools. As he was packing up he added, "Tell me if Amity has any headaches. I worry about her. Th mountain lions, her sister dying, and then . . . well, she let Montgomery lie to her."

Colton's primal instincts roared back to life. "How so?"

Dan grinned. "Some people have the sort of destiny that you or I can't explain."

At hearing such words from a flannel shirted bar owner in a middle-of-nowhere town, Colton started in surprise.

"Helluva thing to try to love someone when their heart's already given." Dan shrugged. "Montgomery belongs to the Barrow girls. He did before he was born. Running—on both their parts—wasn't going to change facts. Duty called them home, and Amity got caught into the crossfire."

Colton expected a wink or a grin or some hint that the words were a joke. Instead, Dan added, "Compulsion to come home. Duty. Sometimes that's the lot of people."

And there was enough of a pause that Colton was damn sure they weren't talking about Byron Montgomery now.

"You got something to say to me, Greeley?"

Dan shook his head. "Thanks for handling the situation last night. Think about the council."

Then he walked off humming.

"Sheriff called. I told him you'd been by and didn't need either of you to follow up," Dan said, back still turned.

Colton shook himself out of his surprise and called, "I'm going to check around outside. See if I can find any clues as to who was out here."

"Suit yourself." Dan shrugged, and then he resumed he tossing wood scraps into the bed of his truck. "Nothing to find. No reports to file. Probably just kids being rowdy. Amity is tense, and she misunderstood."

"I'll be around back." Colton walked around to the area behind the bar where he could've sworn he saw someone. The ground looked mostly undisturbed, but here with the aid of daylight, he could see several footprints.

He took a piece of paper to place next to it for measurements and snapped a few pictures. Then he used the measurement app on his phone. It was quick and not as precise as he'd like, but he wasn't a forensics man.

"I wouldn't have hurt her," a voice said.

Colton was on his feet, gun in hand, and turned around quicker than he'd had to be so far here in Claysville. Until now, no one had managed to sneak up on him or catch him off-guard.

The speaker was younger, not a kid but not much off. He had on boots, the sort that would likely match the tread.

"I'm going to need you to answer some questions." Colton trained his gun on the man. "We'll go to the station and—"

"I can't."

Colton nodded. Nice and easy. That was how he'd handle this. He took a few steps forward and the guy shook his head.

"Probably ought to stay back. I bite." The man started laughing, but in a way that was creepy as fuck. "I *bite*. Get it?"

Colton reached out.

And there was nothing there. No man. No back side of a person as he fled. It was, as with last night, as if he was capable of completely disappearing. That, of course, made no sense at all.

He had no answers, just a visual of a man with nondescript hair, eyes, and build. It wasn't much at all.

17
AMITY BLUE

When Rebekkah arrived at Bonnie Jean's grave, Amity had only been standing in the rain waiting for under an hour. It seemed strange to corner her here instead of at the Barrow house, but it made an instinctual sense to Amity to talk to Rebekkah at the graveyard—even if Amity wasn't sure if she was able to ask her questions without sounding like a madwoman.

It would make more sense with Colton here, too.

That was ludicrous, though. Whatever made her feel pulled to him, it was temporary. She just needed to stay clear of him. He'd been the first man in a while to make her feel wanted, to look at *her* like she was amazing. Plus, he'd shown up like her knight in armor when she was alone at the bar and someone was trying to get in.

It's nothing more than hormones and stress.

Amity adjusted the skull-covered scarf that she draped over her hair in lieu of a hat and wished she'd remembered to grab an umbrella. If the light rain turned to a proper storm, the scarf wouldn't do much to keep her dry, but it worked fine in the light drizzle they'd had the past few days. She tucked her hands into her pea coat and watched Rebekkah kneel at Bonnie Jean's grave for the fourth day that week. If Bek and Bonnie Jean had been friends, Rebekkah's visits would make sense.

They hadn't been.

Up until the past month, Amity would've said Rebekkah was *her* friend, but lately they'd stopped talking.

A voice behind Amity said, "Are you going to talk to her today? Or leave before she comes over like every other day?"

Amity steeled herself before she turned to face the man who'd crept up behind her. Byron Montgomery looked like he did most days when he was off work: a pair of jeans, basic shirt, boots, and a well-worn leather jacket. His hair brushed his collar, and his green eyes glinted a bit more than they used to do. If she'd had to label it, she'd say he seemed more dangerous than he used to be. Half a year ago, that would've thrilled her. Byron wasn't *hers*, maybe he never had been. He'd left her without a second glance the day Rebekkah returned to Claysville. She didn't miss him, either, so it was hard to be upset over it.

And he's not Colton. Whatever she'd felt with Colton, it was already more than she'd had with Byron. Byron had simply been a friend who she'd also enjoyed naked. That was it.

Amity met Byron's gaze and said, "I don't know what you mean, Byron. Why would I be here to see Bek?"

"You're a lousy liar, Amity. Come here." He stood with an umbrella in his hand. It was an absurd thing covered in cartoon cats and dogs, and she didn't have to ask why he had it. It was for Rebekkah. Still, he opened it over Amity's head.

Amity concentrated on the snick of the opening umbrella, the patter of rain on the bench beside them, the slick mud under her boots.

Byron stood half-under the umbrella, keeping his distance in a way that he wouldn't have if they hadn't recently been *more* than this. "Are you doing okay?"

She forced a smile and shrugged.

"Bonnie Jean's seat on the council is still open," he said.

Any lingering doubt that she may have held as to whether Daniel and Byron both knew something evaporated with those words. They were too keen on her joining the council, too evasive in their words, and she started to wonder how many people were involved in whatever conspiracy they had.

Colton hadn't suggested the council. That made her trust him a little more.

All she said to Byron, however, was "No."

"It might help," Byron suggested in that gentle tone he'd never used with her before Rebekkah's return. *Then* he was the sort of man who didn't quite care, not that he was cruel, just that he wasn't so cautious with her—or maybe she wasn't so sensitive to it. He'd somehow become both more dangerous and kinder all at once.

"No," she repeated. Then, after a moment, she added, "I didn't know you were a council member."

"I am now—since Dad died. Honorary member and all . . . because of my job." He looked uncomfortable as he dodged whatever admission he—and everyone else—seemed unable to make. Instead, he offered the weak explanation that Daniel had: "It helped me; it might help you."

"Help me *what*?" Amity realized she'd had two people suggest she join the council in as many days. She met and held his gaze. "What would I learn if I joined the council, Byron?"

He paused. "I can't rightly say."

"Really?" Amity folded her arms over her chest. "What would *help* is if either one of the men I trusted was around, but Troy's dead and you . . ." Her words trailed off. There wasn't any good way to finish that sentence.

"Amity . . . there are things I can't say, things Bek can't say," he started.

"And my sister?"

He nodded. "Join the council."

They stood awkwardly for a few moments, both pretending they weren't uncomfortable, both carefully not watching the woman who'd thrown their lives into chaos. Rebekkah hadn't looked their way, but Amity was sure she knew they were here. Her sense of her surroundings had always been downright creepy. She'd come over sooner or later, but Amity didn't feel like waiting for her to join them before she asked what she needed to know. She was overdue for answers.

Amity straightened her shoulders, caught Byron's gaze, and said the words she'd been trying to get the courage to say. "I remember Troy biting me."

Byron stared at her for a moment too long before asking, "*What?*"

"He was dead, and he bit me . . . but *you* know that already. You were there, and then you and Bek followed him. I remember all of that, too." Amity felt herself start to shake. Whether it was nerves or anger, she wasn't sure. "I think it's why my head hurts all the time."

She laughed in embarrassment and added, "Or I'm going crazy."

"You can't remem—"

"Don't lie to me, Byron," Amity half-begged, half-demanded. "A dead man bit me, and I want answers. You know something; you were *there*."

The usually unflappable undertaker opened and closed his mouth without actually speaking. Amity felt a twist of guilt and satisfaction spiral through her as he stared at her in silence. They might not be bedmates any longer, but that didn't mean she'd forgotten all she'd learned about Byron Montgomery in the half year that they'd spent together: he would've objected with some sort of exceedingly logical explanation by now if she were actually wrong. He wasn't arguing, simply giving her the careful study of someone who had shocked him.

Still silent, Byron lifted his arm and motioned Rebekkah to them.

At his gesture, Rebekkah stopped pretending she hadn't noticed them. She rubbed her hands together, wiped them on her jeans, and trudged across the cemetery toward them. Neither Byron nor Amity spoke as they watched Rebekkah's approach. Amity's mouth was so dry from nervousness that she considered tilting her head back to let the rainwater fall on her tongue. Instead, she licked the droplets from her lips, swallowed, and waited.

"Hi," Rebekkah said quietly as she joined them. Her voice hitched, making her sound too much like a child afraid of rejection.

Amity suppressed a moment of sympathy. She was hurt by Rebekkah's secrecy. It had started when Rebekkah came back to Claysville, and it needed to end *now*.

"Bek," Amity said in greeting. She straightened her shoulders like she was about to enter a bar fight.

"How are you?"

"I came to see my dead sister," Amity interrupted. "Just like you do. I knew you'd be here, Rebekkah." She stepped out from under the umbrella and gestured up at it, trying to be a little less aggressive and maybe buy herself a moment to get her emotions in order. "Here. Byron brought the umbrella for you. Not me."

"I'm good." Rebekkah was wet clear through her jeans and sweater, but she wasn't shivering with the cold. She tucked one muddy hand into her pocket and smiled.

Byron stood there holding the umbrella as both women stood in the rain. It wasn't the most awkward encounter they'd had in the past couple of weeks, but it wasn't anywhere near comfortable.

"Bek?" he said, drawing both of their gazes to him. "Amity remembers."

Slowly, Rebekkah looked from one to the other. "Remembers . . . ?"

"Being bitten by a dead man," Amity supplied. "Troy. I *remember* a thing that couldn't have happened, Bek. And I know damn well that mountain lions aren't prone to killing people like everyone here thinks—like I used to think."

"That's not possible." Rebekkah stepped backward. "She must have—"

"Don't! I *thought* I imagined it. I *thought* I was losing my mind." Amity stared past them, remembering the fear that she'd well and truly snapped. She hadn't, though; she remembered those impossible things about Troy, the vanishing girl, and Bonnie because they'd really happened. She was even surer of it now that she stood facing Rebekkah and Byron.

"Troy was here, and *you*"—Amity pointed at Rebekkah—"knew. You weren't surprised." She stepped back so her glare could take in both of them. "You *both* knew, and you know now that I'm not lying."

"Let's sit down and . . ." Byron started.

Rebekkah grabbed Amity in a fierce hug. "This is wonderful!"

And Amity wasn't sure whether it was better or worse that she was right. A small part of her had hoped that she was wrong, that there was a reasonable explanation for everything, but Bek's reaction made it clear that she was not imagining things.

"*Explain*," she ordered, squeezing Rebekkah back.

18

REBEKKAH BARROW

AMITY WAS IMMOBILE IN HER ARMS, BUT THAT DIDN'T MATTER now. Rebekkah knew that Amity was, obviously, destined to be the next Graveminder. Rebekkah didn't need to worry about what would happen if she failed and died. There was a plan. She had a replacement.

And she'll be prepared. Unlike me.

That was huge progress.

Rebekkah could tell her everything. She could explain how Bonnie Jean died, that Bonnie Jean had known about the dead because she was on the council. Rebekkah could explain that Troy was doing well in his afterlife, not in a "maybe" way but in a "I took him there" context. The answers she hadn't been able to share, she now could.

"This is such a relief," Rebekkah said.

"For whom?" Amity jerked away. "Explain how this is a good thing, Bek? Because finding out that my former friend and fuck-buddy are both liars, finding out my ex and friend bit me, not like in a I-read-too-many-books way but for *real*..."

Quickly, Rebekkah caught Amity's hand and started, "Not too

long ago when I thought I was going to die, I said '*Amity Blue. I want Amity Blue to take this task.*' That's exactly what I said. I picked you to be the next Graveminder. I thought Cissy was going to kill me, and—"

"*What?*" Amity shook her head.

Rebekkah felt a wash of empathy. She remembered this feeling, the sense that it was impossible, madness even.

"I picked you because I needed someone I could trust to watch over the dead," Rebekkah said, adopting a calming tone suitable for mourning or bar fights. "You are the person I can trust. Not my cousin or . . . just not anyone else here. You're it, Amity."

And then Rebekkah quickly summarized the events of the last few months: that her aunt had attempted to murder her because she was the Graveminder; that there were dead folks who'd been allowed to wake; that the dead had killed members of their town, including Bonnie Jean; and that, as the new Graveminder, Rebekkah had led the dead to their rest and was doing her work to assure that the recent dead stayed where they should.

Amity listened with an expression somewhere between disbelief and acceptance.

Then Rebekkah added, "I had to name a replacement, and you were—*are*—the only person I knew who I was sure could handle it. You can turn it down, and you'll forget all of the things connected to the Hungry Dead, but . . . there's no one else here right now suitable for it. No one stronger or wiser or calmer."

"So . . . you're telling me that you hang out in cemeteries and catch zombies?" Amity asked in a tone that made clear that she wasn't entirely sure of Rebekkah's sanity.

"They're not zombies. Zombies are created by a *bokor* using zombie powder. That's different. Sometimes the dead just don't stay dead in Claysville," Rebekkah clarified.

"Okaaay . . ." Amity looked at Byron.

He gave one short nod, but he didn't speak. This wasn't his responsibility. He could choose an Undertaker if Amity didn't fail, and fate would assign the Graveminder role to the best choice. Or Amity could accept it, and they'd sort out the Undertaker. It was still a little nebulous to Rebekkah, but she was hoping that this, at least, was in order.

Then, they'd figure out what—or *who*—had enabled someone to kill Marie in the land of the dead, and shoot Charles, and talk to the town council and patrol and. . .

One thing at a time.

For a moment, Rebekkah wasn't sure what Amity would do. When Rebekkah had learned the things Amity was now hearing, she'd had more than a few questions, too. Mostly, she'd only believed the truth of the situation after she'd been to the land of the dead.

Before Rebekkah could figure out what else to explain, Amity said, "Suppose I believe you. It's better than my maybe-Troy-was-a-vampire theory, I guess. So, now what?"

Byron gave them both a tense smile, and then pointed out, "We'll need to tell the council a new Graveminder has been selected."

"The council?" Amity asked. "Is *that* why everyone says I need to join?"

"They all know about the dead," Rebekkah said, trying to resist the urge to hug Amity again. They had been friends so long, and she'd missed Amity—and *hated* lying to her. Amity had lost more than most folks in Claysville during the recent events with the Hungry Dead, though, so Rebekkah was trying not to spook her.

Byron's next works were delivered with as much joy as news of upcoming dental surgery with no anesthetic. "And we'll need to introduce her to the old bastard. Maybe not now, but—"

"What bastard?" Amity interrupted. "And again, the *town council* knows about all of this? That's why you and Daniel both suggested I join?"

Byron nodded.

"So, you're saying Bonnie Jean knew all this too?" Amity's voice sounded strained now. "How could she—could all of you—keep secrets from me? She was my sister."

"You wouldn't remember," Rebekkah started.

"You were my friend, and you"—Amity glared at Byron—"were my. . . fuck buddy. No one told me. *No one*?"

"I'm sorry," Byron said. "I didn't know until right before Bonnie died, but even if I did, I couldn't have told you. None of us could've. If people hear or see things that they aren't supposed to remember, they get migraines. It's—"

Byron's phone rang, cutting his words off.

He stepped away to take the call, and Rebekkah continued on where he'd left off: "The only people who don't forget are the council, the religious leaders, the Undertaker"—Rebekkah pointed at Byron and then at herself—"and the Graveminder."

"So why do I know? And *still* have these fucking headaches?"

Rebekkah paused, sucked in a deep breath, and added in a rush of words, "The only other people who can remember are our replacements. The man and woman next in line to be Undertaker and Graveminder. That's traditionally one of our kids when we are getting too old, but . . . I picked you. You remember because you're *next*, but because you didn't accept the calling, you still had headaches."

"Why me, Bek? Why—"

Rebekkah grabbed Amity's hand and held tightly to it. "You're one of my best friends, Amity, and I didn't come home expecting that you and B were . . . No one told me. I didn't know Bonnie was in danger either. I didn't know *anything* when I came home. Maylene died before telling me."

Maybe Amity was in shock or she was taking this all far better than Rebekkah had. Maybe it was easier if you'd already seen the Hungry Dead walking around; maybe Amity was just hard to shake. Either way, she simply looked at Rebekkah and said, "Okay."

Byron disconnected his call and rejoined them.

Rebekkah knew that look, that indescribable shift. "We missed someone."

He dipped his head in a half-nod. "Maybe or maybe t's tied to recent things *there*."

Rebekkah felt her body start to send out some kind of nonverbal questions, as if she could summon the dead. It wasn't that simple, but her very essence started to seek for a lost one, for the woken dead. The duly buried dead she could manage, but the ones that fell outside the norm were the risks. Sometimes people died alone, lost or murdered, and those were the ones she feared.

"Why don't we meet tonight to talk more, Amity," Byron suggested. "We can come by Gallagher's and—"

"No." Amity straightened her shoulders and stared at him in a way that Rebekkah recognized all too well. "You said you 'missed one.' Like a dead person who's out there killing people?"

"This isn't your problem yet," he said gently.

At that, Rebekkah's fears were confirmed with that statement. The only way there was a problem was if there was evidence that the dead had woken. Someone had woken hungry. That was the point of the call.

Typically, the dead sought the Graveminder the moment they could. They found her, and she felt them, knew their presence. That's how it worked. She hadn't been Graveminder long enough to know everything, but that much she did know. She closed her eyes and tried harder to feel for any tendril of connection, any pull to the dead.

Nothing.

She opened her eyes and met Byron's gaze. "I don't feel anyone. Are you sure?"

"Maybe it's nothing," he said, but his tone was the perfectly level one he got when he was trying to be comforting. "The council could be wrong this time."

"What happened?" she prompted, because as much as updating Amity mattered Rebekkah's first duty was to the dead. It had to be. She was the current Graveminder.

"It might just be nerves, Bek, but after everything that happened, the council is asking us to investigate," Byron said softly, voice intentionally gentle so as to keep her calm even as he scanned the graveyard for threats.

Amity watched, and Rebekkah realized that he was being evasive because of Amity's presence.

"She'll learn sooner or later," Rebekkah reminded him.

Byron glanced at both of them briefly. "Some people are missing, so Mayor Liz wants us to take a look around."

Rebekkah nodded. She didn't think she'd missed any of the bodies her aunt had hidden, but she couldn't swear to it without a doubt.

Could there be dead that had been trapped all this time?

The longer they waited, the worse they were. That wasn't the sort of experience she wished on a new Graveminder. It was what Rebekkah had faced, and she still had nightmares.

"I don't know how long this will take," Rebekkah told Amity. "I promise you that the moment we can, we'll come to you, but this can't wait."

Instead of answering, Amity lifted her phone to her ear. "Daniel? Listen, I might be late tonight. It appears that I'm the next Graveminder." She paused as he said something that only she could hear. "Yeah, I know I can't tell everyone, but you're on the council." She smiled at whatever he said and then locked gazes with Rebekkah. "Right. I'm with them now . . . Of course, I can . . . I will."

When she was finished, she tucked her phone away. "Daniel says I'm to tell you to keep me safe and 'explain the rules carefully.' Apparently, he thinks I'm a little reckless."

In spite of everything, Rebekkah laughed. "Oh, I've missed you."

"Whatever," Amity said, but she had a slight grin now.

Byron shook his head and motioned toward the street where a battered truck was parked. A dead girl had given it to them, and as much as Byron didn't like the dead, he appreciated having a truck for days when it was too wet for his Triumph and the hearse was too conspicuous. He didn't say anything: he'd already slipped into whatever mind space he went to when they were hunting.

While Rebekkah felt a kinship for the dead, Byron saw them only as threats.

19
MICHAEL

This time when Michael woke he realized that he'd been inside the garage for several days, and that he'd been lucky that the food kept coming to him, but the first three bodies weren't tasty anymore. Only Courtney was still edible, but that would only last for another couple days. He needed to find food; more importantly, he needed to find *her*.

He couldn't remember where *home* was anymore, but the urge to find the woman with the answers had evolved into a need as powerful as the hunger-thirst-craving that kept pulling him to wakefulness. The panic he'd known for years had lessened since he'd woken up from his apparent overdose. Not only had he stopped feeling the tightened sensation in his lungs, but he felt like he didn't even need to breathe.

What was unchanged, however, was his sense of confusion. There were answers, explanations to be had, and he knew that. He also knew that those answers were held by a woman he needed to find. She could free him from the haziness in his mind.

The other one wasn't her.

They seemed alike, but it was a rose and a lily, or a line of coke and a rock of coke. They were just different enough that they weren't interchangeable. He needed the *Graveminder*.

Michael walked out of the garage and toward the center of town. It was a long walk, but everyone he knew with a car was dead and rotting in the garage. His stomach growled at the thought.

"Maybe over at the bar," he muttered.

He didn't know how he was sure of it, but he knew that the only people who could help until he found *her* were people who knew him before he died.

Claysville had an abundance of bars, which Michael had always appreciated. He'd discovered the joys of bourbon when he was in high school. It didn't make it easier to get a girl, but it made it easier to forget that he didn't have one.

He wasn't ugly or mean; he was, however, both shy and poor. Somehow, girls went for mean before shy, and while they didn't always go for ugly before poor, they went for ugly with money before average but poor. At least, that had been his experience.

It wasn't until he had money to throw around that he was able to get laid regularly. Then he discovered drugs. Some girls would do anything for a share of what he bought. He felt a twinge of loss at the deaths of Courtney and Jilly.

He was sullen by the time he reached McCormick's Pub. It was a little hole in the wall that had seats for ten or so people at best. Mostly, it was a front for Jenni McCormick's side business. Like a lot of people in Claysville, she had to make do on less than she needed, and since no one really left town, Jenni had to find ways to supplement her income. She was a "connector." She hooked people up with coke, heroin, and sex. Admittedly, the sex wasn't terribly creative, but Jenni was a good-looking woman. She kept herself fit, and in the low lights, the wrinkles she was starting to get around her eyes weren't that obvious.

He opened the door and walked into the dim interior of the house-turned-bar. There were two men sitting at one of the tables. A football game on the little television mounted in the corner held their attention, so that they didn't even glance his way when he walked up to the bar.

Jenni turned and looked at him. Her mouth opened in surprise before she managed to say, "Michael? Where have you been, boy?"

"Hey," he said. He shrugged. "I don't know. It's hazy in my head."

"I was worried." She reached out to squeeze his hand, but he stepped out of reach. Hurt flashed over her face.

"I have a head cold or something, Jenni. I don't want you catching it," he lied. There was no way he was going to tell her that he was either dead or crazy. Eating people wasn't something he expected most folks would forgive.

"You poor baby," she murmured. "Well, once you get right, you come see me. I've worried."

Her affectionate tone made him uncomfortable, especially considering the things they'd done over the years, almost all of which he'd paid to do. It was confusing when he paid people to touch him or bribed them with drugs, only to have them talk like he mattered to them. He shook his head. "I need a ride."

"I can get you whatever you need. You don't need to go anywhere if you're sick." She looked past him and called out to the two men at the table, "I need to get Michael settled. Do you need a round before I go?"

"I don't want to stay," he started. "I need to—"

"Miller Lite and bar mix," one of the men called.

Jenni muttered, "Like I'd forget what they're drinking when they're the only two geezers in the bar."

Michael smiled. Being around her helped. She was familiar. Maybe he could rest here a little longer. "I'll stay, but you can't touch me at all, Jenni."

She looked away from the draft beer she was pulling and grinned. "Your call, babe. I can help you sleep without catching your cold. On the house even. I really was worried."

Neither of them mentioned the odd fact that he was claiming that he *had* a cold. No one in Claysville got sick, not really, and he had no symptoms. He didn't know how else to explain what he felt. Hunger for human flesh didn't seem healthy. That meant he was sick. Some bad drugs and he was reacting—because if it wasn't that, he was dead.

Dead folks didn't get up and talk, though.

"Maybe later," he said.

"You *must* be sick," Jenni teased. "Turning down a little TLC isn't like you."

He shook his head. "Just talk to me. That's all I need right now."

With a frown, she led him around back to one of the three bedrooms that were on the private side of the house. He'd spent more than a few nights here over the years. He'd even taken on a few customers for her when he was younger. It was a way to earn some money, and getting paid *and* orgasms sounded like a win-win situation at the time.

Jenni opened a door and stepped to the side. "I'll be back in a bit to see to you . . . tell you stories or help you sleep if you change your mind."

Michael had to concentrate on not touching her. The familiarity of it all helped his mind clear, but he knew that having a bite to eat would help even more.

"I need to sleep," he told her. "I'll be back out there when I wake."

"Okay. I'm here if you need me," she said.

He couldn't speak, but then she smiled and left. And he was left trying to figure out what to do next. He didn't want to kill Jenni, but he had noticed that the more he ate, the clearer his mind was. The urge to find *her*, the woman who had answers, pressed on him—and so did his hunger.

He started to reach for the door to call Jenni back, but as he lifted his arm, he realized that his body had turned to smoke and was drifting away.

"What the hell?" he muttered, and then he was gone before he could try to make sense of this latest oddity.

20

AMITY BLUE

THE THREE OF THEM WERE ALL CLIMBING IN THE FRONT SEAT OF the old pick-up; Byron was driving and Amity was in the passenger seat. It was the only thing that worked because literally being between them seemed like a terrible idea.

"Do we want to take a different car so Bek can drive?" Amity asked. "One with a backseat?"

Byron calmly said, "Bek doesn't drive when we do this."

"One accident, B. *One*."

"She just parked in the middle of the street and went chasing after a corpse." Byron shook his head and eased into the nearly nonexistent traffic. "I expected to protect her from dead folks, not perfectly avoidable things like oncoming traffic."

Rebekkah folded her arms. "Amity can drive."

"Nope." Byron shook his head. "Until we know how she reacts to the dead, that's not happening either. One time plucking you out of traffic was enough for me for a lifetime. I drive. You two do your dead-finding thing."

Amity rolled her eyes. "Does he think we're tracking dogs? Maybe I should ride on the bed of the truck."

Despite the awkwardness they usually had these days, Rebekkah laughed and said again, "I've missed you."

"Same," Amity admitted. "It would be good if we could all . . . get along?"

Rebekkah and Byron both agreed, and a few minutes passed in silence. The last time they'd ever been around each other comfortably was . . . never. Amity was a little younger, and when they were kids it was always Ella, Byron, and Rebekkah. There was no room for others. Amity wondered now if it was because of what they were. Had they always been this?

"So is he the down to your up because of what you are?" Amity asked.

Rebekkah sighed. "He was always going to be the Undertaker. Me or Ella Mae. We were supposed to choose, but after Ella. . ."

Byron squeezed her knee. "Died," he said. "After Ella died, Bek was the one who was going to replace Maylene. What Bek is trying not to say is that she worries that if Ella lived, I'd be in love with her. Not every Undertaker and Graveminder are married."

"You're getting married though?"

Byron's answering smile was the sort that used to mean he'd heard a joke or something, not a laugh but right next to it. "Good question. Bek?"

"Sooner or later," Rebekkah muttered. She sighed and asked, "Do you really need to put me on the spot, Byron? Seriously?"

"*So*," Amity said, forcing the conversation somewhere that wasn't going to piss off Rebekkah. "Undertaker . . . do I need to consider every date's potential for that? Or am I going to be maybe-marrying some rando chosen by the curse?"

Rebekkah's sigh was louder this time. "Honestly? I don't have an answer to that. Usually one or the other is the child of the current Undertaker and Graveminder if they marry, but—"

"Umm, no. I'm not marrying your kid, guys. There's weird and then there's that. I mean, no disrespect to cougars—the human kind

—but that's a level of wrong when I . . . when Byron and I had a . . . you know."

Byron nodded.

But Rebekkah said, "Honestly, I'm not even sure I want to have kids. Not every woman does, and the idea of raising a kid *knowing* they might be this . . . or what if they're gay? How confusing would that be to have feelings and stuff for someone you aren't attracted to? The curse is antiquated."

Amity had no disagreement with her, but that didn't answer her questions. "Okay, but . . . in the right now. . . what am I to do if you die? No one knows how to do this. You die. I'm next. We're *fucked* then, so we need a plan because this 'figure it out or the town gets eaten alive' plan is not cool. Who has the answers? Where?"

"Mr. D. Land of the dead." Byron's hands tightened on the wheel.

"We aren't to go over tonight now because there were some troubles and—"

"Fuck that. You want me to do this, we go get answers." Amity scowled.

"She's right," Byron said quietly.

For several moments, it was quiet other than the sounds of the engine and the hum of tires over asphalt, then Rebekkah said, "Tomorrow. We look tonight, and tomorrow we try to go over to see Charles."

"*Who?*" Amity asked.

"Mr. D, Charles, Charlie, the old bastard, Death," Byron said. "Pick your term."

Then, plan in place they drove around looking for—and not finding—a walking corpse. Maybe there wasn't one to find.

Come evening, Rebekkah's phone rang. Sheriff McInney updated her that there was a body. Several bodies, actually.

"We'll go see to them," Rebekkah said.

Then she disconnected. "We'll drop you off and go out to—"

"I can come," Amity interrupted.

"Actually, you can't," Byron said. "There are crime scene rules. We'll drop you at the bar and then tomorrow, we'll pick this up. Trust me, you'll see plenty of dead bodies tomorrow."

21
COLTON MCINNEY

By the time evening rolled around, Colton was ready to see Amity. He wasn't on duty, and there was no reason at all that he couldn't just spend the evening listening to music at Gallagher's.

Is that stalkerish?

He'd been there an hour or so when he decided he was about to give up. Maybe he'd stop by her house. He motioned to Daniel, who was bartending. "Let me settle up, Greeley."

"Not going to wait for her after all?" Daniel asked.

"Never said I was waiting for Amity."

Daniel chuckled. He was about to answer when instead he inclined his chin toward the door. "She walks in beauty like the night," Greeley murmured.

Seeing Amity walk in with Byron Montgomery did unpleasant things to his mood. He knew damn well that Montgomery was off the market, but he'd been in Amity's bed—and Colton hated him for it. Never mind that Colton was not even living here then.

Amity looked up and met Colton's eyes, and she looked like she needed rescuing. Maybe he wasn't the only one not pleased that she walked in side-by-side with Montgomery. That thought did a lot to improve Colton's mood.

He was off his stool and across the bar before he realized what he was doing.

Amity grinned at him. "Aw, shug, you here waiting for lil ol' me?"

"Never know when ghosts"—he shot a look at Montgomery—"or other threats might crop up. I am here to offer my services, Miz Blue."

With a feigned swoon, Amity threw herself into his arms. "My hero!"

Colton felt more foolish than not, but then Amity snuggled into Colton's side like they were a whole lot closer than he thought they were—not that he minded—and he saw an assessing look in Montgomery's eyes.

"You putting down roots, Colton?" Byron asked.

"Maybe," Colton admitted.

"When did you feel the urge to come back to Claysville?" Montgomery asked. "Was that around when Bek came home? Or before? Or later?"

Amity tensed, as if the question was loaded.

"You were already with Rebekkah when I came home," Colton offered. "Be careful, Byron. You might be her ex, but that doesn't give you room to accuse her of—"

"Not saying that." Byron smiled, wide and warm, and then he looked at Amity. "A few things changed right around when the mountain lion was plaguing the town."

Amity sighed. "Go away, Byron. I know what you're asking, but he doesn't. So, just shut up."

"Talk to Dan about the council," Byron said, looking at both of them in turn. Then he bowed his head to Amity in a rather old-fashioned way. "Bek will be in touch."

And he was gone, leaving Colton with an armful of woman, a sigh of relief, and a considerable confusion. Whatever they were discussing, he wasn't in on the secret. It was irritating.

Then, Amity looked up at him. "I don't have work tonight. I know you mentioned coming by, so I should've called you. It's just been a day, so I called off. I'm free."

"Me, too." Colton tried not to grin when she sniffed him. He wasn't insecure enough to think he smelled bad. He'd showered before coming to the bar.

After a moment, she said, "Will you trust me? This may seem odd, but . . . just . . . will you?"

"Sure. Can't be much more unusual than the caveman feeling you bring out in me." He chuckled at the admission. "If Montgomery had been any closer, I might've had to arrest myself for punching him."

"Did I miss that punch?" Amity grinned. "Lightning fast or something?"

"Nah. Once I had an armful of you, the urge to hit his smug face wasn't quite as important." Colton steered her to the bar where his beer was waiting. "Have a drink or head out?"

Amity was quiet in a way that he already realized meant she was thinking before speaking. So, he waited. Whatever was on his mind, he could see that she was weighing out her words.

"Give me a minute?" she asked.

"I've just been sitting here nursing a beer and waiting on a pretty girl," Colton said. "I've got all the time in the world tonight."

She brushed a quick kiss on his cheek and walked to the bar flap. After lifting it and letting herself back behind the bar, she grabbed a glass and poured herself a tall glass of vodka with a little bit of sours and cranberry. It was the opposite ratio of how most drinks were to be mixed. More liquor than mixer was never a good sign.

Then, for reasons he didn't know, she grabbed a big thing of salt and shoved it into a bag.

Colton was bracing for something awful when she sat down next to him with a stiff drink and bag of salt. "You want to fill me in?"

Amity grabbed a bar napkin and what looked one of those make-up pencils for under eyes or outlining lips. Colton had watched enough women draw their faces on that he knew more or less what it was.

Amity carefully started to write something or other, and then as she wrote, she read it aloud, "I hereby join your damned town council, you liars. Amity Blue." She finished and slid an empty napkin to him. "Like this. I *need* you to join."

"The damned council?"

"Yep." She glared at her boss as he walked over toward them. "I can't tell you why, Colton, but I want you at my side. Please?"

As they were sitting there, Daniel Greeley came up to them. There was no need; they both had drinks.

"Colton. Amity." The way Daniel looked at Amity was odd, but not as much as his next words: "Saw you come in with the Undertaker."

"He cleared a few things up for me. *You* could've." Amity tapped her napkin. "I will have words for you, boss, and if you're smart, you won't fire me after I say them."

Whatever was going on, Colton knew he wanted to be at her side. He took her make-up pencil and scrawled on her napkin. "'What she said. Colton.'"

Then he held it up to Daniel. "Where she goes, I go."

Daniel looked at Amity. "So, it's like that? I wondered with the way these *feelings* hit you. It's a helluva thing. Took Rebekkah a minute to—"

"Stop." Amity shrugged and poked him in the chest. "I'm not ready to talk to you. My fucking headaches were *hell* and you—"

"I suggested the council."

Amity downed her drink. "Fuck. You. Danny Boy." Then she grabbed Colton's hand and tugged. "Let's get out of here."

"I go where she goes, Greeley," Colton stressed. "I don't know what I'm missing, but I'm sure of that."

"See you both at the meeting," Daniel called out from behind them. "If you have questions, we have answers."

Colton made a dismissive gesture. What kind of answers could he have? The folks on the Claysville town council often acted like they were so high and mighty, but it was a bit ridiculous, if you asked Colton. It was a small town, with a small sheriff's office and a small council.

Amity raised a hand and flipped her boss off over her shoulder, but that was her only response.

And Colton was increasingly sure that what he had were questions for her. Amity Blue was a bundle of temper and sass, and he found it damn near irresistible. He left the bar with her, and once they were outside, he glanced at her. "Want to tell me what that was all about?"

"Not on the doorstep," she muttered. "Do you still want to drive me home, Colton?"

"I do."

"Then we'll talk there." She stopped at the door of his truck.

Once he opened her door, Colton looked at her and asked, "Are you hurt? Did he harass you or . . .?"

"No." She sighed. "I don't want to deal with it tonight. I swear I'll tell you, but can we just put a fucking pin in it and go home?"

"Home?" He grinned at her. "So, then, you want to shack up, Miz Blue?"

She cocked her head at him and said, "Darlin, do I look like I'd buy a horse I haven't test driven? Until you demonstrate those boastful things you said, we're strictly on a 'if I can find time for you' schedule."

Colton laughed. Her arrogance was a disguise, and he was starting to see through it. Amity was worried and tired, and it made her more smart-assed than usual. But even in the middle of the mask, she was leaving a crack in it for him. She wanted to be with him, and that made him feel like the hero she'd called him jokingly.

Where she went, he went, indeed.

And whatever he'd just agreed to on that bar napkin was fine because it meant he had more time with her—and more time with Amity Blue was worth whatever cost he paid. Colton's longest relationship was maybe a month here or there, and that was more about drinking his fill of a woman's charms. This thing with Amity was different, like something had burrowed into his brain and demanded that he stay near her, protect her, whatever it took for her to smile.

If he thought about it, Colton suspected he'd be packing his truck and headed anywhere but here. So, he wasn't going to think about anything other than the fact that she seemed to be struck by the same madness.

They left the bar side-by-side, and maybe it was being away from the audience, but Amity deflated a little.

"Are you okay there?" He draped an arm over her shoulders.

She gave him a tight smile and then asked, "Do you believe in fate? Like soulmates or any of that?"

Colton had always been the sort of man to run from commitment talk, and he knew damn well that what she was talking about was them. Instead of ignoring it, he said, "Until you? No. Today? Maybe."

"Do you . . . *want* that?" Amity Blue, who usually seemed bolder than brass tacks, sounded small and anxious in that moment.

"I want you." He kissed her, and she was as willing as a bride on her wedding night.

But she pulled back too soon and said, "I need to tell you some things before we do that. I want you, but I'm not sure it's *us* doing the wanting or it's the curse . . ."

"The what?"

She opened the door of his truck and climbed in. "Take me home, Colton. That napkin we just wrote on means we signed up for being able to talk about some things that I couldn't tell you just yet, and until you know, any more kisses ought to wait."

"You're not making much sense," he said.

"Take me home so we can talk."

Colton didn't particularly like the tone she had. He'd heard it in his mother's voice and plenty of his friends and relations' wives. Talks with *that* tone always meant trouble.

22
AMITY BLUE

"Tell me if I ought to be worried?" Colton asked as he drove her home. "I mean, if not for the fact that we kept our trousers on, I'd be thinking you were about to tell me I was going to be a daddy."

He glanced at her, clearly expecting a laugh or something, but Amity wasn't at a place where she could laugh. Dead people killed her sister, Miss Maylene, and from the sounds of it, a lot of others. She wanted to think about what this meant. She'd wanted a purpose, a reason, but some people already had that—maybe Colton did. She couldn't leave this town, but he could. Being born outside the town meant he had choices she didn't. Was it better to be trapped here and unable to realize the threats? Or was it better to be the one fighting them? Could she ask it of him? To be bound to her? To deal with all of this?

Even as she thought, Amity was pretty sure she was going to do it, but could she expect him to do the same?

"You felt called to come home," she said. "What happened?"

He shrugged. "Woke up one day. Knew it was time. It's not that odd. I got home, and Chris gave me a job. He's been offering for years, says he has money enough put away and just wants to be home." Colton glanced at Amity. "Expect he's planning on me being sheriff in time. Got to get my sea legs and all, but . . ."

"Do you want that? Being here?"

Colton didn't answer for several moments. When he pulled in outside her home, he cut off the engine and turned to face her. "What's going on here?

"What if I told you it wasn't mountain lions that killed folks here in town?" she hedged.

"What? Like a serial killer?"

"Kind of," Amity said.

He took her hand in his. "And that's who was at the bar? Do you know something? Do I need to call on the staties? Because I'm not sure Chris and I are prepared for serial killers."

Amity paused, unable to think of how to say it. Maybe it would be better if she just called Bek and Byron. They could explain.

"Are you in danger?" Colton asked. "You can trust me, Amity. Whatever we are or aren't, I'm here. If you're in danger, I'm—"

Whatever else he was going to say was lost as Amity's door was jerked open. She gave a yelp as she tumbled out of the truck and landed in a tangle on the ground. Beside the truck was a skinny young man with deep carved lines under his eyes, and cheek bones so pronounced that he looked like he could injure others by getting too close.

"Are you *her*?" The young man stared down.

Amity knew in her heart that this was him. The Hungry Dead that had been at the bar, but he ought to seek out the Graveminder—not the woman who wasn't the Graveminder *yet*.

Amity crab-walked backwards as Colton came around the truck. He had a pistol in his hand. "Back away from her."

The man stared at Amity, not moving, not even acknowledging Colton. And some part of her wanted to fix it, help him, make Rebekkah appear instantly. She couldn't any of it. She stared, helpless, think about how strong Troy had been—and how one of the Hungry Dead had killed Maylene Barrow.

"Do you hear me?" Colton's voice startled her. He took another two steps closer. "Raise your hands."

The young man stared at Amity, ignoring Colton. "I'm lost, and I'm just so hungry. I thought you were her. Are you her?"

"The Graveminder?" Amity whispered.

"Feed me. Please, just feed me." He reached down to grab her.

And Colton shot.

The man looked betrayed, but then, in a blink, he was gone. Nothing but mist remained. No blood droplets. No injured body. Simply empty air.

Amity scrambled to her feet, looking around in case the Hungry Dead materialized nearby.

Colton was at her side, gun raised, scowling. "What the fuck just happened?"

"That, Colton, was a dead man," Amity blurted out, voice shaking. "He was here because my fate, or curse or whatever, is that I'm going to be the one to handle the dead in Claysville. Like Rebekkah does now."

Colton stared at her.

So, she added, "And, you felt called to come home, to be here, and feel all mixed up in wanting to protect me and be near me. The *reason* for that is, because if you want to, you're the one who will be my partner in this."

Instead of answering, Colton looked around and asked, "Is that guy coming back?"

"Fuck if I know," she admitted. "Probably not. I've only seen one other walking dead guy, and he bit me. So, your guess is as good as mine. Maybe?"

He scanned the lot again and motioned to her house. "I need a drink and answers."

"Yeah, that was my day, too." She grabbed her keys from where they'd fallen and led him to her door.

The adrenaline rush was making her tremble and feel like puking. A not insignificant part of her wanted to call Rebekkah and refuse this fate. Another part was whispering that she needed to figure out how to handle this because damn was she unprepared!

Colton didn't lower his gun fully until they were inside. He still held the gun at the ready as she locked the door. "It turned to smoke. I'm not sure deadbolts help."

"I have a magical deadbolt, too." Amity pulled out the bag of salt she'd grabbed at the bar.

The look Colton gave her was somewhere between doubt and hope. He carried the pistol with him as she went around and poured it on the doorframe and window sills.

"It keeps them out," Amity said, explaining what she'd thought was a superstition. In the past, her sister had done it when she stayed over and tried to get Amity to do it. Now, she understood.

It didn't save Bonnie.

Amity rubbed the salt between her fingers. It was a silly thing to think that it saved lives, and she had a brief flicker of wonder that some people *knew* about the Hungry Dead and left their homes. Bonnie Jean had been braver than Amity had known.

Am I brave enough?

"So . . . that was a dead guy?" Colton prompted.

She took a big breath, sat down, and told him everything she knew now. Amity explained how the dead stayed dead if they were "minded," but if not, they rose in a year. She explained that if they *did* rise, the Graveminder was the one to stop them or they ate folks.

And Colton said nothing until she was done. He stared at her intently, not saying a single word. After several minutes, Amity began to worry that he was mentally injured by the revelation.

"Colton? Hey?" Amity touched his hand. "Are you . . . it's a lot, but . . . say something?"

He nodded. That was it. She didn't know him well enough to know if that was odd, so Amity called Byron while Colton was still staring at her in silence. She put her phone on speaker.

"Hey, is Bek there too? Put me on speaker on your side." She paused while Byron did, and when she heard the tell-tale shift in volume and background noise, Amity added, "Colton's here with me. Doors are salted. We're inside, but . . . one of the Hungry Dead met me in the parking lot. Asked if I was the Graveminder. So, since Colton's on the council now and the likely pick for my partner, I told him everything."

"Is he okay? Are you?" Rebekkah asked, voice more maternal than Amity was expecting.

Amity looked at Colton. "He's just staring at me. I maybe broke him or—"

"I'm fine," Colton said. "Is this all real? Seriously?"

"Sorry, Colton." Byron's voice was as comforting as the best of morticians. "It is."

"Tomorrow," Amity stressed to them. "Tomorrow we meet and go and—"

"He can't," Rebekkah interrupted. "If he does, he or Byron will die tomorrow. Just you, Amity. Until the time comes, he can't cross over. He has to take it on faith."

Colton was staring at Amity now. He took the phone and disconnected after a quick, "Amity and I need to talk."

Then he put the phone next to the pistol and stared at her.

Amity waited. For all the reasons she'd already said to him, this was different for him. He could leave here. Outside Claysville, the dead stayed dead. He could avoid this. Amity didn't have the same options. She could stay and fight, or stay and not fight.

Colton had a third option.

After a long silence moment, he said, "I want to just say yes. My body, my heart, but my mind is telling me I need space to think."

Amity nodded.

"When do I need to decide?" he asked, reaching for her hands. "And can we still . . . I mean . . . I still want to get to know you, Amity. I know you think it's this, but—"

"It *is* this." She pulled away. Tears threatened, and Amity was sick of crying. She'd wept over Maylene and Bonnie Jean and Troy and ending things with Byron and her headaches . . . She forced herself to close her eyes and not-cry.

"So you're part of the package, then?" he asked. "No agreeing to dealing with the dead is no on being with you?"

Amity paused. "Not necessarily. Graveminders and Undertakers aren't always together. Maylene and Byron's dad weren't a couple, but . . . I need to know before I decide how close we are to be. I think I want the whole package. That doesn't mean we couldn't be something casual—"

"Not what I want," he interjected.

Amity continued as if he hadn't spoken, "But I want a partner in every sense of the word. Maylene and I talked about how she and her husband had difficulties with the time she spent with Mr. Montgomery. I don't want that."

"I'm not ready to talk about *marriage*."

"Me either." She gave him a small sad smile. "But I want to know if the dealing-with-the-dead part is off the table. If it is, I need to think about that."

"It's a lot." Colton reached out again.

Amity didn't pull away this time, but she didn't move closer either. "Take your space, Colton. Once you had time to think, we can talk or something. I can't . . . blame you. If I could leave, maybe I would."

"You wouldn't."

She pulled her hands away from his. "You know where the guest room is. . . if you want to sleep here."

"Do you want that?"

Amity smiled at him. "I want a lot of things, but what I want is rarely what matters." She stood. "If you're leaving, let me know so I can lock up. If not, I'll see you in the morning."

Then she walked away, chin up and no tears. She couldn't *blame* him, but it still stung.

23
REBEKKAH BARROW

"HOW DID WE MISS HIM?" REBEKKAH ASKED BYRON AS THEY walked toward Montgomery Family Funeral Home the next day. She felt like she'd had it all under control, but obviously she was wrong. There were several badly mutilated corpses in a garage. The teeth marks on them were clearly human, so they either had Hungry Dead or a cannibal outbreak.

Byron frowned. "We got everyone that was in that house, Bek. Maybe Cissy stashed this one somewhere else . . . or maybe this wasn't one of the ones Cissy raised."

Rebekkah rolled the thought around in her mind. A couple of months ago, her aunt had murdered a number of innocent people so they'd wake. She'd had some twisted plan that she thought justified her crimes, but nothing justified senseless murder—or using the innocent.

Was it possible that there were others in another location?

It seemed the mostly likely answer. Cissy had hidden them, using the knowledge of the Graveminder to create barriers. Salt lines. Seclusion. The dead had been hidden away. Maybe this one was, too.

"Maybe someone died, and we didn't know about it because we were dealing with the rest," Byron began.

"I'd have felt them," she said.

Together, Byron and Rebekkah walked through the door into the funeral home as they spoke.

Amity was waiting at the lobby, looking surprisingly calm considering the revelations of the last day. It reassured Rebekkah that she was the right person to become the next Graveminder.

"No unwelcome guests this morning," she said as she saw them.

"Good." Rebekkah held out a hand to her. "You're okay? Colton?"

"We're fine," Amity said, but her voice was tight.

Byron paused to check in with Elaine—the manager, receptionist, and general assistant at Montgomery Family Funeral Home. She handled the daily business with a thoroughness that would intimidate military generals.

Rebekkah glanced first at Byron. They *had* to figure it out. The town was still trying to heal after the first round of murders. And Amity was one of the people who'd lost a lot.

If, for some reason, the dead woke, it was because they hadn't been tended properly. The only time that she should have to deal with the Hungry Dead was either accidental deaths or those who died alone and forgotten. What Cissy had done was an aberration, one nearly impossible to repeat because to know about the dead waking meant being one of only a select few people.

"He should've found us, found *me*, unless he was trapped." Rebekkah hadn't had the experience of an accidentally lost Hungry Dead arriving at her door, but she'd heard Byron talk about strangers showing up at the house when he was younger. Talking to herself as much as them, she added, "If he was trapped, where is he now?"

The dead knew innately that they must find those who could set things to rights, that they had to seek the Undertaker and Graveminder. That was her and Byron now. The dead would wake starving and confused, and then in that dangerous state, they'd find her. He shouldn't have gone to Amity.

"We'll figure it out," Byron echoed her promise. "It's new and . . . We need to introduce Amity to Charlie anyhow. We'll take her over, make introductions, ask questions, and then we'll come find the dead guy."

Rebekkah wanted to believe it was really that easy. She knew Charles had said the passage was closed, and if it was they'd turn back, but she needed answers and she knew that he had them.

She nodded and followed the Undertaker to the basement of the funeral home.

"What exactly are we doing?" Amity asked. "How do we do this?"

"I open a passageway to the other world," Byron said, as calmly as he did most things. He opened the door to a small room and ushered them inside.

"Oh, *sure*."

"I'll lead you there. It's fine," he reassured her.

"So you're a ferryman to the afterlife? Seriously, Byron, why were you so boring before if you could do things like *this*?" Amity said, eyes rolling and lips turning into a small grin.

Rebekkah knew she had to be afraid. Who wouldn't be? But Amity handled weird exceedingly well.

Byron and Rebekkah exchanged a look as they prepared to open a doorway that no one else alive now knew even existed until this moment.

After leading them to the room where the gateway was, Byron locked the door. The sound of the bolt being thrown seemed unnaturally loud in the stillness of the room. "On this trip, Amity, I swear to you that I will die before I let danger touch you."

Amity snorted. "Melodramatic much, ferryman?"

"It's incredible there," Rebekkah added. "He doesn't like it, but. . . you will."

"A bunch of walking corpses who find the woman I love—and now my ex too—irresistible? What's not to love?" Byron scowled. "Just be aware that you are rare. Living beings attract undue attention."

I'll keep Amity safe.

Rebekkah reached a hand out toward Amity, touched her carefully on the wrist, and promised, "It'll be okay. It's a strange place, but it's just another city in some ways."

"I've never been to a city," Amity said quietly. "*Most* of us can't leave Claysville."

Rebekkah didn't know how to respond. The truth felt like a slap. She'd been privileged, able to flee the town because she wasn't tied there, wasn't *born* there. She'd have always had to come home because of the curse, but she'd been able to leave Claysville for several years. It had meant moving to try to find a way to assuage the discontent she never could quite shake, but she'd done it.

So had Byron. Being the Undertaker gave him that ability.

So had Colton. He'd been born to a Claysville resident but not born *there,* so he'd been only half-tethered to the town. Either the magic found a way to draw him back, or he'd been drawn there for Amity.

Amity could leave now, and maybe she would. Maybe she and Colton ought to take off until it was time to assume their duties to the town.

"It'll be okay," Rebekkah repeated to Amity. "I'll be at your side in the land of the dead, and you can ask me anything."

Amity nodded. The only hint that she was anxious was the widening of her eyes as Byron walked over to a battered blue metal cabinet. He reached behind it and pulled it toward him. For a moment, no one moved.

Rebekkah couldn't speak. They'd only been aware of the passage for a few months; the entwined fear and excitement of opening that hazy doorway was still new to Rebekkah.

Amity stared at the glimpse of the tunnel in silence, and Rebekkah fisted her hands at her sides to keep from reaching out. She knew Byron didn't share her joy, knew that he had weapons secreted on him somewhere, and she didn't need to look at his face to know that he looked angry. He resented the allure the dead had for her.

Through this tunnel was another world entirely, one where the dead continued on as if they were alive. If they woke in Claysville, Rebekkah and Byron's job was to deliver them to the land of the dead, but it was a job they were still figuring out. Their predecessors hadn't warned them of their destiny, hadn't told them of the monumental task before them. By the time they knew, Rebekkah's grandmother was dead, and Byron's father was injured, and the town was beset by the Hungry Dead.

We won't make their mistakes. Her replacement—Amity or someone else—would know, would learn, and when Rebekkah died, Amity would be ready.

Byron glanced at Rebekkah once again, asking wordlessly if she was certain.

"I'm ready," she said.

Even now, only willpower kept Rebekkah from racing to it. Amity had only managed to take one step before Rebekkah caught her hand.

"We can't go in without him," Rebekkah murmured.

Amity reached forward—and hit the invisible barrier. "Can you hear them all the time? The voices?"

"Here? Yes. I hear them in the passage, but not out in town," Rebekkah said. There was a song, a swell of voices and rhythms that she recognized as audible only to the Graveminder. In the song, she heard her name and now Amity's, too. The voices of the lost dead were entwined together for them. They called out, cajoling and tempting.

Byron took down the torch that hung just inside the tunnel. As he grasped it, it flared to light.

With effort, Rebekkah managed to tell Amity, "Only an Undertaker can open the gate. Only with him can you go to the land of the dead." She pulled her gaze from the tunnel and looked at Byron. "He will be your anchor: your feelings for him will keep you tethered to *this* world."

Byron's voice was bitter as he broke into the lingering pause that followed her words. "What you feel right now, Amity, is mild. I ***know.***

I watch her try to pretend that the land of the dead isn't where she'd rather be. When Bek and I die, you'll have someone here to anchor you. Today, I will see you to the other side so you can meet Mr. D, but after this, the only one who will take you there is your Undertaker."

"So, it's just you for now?" Amity's voice sounded like she was trying to provoke him as she asked, "We share you?"

"No," he said, obviously ignoring the teasing in her voice. "After today, you will stay in Claysville until Bek and I die."

Amity nodded, and Rebekkah knew from experience that they wouldn't get much more out of her. She wondered briefly if Amity had *always* been the inevitable next pick. Was that part of why Byron was drawn to her? And her to him?

"Take my arm," Byron said to them both. "And no matter what you hear or feel, don't let go of me."

Amity and Rebekkah both took one of Byron's arms, and together they entered the tunnel.

Strange soft hands brushed against them as they walked. Fingers grasped, and lips sighed. The dead in the tunnel were bodiless, nothing more than spectral remnants. They slid against her as if trying to caress her. Rebekkah suspected that their cold touches would unnerve most people, but to her they were a soothing welcome. She belonged to the dead, and they belonged to her.

Absently, she wondered if Amity and Byron had been speaking. Her ability to focus tended to vanish as she crossed through the passage. She concentrated on the caress and whisper, the slap and snarl of the dead. These were the ones who had been lost in the tunnel by past Graveminders. Someday, she hoped to find a way to rescue them, a wish she whispered to them every time she passed.

I will not forget you, she swore.

Too soon, she was stepping away from the souls lost in the tunnel. Her heart ached for them, even as it felt like it would thunder out of her skin at the excitement of being back here. Nowhere in the living world had felt like home, but here she felt as if her soul fund quiet, as if every urge to flee vanished.

In front of her, the land of the dead sprawled like a city with too many personalities. Spires and turrets shared the sky with high rises; a cacophony of modern engines and animals' cries greeted her ears. A wooden walkway twisted off to one side; a cobblestone walk intersected it a short distance away. To her left, a dirt path and a paved city street extended into what looked like different neighborhoods.

And there was the man-shaped entity who stood grinning at her. He might look like any number of dark-haired, decidedly fit, well-dressed men, but he wasn't even human. What manner of creature he was, she wasn't sure. All she could say for certain was that he was the ruler of this place, the entity who'd made that long-ago contract with Claysville, and as a result, he was either her nemesis or her ally. The jury was still out on which.

Her gaze swept him, seeking lingering injuries. She saw none, but she did see him noticing. He opened his suit jacket to show that he was well. "I'm fine, Miss Barrow. You, however, seem to have ignored my note that the door was to stay closed for now. . ."

"Am I not allowed to worry? Or do my job?" Rebekkah asked, trying to keep both her worry and her temper in check.

"Far be it for me to argue," he said, smiling. "But . . . this young woman appears to be alive, my dear. That's not your duty."

Rebekkah rolled her eyes. He, undoubtedly, knew why she would bring a living woman here. Sometimes she suspected he knew far more than Rebekkah hoped to ever realize. She made a sweeping gesture at Amity. "Charles, I want you to meet my replacement. I needed . . . Amity needed. . . . that is to say that she's my replacement."

Charles embraced Rebekkah and murmured so low that his words were quite nearly a purr, "My dear, you are just filled with surprises, aren't you?"

Then he caught Amity's hand in his and pulled her out from

behind Rebekkah, stepping backward so the two women were side-by-side.

Amity was uncharacteristically silent as he studied her. "Another lovely, *living* Graveminder here so soon."

Neither Byron nor Rebekkah spoke.

Charles might pretend to be a chivalrous gentleman, but that was a guise. He was Death, and no matter how often they stood at odds, there were times when it was all too easy to remember than Death himself was something to fear.

"And you are?" Amity said, her voice no more than a whisper.

"Mr. D or Charles if you prefer, my dear." He bowed with the sort of grace that belonged in long-gone ballrooms—or in the parts of the land of the dead where the past was still present. "This is my domain, and as you are here, I gather that you are my next Gravem—" He cut himself off and spun sharply to face Rebekkah. "Are you ill?"

"No, I'm *fine*, Charles." Rebekkah was shocked by the raw look of worry on his face. "I had picked her when Cissy . . . when I thought that I—"

Her words were stopped by Charles' sudden embrace.

Byron, usually eager to quarrel with Charles, said nothing as Death held her in his arms again.

"You frightened me, Rebekkah," Charles whispered in her ear. "You'd better have years ahead of you before you die. I'm still reeling from the loss of your lovely grandmother, and after the events here . . ." And then, as if nothing particularly odd had happened, Charles stepped back, straightened his tie and said, "Well, then. Where were we?"

24

AMITY BLUE

AMITY SUPPOSED THERE WERE ODDER THINGS POSSIBLE THAN meeting Death dressed in a pin-striped suit, but she wasn't sure what those things could be. She hadn't expected the embodiment of Death to be . . . well, *attractive.* He was, though: dark hair that was just long enough to have a slight curl to it, dark eyes that stared at her intently, full lips that seemed meant for kissing, and a form that hinted at good things if he were to shed the suit.

I'm lusting on a dead guy.

She yanked her attention away from Mr. D and studied her surroundings. Behind him, a city stretched into the distance. Directly in front of them was what looked like the edge of a Wild West theme park, and beyond that, she could see tall brick buildings. The street itself had 1900s automobiles, a Harley-Davidson, and a horse drawn carriage.

"The rabble didn't know you'd be visiting, but undoubtedly they'll be drawn out to the streets to gawk and dither." Charles frowned at Byron. "You could've given me time to prepare a proper welcome. I believe we spoke of the reasons to not visit here for a while . . . ?"

"It was Rebekkah's call, but I can look after both of them." Byron tucked his jacket back, revealing a handgun that Amity hadn't known him to own—much less carry. He didn't draw the gun, but there was an implied threat in his gesture that she hadn't expected.

"You already have *your* Graveminder, Montgomery." Charles narrowed his eyes in obvious displeasure. "I may have to share Rebekkah with you, but this one"—Charles flashed a warm smile at her—"is *only* mine right now.

"Excuse me?" Amity said.

"I protect what's mine," Charles announced with a strange edge to his voice.

"She's human," Byron said. "And living. And not *yours*."

"Surely, you don't think that they are *yours*, Mr. Montgomery. I know you've enjoyed the love of Ella, Rebekkah, *and* Miss Blue. That makes three of my Graveminders and the maternal love of a fourth." Charles' tone was needling. "Do not make the mistake of thinking that the pull Ella, Rebekkah, and Miss Blue felt for you is any less than the draw they feel for me."

"You bast—"

"Enough," Amity snapped.

Some part of Amity's logical side remained alert enough to be offended, but another, slightly less evolved, part of her preened. Byron no longer had a right to be possessive of her. Plus, Charles had the sort of glint in his eyes that promised trouble—and he was looking at her with the same sort of approving assessment that she'd given him moments earlier.

"Did you have a question for me, Miss Blue?" he asked.

She had a lot of questions, but the first one that popped into her mind was, "How old are you?"

He laughed, a sound far more tempting than she'd have expected from Death.

Amity blushed. "I mean, have you always been . . . *Death*? You look young, aside from the suit. Is it like the Graveminder? Like you get replaced?"

"No. This is what I am, and I've bever been replaced. Age,

however, is a human construct," Charles explained. "No one ages in the land of the dead."

"Because they're *dead*," Byron interjected. "You might want to consider that, Amity. They might not look like corpses, but they are. Don't forget that."

Charles ignored him as if he hadn't spoken. "As their ruler, my dear, it would be odd for me to age. I am forever young."

He moved close enough to her that she wondered if he was going to touch her. She wanted him to. She wanted any number of things that seemed exceedingly wrong to want with Death. He inhaled sharply and gave her a look as lust-filled as her own undoubtedly was.

A flicker of a thought of Colton nudged at her, but she quickly reminded herself that they'd barely just begun to be anything, and that Colton very clearly said that he wanted space.

Charles lifted his gaze to the street and surveyed it. His actions reminded her of exactly how Byron had changed. This was it. Byron had become more alert to threats, more protective of Rebekkah. He'd become exactly the way that Charles was acting toward *her*.

Several men and women headed their way. Many of them were all armed in a curious mismatch of styles. One woman carried a pair of swords on her back; another had a shotgun resting on her shoulder and a pistol at her hip. There were men with similar weapons, and both men and women who had no visible weapons, but they all looked very much like the sort of people one shouldn't antagonize. If they'd walked into her bar back in Claysville, she would've suggested her regulars quietly leave.

"Ahhh. Our escort has arrived." Charles strode forward.

The armed men and women seemingly didn't react to his approach; they watched the area around them with the vigilance that spoke of training—and of the probability of threat.

"Come on," Rebekkah urged.

Byron, like many of their armed escorts, had a gun in his hand now, and Amity realized that he wasn't the man she thought she'd known at all. They'd shared a bed for months, but between yesterday and today, she'd glimpsed a side of him that she'd known nothing about.

It didn't surprise Rebekkah. She *knew* him. Watching the two of them here made her admit to herself that they fit together in a way that was freakishly right. It wasn't that she ever thought he'd fit with *her* that way, but it was embarrassing to be forced to face the fact that she'd never been anything more than a stand-in for the woman he'd wanted—and not a very good stand-in at that.

A brief a thought of Colton came over her. He was, if she chose him, going to be her protector, doing as Byron did for Bek. Colton would be her partner in the land of the land. She wasn't quite ready for forever, especially a forever someone else selected for her. Despite that, she knew—and *would* have known even without Byron and Rebekkah's heavy-handed intimations on the subject—that Colton was her fate.

Could she do that? Decide his fate? Believe he was going to stay in Claysville for her? A few kisses and longing touches did not a forever make, and when she talked to him, he asked for space. Space wasn't being together.

For now, though, she was not convinced there was going to be a man in her life—and an eternal, remarkably attractive being was looking at her like she was fascinating.

Amity walked up to the left of Charles, who promptly cut his gaze her way.

"Step back, Miss Blue," he said in a low voice that would allow for no argument. "They may be my ruffians, but they *are* still ruffians."

"I'm not afraid," she insisted.

He shook his head, a hint of a smile on his lips. "Graveminders never are." Then he stepped in front of her before adding, "I'd be crushed if something were to happen to you, so humor me for now."

"Can't everyone die?" she asked.

Charles didn't look back at her as he spoke. "I am invulnerable."

"Really?" Rebekkah prompted.

"Are you, Charlie?" Byron added.

Charles brushed their questions away and looked at Amity. "I am invulnerable," he repeated.

"Good." Amity rested one hand on his back, her palm flat against his suit jacket. She felt him tense under her touch. "Killing Death seems like a thing that ought not be possible."

Byron snorted.

At a word from Charles, the armed escort re-organized and a wall of bodies pressed so tightly together that she was impressed that they could walk. Once she was shielded by them, Charles pulled her forward to his side.

"You're not intimidated in the least bit, are you?" he said in a voice too low for anyone else to hear.

"Should I be?" she replied just as quietly.

"I'm *Death*, my dear. Most people find me unpleasant." He gave her a bitter smile, and Amity realized that she felt sympathy for him. He was beautiful, powerful, and eternal—and she felt sad for him. Whether he said the words or not, Charles was lonely.

"I'm not most people. From what I hear, I'm a girl who can handle the dead. You're a dead guy." She gave him a cheeky grin. "Shall I handle you?"

His eyes widened in surprise for an instant, and then he laughed. "Someday, I shall hate the living man who has your heart."

They walked through the land of the dead, Amity wasn't sure whether she was more intrigued by the city or the man at her side. Both drew her attention in equal parts. She half-listened as Charles and Rebekkah talked about the difficulty of finding the current walking dead man in Claysville.

"He should've come to me," Rebekkah was saying. "Not to Amity. She's vulnerable."

"We'll sort it out, my dear," Charles murmured. "First we deal with introducing Miss Blue. Then, after our business is concluded, I'll tell you what I can about your dilemma."

25

REBEKKAH BARROW

THEY WALKED FURTHER FROM THE PASSAGEWAY THAT CONNECTED the land of the dead to Claysville. Charles was now between Amity and Rebekkah. They were speaking quietly together, and Rebekkah didn't have the right to interfere. At the same time, she couldn't quite see her way to letting him have *too* much privacy with Amity. In Rebekkah's impulsivity, she'd failed to warn Amity about Charles—or maybe she simply didn't know how to warn her. It wasn't that he was necessarily bad, but he wasn't altogether honest either.

What he was, unfortunately, was damn near omnipotent in his domain.

Rebekkah had spent a great deal of time over the past few months—after she'd delivered the Hungry Dead to this world—reading about theories of death. None of them matched the world and the man she knew to be real. Charles might wear a human shape, but Death was an inevitable state, a loss of life, a transition, an ideal—everything in philosophy and religion told her as much and more. It didn't mention that he was also a romantic, if he was to be believed, or that he had exquisite taste in food and fashion. It never mentioned his obsession with music. Charles was a person in all that ways that she understood; he just happened to also be ruler of the land of the dead.

At least this *land of the dead.*

She had hoped that they'd be able to discuss it further. He answered questions as the whim struck him, revealed tidbits and ignored questions if he felt like it, but now they had this new development to address.

As they walked through the land of the dead, their escort moved in a way that obviously made sense to them, but not to her. Some of them were in front, behind, and to either side of the living. Others disappeared down streets, only to return.

"You expected us," Rebekkah half-accused, drawing Charles' gaze to her. "Why else would you have the guards meet us?"

Charles held his hands up disarmingly. "How could I expect you?"

"You can see more in my world than you admitted," Rebekkah said, stunned as the realization washed over her. She gaped at him. "You *always* know. Who will wake. Where. All of it . . ."

Charles nodded once.

Rebekkah slapped him. She slapped *Death* in the face as if he were nothing more than a man who'd lied to her. This was worse than a lie, though, and he was not a man.

"Miss Barrow," Charles said, voice far from the light cordiality he usually adopted.

Byron and Amity were staring at her.

"Bek?"

Rebekkah held up a hand. "It's fine. We're just discussing a few things." She smiled at Amity. "Nothing for you to be worried by."

And maybe it was just the wonder of the world, but Amity's attention flitted over everything they passed, and Rebekkah had to admit —silently, to herself, at least—that she was glad the guards were there. Her first visit to this world had included being shot. She didn't want Amity to have to deal with that, at least not yet.

"I don't trust him," Byron muttered beside her.

"You wound me, Undertaker." Charles sounded more amused than hurt, but he and Byron had a contentious relationship at the best of times.

Quietly, she asked, "Why the dramatics if you know the answers?"

Charles glanced at her. "Rules, my dear Miss Barrow. Your great-grandmother often struck me for the same reasons, so I ought not be surprised. And Bitty"—he smiled the smile of a man remembering good times—"she once jabbed her hat pin right into my neck when I hugged her. My Graveminders are always fierce."

"Not yours," Rebekkah muttered.

He chuckled. "As you say. Maybe you are not wholly mine. Your replacement, though, is unattached."

Rebekkah glared up at him. "Who killed Marie? What does that mean? And why were *you* able to be shot and bleed last time? You owe me answers, Charles."

Byron and Charles were supposed to be impervious to actual *death* in the land of the dead—Byron because of some contract clause Claysville's first Graveminder and Undertaker had asked for centuries ago, and Charles because he was, as clear as Rebekkah could understand, *Death* himself . . . or, at the least, one of the entities that were Deaths.

"Can Byron be killed here now?"

"No." Charles sighed. "And the culprit would not harm him. Or you." Louder, he added, "The 12:06 train should pass in a moment. Wait."

Charles watched for the train, and Rebekkah watched him. "*Why* are we safe?""

"Because the culprit would not harm an Undertaker or you," Charles said in a near-whisper.

"Is Amity like me or like B?" she asked in an equally low voice.

"Like him until you die," Charles answered just as quietly, affirming that she could not die while here.

He caught Amity's hand and pulled her closer. Once she was at his side, Rebekkah had to stop asking thing. Charles met Rebekkah's gaze as he tucked Amity's hand in the fold of his arm. Amity didn't object—or ask why.

"The train's coming," Rebekkah explained.

Beside her, Charles tensed. At the same time, Byron's arm wrapped possessively around Rebekkah's waist.

"I'm fine," she said softly to both of them. There weren't any people even near enough to hurt her, but after one incident in which an angry woman tried to shove her into the path of the train, the walk through the center of town had become more cautious. Having Amity with them today increased everyone's tension.

And although Charles seemed to know who was responsible for his injury, Rebekkah had no idea. He was still watching for threats, and Rebekkah couldn't help but feel safer as a result.

She followed Charles' glance to the world be beyond her. The clash of colors, sounds, and scents had become more familiar as she'd visited Charles' domain, but it was still disquieting. Statuesque women in what appeared to be period costumes mingled with young men in jeans and weathered denim jackets. A girl no more than ten years old sat on a wooden railing outside a saloon watching the throng of people moving along the wooden sidewalk in this part of town.

The girl hopped down with a squeal when she saw them.

"Mr. D!" She ran toward them, barely avoiding a horse and all but toppling an 1800's bicycle.

As she neared them, Charles swept her up into his arms before she could cross the path of the oncoming train. With a scowl, he looked from the child to the train that cut through the city with neither track nor noise.

The wind of the train caused tendrils of Rebekkah's hair to lift and her shirt to press tightly to her skin. Beyond sensation and the sight, there was no other way to know it was passing. On occasion the conductor allowed the scream of metal wheels on invisible tracks, and rarer still, he made use of the whistle. Today was not such a day.

"What did I say about caution?" Charles lectured as he lowered the child to her feet. “Especially when Miss Barrow is with me—and with a guest today. The Undertaker might’ve shot you.”

The girl giggled as Byron sighed in frustration.

Charles continued, “Miss Walpole could show up at your bedside with a switch the way you unsettled her running out to me.”

“But—”

“No,” he tapped her once on the nose. “You need to be more careful, munchkin, or I’ll stop letting you in the back to hear the singers.”

And in that peculiar way of the dead, the threat of losing her favored entertainment worked where threats of being shot didn’t.

“Yes, sir. I’ll try harder.” The little girl ducked her head. For all of a moment, she was contrite, then she looked up, “But you like *my* singing too much to kick me out for long.”

Charles stared at her, expressionless for several heartbeats, and then he shook his head and grinned. “Imp. Get on with you.”

And, *that*, Rebekkah thought, was the side of Charles that he wanted her and Amity to see. She was never sure if he arranged strange experiences to make her see him as something other than the monster that had made the bad decisions that created the need for a Graveminder. If not for his actions centuries ago, the dead would stay dead in Claysville, and there would be no need for a Graveminder.

26
AMITY BLUE

CHARLES HAD LED THEM TO A BUILDING THAT WAS EVEN MORE impressive than the mish-mash of architecture in the city. Marble steps, columns, and an enormous door all assured that this house wouldn't be missed. Above the third floor a rooftop garden held towering trees and plants that draped over the sides. And on the second floor, a long balcony stretched half the length of the building.

His voice was a low rumble as he leaned toward Amity and murmured, "Welcome to my home, Miss Blue."

She raised both brows at him. "A bit over the top, don't you think?"

He lifted one shoulder slightly. "I like beautiful, complicated things."

Amity snorted at his tone, and he gave her a strange look.

"What?"

Charles shook his head. "You're unusual."

"So are you." She gestured to the house. "Lead on, or are we waiting for a red carpet to roll out to greet you?"

His lips quirked in a small smile, and he turned to Rebekkah.

"You and Montgomery can go freshen up in your rooms, my dear. I'll show Miss Blue to hers."

Byron gave Amity a look that she knew was intended to ask if she needed help of any sort.

"I have a room?" she asked.

"Of course." Charles covered her hand with his and escorted her up the absurdly beautiful steps and into his home. "Rooms. A sleeping room, a sitting room, and a bathing room. There are dresses and shoes and—"

"Not a dress girl," she interrupted.

"We'll have trousers made for you then. Whatever pleases you, Amity. You only have to say the word, and I'll do all I can to make it so." He'd stopped in the foyer inside his home.

At the foot of the staircase, several people waited. One man looked like security, and the other two were maids in some sort of old-fashioned black and white uniforms. After a lifetime of modest means and normal people, this was a lot to take in.

"Patricia will look after your needs, Amity. After you've changed and perhaps enjoyed a good soak, we can dine."

"Rebekkah tells you there is a dead guy killing people, and you want to go to dinner?"

"There are always dead men to attend, and there are always crises looming," Charles said reasonably. "You will only have one first day in my world. We will relax, enjoy an evening out, and then I will tell Rebekkah what she wants to know." His voice was gentle already, but it became more so as he added, "She expects as much, as does Montgomery even though he despises it; that's why they've gone on to Rebekkah's rooms with Cora already."

Amity looked to the staircase where, indeed, her friends were already vanishing. Today had been long and filled with surprises she could never have guessed. Taking a moment to pause and think certainly *did* sound appealing. Quietly, she followed the remaining maid, Patricia, to her rooms to bath and perhaps change.

. . .

AFTER SHE WAS ENJOYED A SOMEWHAT RELAXING SOAK IN THE oversized slipper tub in her bathroom, Amity rejected most of the clothes in her wardrobe. . . only to find that the jeans and shirt she'd been wearing were now missing.

"Where are my clothes?" She'd dried and pulled on underthings, but had no idea where her actual clothes were.

"There are other options!" The maid, Patricia, followed her

Amity stomped into her so-called "sitting room"—only to find Charles there waiting for her.

"Where are your clothes, my dear?" he asked.

"That was my *exact* question." Amity folded her arms across her chest. "She *took* them."

"They're being laundered," Patricia said.

"Miss Blue . . ."

"No." Amity scowled at them both.

Charles motioned for Patricia to leave.

The maid made a small *eep* sound and fled, leaving the mostly bare Graveminder-to-be alone with a suit-clad man who ruled this world. The man, or entity, in question started, "There is a full wardrobe of—"

"Dresses and stuff," she snapped. "Do I seem like a cocktail dress or ball gown woman to you, Charles?"

"You'd look lovely in—"

"I signed on to hunt dead things. I'm a *Graveminder*, right?" She shook her head at him. There should've been something intimidating about talking to him while clad in nothing but underwear and a bra, but the hungry look in his eyes made her feel like she was the one with all the power.

"In theory but right now—"

"I'm a *bartender* over there, Charles. I roust drunks and dodge pinching fingers. I have no desire at all to be dolled up like some old-fashioned lady."

He stared at her for a moment, and just as she was about to squirm, he said, "Well, you can't go out in your undergarments; as delectable as the view is, I'm fairly certain that you would attract far more attention than would be wise."

Amity felt her anger fade as quickly as it had arrived. She laughed at the absurdity of it all and asked, "Delectable, huh?"

"Very," Charles murmured, his gaze raking her from bottom to top. "But as much as I'm sure the citizens would appreciate it, I find that I'm feeling uncommonly possessive just now. What do you say we find something you can tolerate for just one night, and in the future I'll be sure your clothing preferences are better attended?"

Mutely, Amity nodded her assent. She considered letting Charles precede her into the bedroom, but then decided that if she was going to be going toe-to-toe with him, she might as well play it for all she was worth. He liked the look of her, that was clear, and she might as well accept the advantage it offered her in the moment, especially as she figured there weren't a lot of occasions when she'd have the advantage over someone who was at the least centuries-old, and probably eons old if he legitimately was the embodiment of death.

She strode past him with as much confidence as she used when she walked across Gallagher's at home.

Charles made a strangled noise.

"What?" She tried to sound innocent and failed miserably.

"Times have changed," he said. "Underthings used to cover a woman's derriere. I can't imagine that that"—he gestured toward her thong—"is expected to cover anything."

Amity laughed and walked to the wardrobe. The doors were still wide open. "Help me out here, Charles."

He reached past her, his jacket sleeve brushing her bare arm in the process, and flicked through the hanging garments. She couldn't feel anything, simply a bit of cloth brushing against her skin, but as the moments ticked by, Amity felt like she was on the verge of behaving very inappropriately.

"Here we are," he announced.

She shivered as his breath burned her skin. "What?"

He withdrew a simple black skirt that was cut high on both sides.

It wouldn't restrict movement, but it was still a skirt. He handed it to her and then added, "And I was wrong about going out in undergarments. I think a corset top would suit you perfectly. I know they're worn like outerwear over in the living world these days."

As he spoke, he pulled out a dark blue top. It wasn't tragically ornate, just a bit of lace at the top, and it covered as much as most of what she wore to work. It was a lot nicer, and presumably hand-made, but it was the best option she'd seen.

"I'll send a shirt over with Patricia, so you have it in case you get chilled," he added abruptly, and in a moment, he had left her there.

27
REBEKKAH BARROW

VISITING THE LAND OF THE DEAD WAS ALWAYS ODD, BUT REBEKKAH was finding tonight more so than usual. Charles had announced that they would skip the normal elaborate meal in favor of "light fare at one of the clubs."

Rebekkah had been too stunned by the decision and his attire to say much in response. So here they were a few hours later in one of Charles' clubs. It was so different from the places Rebekkah had been with Charles that it was hard to imagine that it was the same world—or that he was the same dapper gentleman she'd met on every other visit.

Even Charles himself looked thoroughly different in a pair of simple trousers and button-up shirt with the sleeves rolled back. He seemed like a stranger as he stood beside Amity while some sort of bluesy rock shook the walls. *This* man was nothing like the visage of Death she'd known until he caught her staring and shot her a knowing grin. That detail was unchanged. He was an enigma refusing to be understood—and well aware that she was trying to understand him.

Rebekkah shook her head.

Charles was explaining something about a piece of art that hung in the room. Rebekkah realized that she didn't know enough about the rules of his world and the living world when he said, "In life, he was overlooked, but in death his paintings have become collectors' pieces. This one"—he gestured at a small canvas that was covered in angry slashes of color—"doesn't exist there. I've let others be taken back to be 'discovered,' but this one is a favorite of mine."

Rebekkah and Byron both swung their gazes to Charles. "Taken back?" she echoed.

"Items can be carried both ways." He gave her a guileless look. "Only people are problematic. Things have less restrictions."

"What kind of restrictions?" Amity interjected.

"Weapons of a newer sort can't be brought in without my—"

"No," she said. "What are the restrictions on *people*? On me?"

The silence was heavier than seemed possible in a crowded club with some sort of guitar-laden music.

"Only the Graveminder and Undertaker can come here without dying. When the next Undertaker comes here, he will accept his duty and return to that world, or he will die. If he accepts his duty, Byron dies. However, the next Graveminder"—Charles stepped closer to Amity as he spoke—"is able to visit my world exactly *once* before becoming the Graveminder. She can come here and discover the land of the dead, the people who are her subjects, and of course, I can have the pleasure of meeting her. I didn't have that chance with Rebekkah before she assumed the mantle, but she brought *you* to me."

"I didn't bring Amity to *you*. I brought her here to see this world because I want her to have a choice," Rebekkah interjected. "I had none. She deserved to decide what she wants."

"Precisely. Choices are very important." Charles looked at Rebekkah then with such affection that she felt like she'd been his puppet, speaking a line at his request.

"And she's seen it now," Byron added. "We can go home."

"Watch yourself, Undertaker." Charles didn't raise his voice, but the threat in it made clear that he wasn't speaking idly. "You can challenge me without repercussions where Rebekkah is concerned. *That* is your role. What happens next is not within your purview."

The music grew in tempo, as if it reflected Charles' flash of temper. Perhaps it actually did. The finer points of the land of the dead were still outside of Rebekkah's understanding.

"I do hate to agree with your Undertaker, my dear, but the boy is right. It's time for you to return to Claysville, Miss Blue. I'm afraid that it can't be helped. Rebekkah needs to return to look after one of the dead," Charles explained to Amity, before he lifted his gaze to Rebekkah. "He is called Michael Garrety. Look for him by name, and you'll find his usual haunts quick enough."

Byron's expression was shuttered, but all he said was, "Let's go."

"Give me a minute?" Rebekkah asked.

Byron nodded and walked over to talk to a few of the men he knew through his time spent with Rebekkah's ancestor, Alicia Barrow. For a moment, Rebekkah marveled at how easily he blended with the Wild West gunslingers, but then she turned her attention to her friend.

Amity looked devastated, as lost as she'd been at her sister's funeral, and Rebekkah wished they had more time here. Byron might not like the land of the dead, but Rebekkah understood the feelings Amity was experiencing. Being here made her feel alive—and although Amity was only Graveminder-in-waiting, she undoubtedly felt some measure of the rightness of this world, too.

Rebekkah knew without asking that Amity wasn't going to refuse the duty. She hugged her and whispered, "I understand. You'll come back again on day."

Amity walked away with Byron, and Rebekkah glared at Charles.

"Yes?"

"Fill me in," she ordered. "I see how many guards you have here, and I know Alicia's people are here."

"Everyone in the club, my dear," he said softly. "There is trouble afoot."

"Then why not tell us to turn around—"

Charles gave her a look. "I told you not to come, and yet here you are."

"I needed the name, and it was Amity's right, and . . ." Her words faded as he lifted her hand.

"And you were worried," he finished.

"Fine." Rebekkah frowned. "I know you're not supposed to matter to me, your curse is at fault, you're a bad man . . . or being or whatever." She waved her hand around. "I didn't like you being shot."

"I swear to you, my dear Miss Barrow, that I have a plan." Charles stood and offered his arm. "And I have a very strong suspicion who is behind it." He patted the hand she'd rested on his arm. "I am not nearly as young as I look, Rebekkah. You go back to our town and find Michael. I'll handle the culprit here."

Then, Death walked her to her Undertaker and handed her to him. "Watch over her, Byron. She is a treasure to me."

It felt a bit wedding-like for Rebekkah, but for a flicker of a moment Rebekkah wondered if that was such a bad thing.

"Let's go home," Byron said.

28

CHRISTOPHER MCINNEY

JENNI MCCORMICK'S NECK WAS MISSING A GIANT CHUNK OF FLESH. The sheriff looked at her and made the Sign of the Cross. He motioned to the deputy, his cousin Colton, who was staring at her like he'd never seen a corpse.

"Colton?"

"Something ripped her whole throat out," Colton said.

Two techs were gathering a few things, but that was pointless. It was a mountain lion. It always was when the cases were messy.

Colton squatted beside the body. "She has finger-shaped bruises, Chris."

"Jenni made do," Christopher said diplomatically. "Some of the ways she earned her income were things we ignored. Men have needs, and Jenni needed the money."

The sheriff squirmed at the way Colton stared up at him.

"Someone was rough with her, and the door wasn't shut. Mountain lions are a real problem," Christopher explained. "Most town have a lot of crime. We don't."

"Mountain lions?"

Christopher scratched his head, shifting his hat in the process.

"Yes, sir. When this happens, we need to tell the mayor, the town council, and the Barrow woman." He paused. "Of course, we also need to call Montgomery. Can't go leaving a body out like this."

"You think a mountain lion came into her house, ripped her throat out, and wrote on the wall?" Colton gestured to the words "I'm sorry" that were drawn in lipstick on the wall.

"Well, not that." Christopher laughed. "Pretty sure this sort of cat doesn't wear lipstick."

"Did you ever think that there's something wrong with the number of cougar attacks we have here?" Colton asked as he stood.

The techs froze.

Christopher grabbed his cousin's arm and led him outside to the gravel and weed lot alongside McCormick's Pub. "Don't say shit like that! My whole team will be calling off with a migraine if you keep up with questions like that!"

Colton's mouth gaped open, closed, and he just stared at Christopher for a long moment. "And *that* seems normal?"

Christopher took off his hat, turning it in his hands, and thinking of the right words. After a few moments, he said, "This'll be yours soon."

"Your hat?"

"My job," Christopher corrected. "I'm going to retire, and I'm going to live to see eighty. Ev will. My kids will, too. Life here means having no diseases."

"Except migraines," Colton muttered.

The sheriff glared at his younger cousin. "Bring me a bottle of whisky tomorrow because I'll feel lousy after I say this." He paused, took a breath, and said, "Look, Colton. I'm not a fucking idiot. I know damn well that mountain lions don't do this shit." He pointed at the closed door. "Whatever killed Jenni won't let folks think long on it without the pain in our heads. Staying here means the woman I love and my kids are safe from diseases—and yes, that's fucking weird, too. I'm not stupid."

The pain was already shoving at him, so he slid on his sunglasses.

"Chris?"

The sheriff held up his hand and continued, talking as fast as he could to get the words out before he passed out, "You weren't born here, so you can leave. Me? This is my lot in life. Parts are"—he winced as it felt like a small drill in his eye socket—"damned awful. Demons? Something else? Who the fuck knows? Actually, the *council* and their *Graveminder* know."

He closed his eyes and dropped to his knees.

"Chris, stop!" Colton grabbed his arm. "Jesus, man, I didn't mean—"

"Not Jesus behind this," Christopher managed to say. "Or Buddha or Adonai. We have religious leaders a plenty." He stared up at Colton. "Three on the council."

"I joined," Colton said.

"Good. Good." Christopher squinted at him. "You'll take my job by next year."

Colton tugged Christopher to his feet. "Let me drive you home."

"Darby can do it." Christopher wobbled on his feet, clearly not fit to drive with the shards of pain in his head and eyes. He grinned. "Ev would kick your ass if she saw you when I'm like this. We knew you'd ask questions. Just . . . be careful who you ask unless you're trying to torture them."

29
COLTON MCINNEY

WHEN COLTON LEFT THE MURDER SITE, MONTGOMERY STILL hadn't been by to pick up the body. So, he had to leave a tech with a rifle standing outside the house. This wasn't how things worked in normal towns, but every corpse had to go to the Montgomery Family Funeral Home. It was an actual law. Colton had no doubt that it was because of the stuff Amity had told him, but today, it meant that some twenty-year-old young woman with a rifle in her hand and a pistol in her lap was sitting on a plastic lawn chair outside a murder victim's house.

And Colton had to bite his lip when she said, "I'll put that cougar down if it comes back. It's not right to chew on people like that."

"What's your name?" he asked. "I'm still new here."

"Suzie Adams, Deputy Colton," she said, using his first name since there were already two McInneys—the sheriff and a tech.

Colton wasn't sure how long a person needed to be dead before they woke up. Amity said it took a long while, and he was hoping she was right. He looked at the young woman and shook his head. "Ms. Adams, if anything weird happens—"

"Salt shells and regular bullets, sir. I have spares." She met his eyes. "Miss Barrow, the last one, talked to all of us in the department about a journal article that salt shells stop perps as well as buckshot, and the last mayor said it's more cost efficient for the sheriff's office."

Colton stared, mutely, processing the lies that would be necessary to live here and keep the citizens safe. He nodded, thinking of the salt Amity had poured on the floor at her place. "I heard about that article. Practical decision, too, better for the environment."

"That's what I said!"

"Call me if you get spooked or have trouble or hear anything strange," he ordered. "I'm going to run over to the mayor's office and get the key for the hearse."

"It's a nice day, and dead folks don't bother me none," Suzie said with a shrug. She paused before adding, "You ought to get used to calling us by our given names, Deputy Colton. We're a family here. No one leaves the force unless it's to retire."

"Thanks, Suzie." He looked at her, smiling and content, and had to wonder if she'd feel the same way about the dead if she was aware of exactly what gnawed on Jenni, but he wasn't about to ask. Seeing the pain Christopher had been in made him glad he'd joined the council because he was too damn curious to avoid asking questions all the time. It was why he was an officer of the law. People teased that it was on account of his family name, but he was interested in the law because he wanted to understand why things happened and figure out how to keep people safe.

He drove into the center of town and made his way to the mayor's office. He'd not had business with the last mayor, but he remembered him. Seeing Liz Barrow there was strange, but so was seeing messages in lipstick and women with no throats and dead folk that vanished.

"Colton!" Liz was in the reception area with her secretary.

"Mayor Liz." He nodded, hat in hand, and waited to be introduced to the secretary.

"Chelly, this is Colton. Colton, Chelly."

"Ma'am," he said with another nod. He was pretty sure that Miss Chelly wasn't on the council, and he wasn't willing to give her a headache.

"His daddy was one of our townsfolk," Liz was saying. "His mama and him moved on, but Colton has come back and joined Chris McInney in the sheriff's office."

"Mayor Liz, if I could speak to you a moment about a matter of some importance, I would much appreciate it."

Liz nodded.

Chelly smiled and said, "Well, I'm just headed over to grab lunch for us. Can I get you anything Colton?"

"No, ma'am. Thank you, though."

Once she left, he turned to Liz. "Dead person gnawed up Jenni McCormick. I need the spare hearse keys, and if you could notify whoever all needs to know, I'd be much obliged."

Mayor Liz stared at him, blinked, and said, "Well, then. I guess you joined the council if you can keep all that in your head."

"Ma'am."

"Stop that. We're the same damn age, Colton." Liz scowled. "How bad?"

"Throat missing. Just one body. Message on the wall that—"

"In *blood*?"

"Lipstick. It says 'I'm sorry.'" He stared at her, figuring she understood better than him what it all meant.

"So, they've killed at least two others if they can write that." Liz sat down and started taking notes. "Remorse. That's a good two- or three-weeks Hungry Dead. We'll need a census, door-to-door on who's missing from about six weeks back. We ought to find the victims that way, too. At least one should be easy to find. Fresh woken ought not think to hide their leftovers."

Colton stared at her, a bit disgusted. "Leftovers?"

"Colton, this is reality in our town. If you can handle it, there are upsides. If you're squeamish, though?" She waited for him to look at her before continuing, "Take advantage of the ability to get the hell out of Dodge." She scowled. "My mother killed a bunch of people to raise them. My sister's dead. My gran and—"

"Teresa was—"

"Murdered," Mayor Liz said calmly. "She also ate my mother. Rebekkah . . . decided that the dead would get their due, and she didn't step in when . . ."

"I'm sorry. I . . . Amity told me some things, but I . . . seems impossible." Colton sat, feeling a lot less prepared for how calmly everyone dealt with things that were horrific.

"I'd have let them kill her, too," Liz said, looking a lot like Rebekkah in that instant. "She killed my *sister.* She killed her own mother."

"I'm sorry for your loss," he said, feeling awkward but still needing to say it.

"I won't tell you that you'll get used to it," Liz said, lowering her pen finally. "What I'll say is that if you stay, you are safe from every disease but age. Life here is idyllic most of the time, but when it's not. . . you need to be prepared for crowd control, ugly death, and a lot of lies."

Then, Mayor Liz opened a desk drawer and gave him the keys. "Please stop in and tell Miss Elaine that you'll be borrowing the car. I'll notify the others, and then when Byron and Rebekkah are home, they'll handle it."

She was already on the phone by the time he stood and walked away—and all Colton could think was that the trade-off might be too much for him. Whatever the Hungry Dead was, it was monstrous, and the town counted on the Undertaker and Graveminder to deal with it.

Could he do that? Did he want to?

He thought about Amity as he made his way over to the Montgomery Famittaly Funeral Home. The thought of her facing the thing that bit Jenni McCormick turned Colton's blood cold. He needed to talk to Amity, and to Byron and Rebekkah. First though, he had to go pick up a dead woman, so the tech who was guarding her from "mountain lions" could go home.

At least the dead stayed . . . Colton paused. The dead were to stay dead for a year. Not a few hours. Something was off, and damned if he knew what to do about it.

☙ 30 ❧

AMITY BLUE

As she walked to the gate to side-by-side with Death, Amity was saddened that it would be too long until she could return here—and by the reality that when she did, it would be because Rebekkah was dead.

"I had a thought," Charles said, his tone revealing that this thought was far from a surprise. "There is a way to make an exception to the rule."

Amity paused and an uneasy feeling swept over her as she looked up and saw Charles' smile. It was the smile of a man whose machinations were leading to exactly the result he'd hoped.

"The next Graveminder can only *visit* once, but there are no rules as to how long that visit must be." He spoke in a casual tone, as if the subject wasn't of any particular interest to him. "Traditionally, they've always been quite young, far too young for their dear mamas or grandmamas to leave them behind, but you, Miss Blue, are not a child. You could stay a while."

Rebekkah stopped mid-step. "No. Absolutely not. Amity you can't—"

"She can, my dear," Charles said, cutting her off mid-objection.

"Amity is not a child. She's a woman, with the right to choose her own path."

"But . . . What about Colton?" Rebekkah asked. "I thought you and he . . ."

"We talked. He asked for space," Amity's voice had an edge of hurt that embarrassed her. "Apparently, being forced to crave me was a turn-off or maybe it was the dead dude."

"Amity—"

"Don't, please." Amity met her gaze.

Rebekkah stepped up to Charlie. She put one hand on his chest, and he promptly covered it with his own hand. "She's my friend. I need you to keep her safe."

"Don't you trust me, Rebekkah?" Charles' smile was the look of predators before they attack.

"Sometimes."

"Go catch the lost child over there among the living." He stepped backward and beckoned to Amity. "Ms. Blue, would you stay?"

"Maybe." She wasn't ready to decide, so she started walking again. Either way Byron and Rebekkah were going home.

Charles crooked his arm. "I'm sure my subjects would love to meet you. Shall we continue the tour?"

Without a word, Amity laid her hand on Charles' arm. He was dressed casually—for Amity—but he was still every bit the man with the charming old-world manners.

"Bek?" Byron urged as he re-joined her. "What's going on?"

Rebekkah filled him in, gestured as they walked with their very armed escorts. The objection Amity expected didn't come.

Instead he said, "Amity doesn't follow anyone's rules but her own. I almost feel a little sorry for the old bastard."

"But things here—"

"They aren't safe at home either," Byron reminded her. His smile when he met Amity's gaze looked anything but worried. "It's her choice," he said. "We have a killer to stop."

Amity smiled back. He knew her in a way that few did, first as a friend, then a lover, and now a friend again. His regard made her feel brave—just as Rebekkah's worry made her feel loved.

They walked in silence to the tunnel, following a woman who obviously was in charge. The guards all looked at her for orders both here and in the bar. She was pretty but intimidating. She had a pair of tight jeans, a brown button-up shirt, weathered cowboy boots, and an equally battered hat. "What's going on, Undertaker?"

The woman pointed her gun at the tunnel mouth, which was glimmering like a light show was about to erupt out of it. Amity immediately liked the woman

"Someone's here," Rebekkah said, stepping closer. "Tell Alicia, and let's get out of here."

"There's someone in the tunnel," Amity said, drawing the woman's gaze to her. "Bek says we ought to get gone."

"I can see you," the woman, Alicia, said, her eyes widening. "You weren't there earlier, and now I see you . . . Someone tell me *why can I see her?* Charlie? Byron? What's going on?"

"We need to get them to safety," Charles said. "All the answers of this that you want, Alicia, but first . . ." He nodded toward the tunnel mouth.

Every guard raised a gun at the tunnel. Alicia hadn't lowered her gun or relaxed. She met Charles' gaze and said, "I'll be by later."

Then she looked around and smiled at the attentive rows of armed men. "Undertaker!" Alicia stepped closer to him. "What's going on?"

But Byron clearly couldn't deal with both the living and the dead Graveminder at once. He took Rebekkah's hand and said, "Hold on! Once it opens, we go."

"Montgomery is correct. Get out of here," Charles said. "Amity?"

"I'm staying in the land of the dead," she decided, and since no one had offered her one, she asked, "Gun?"

Alicia tossed one her way, a silvered pistol that looked like a Wild West prop. "Fully loaded," she said, not lifting her gaze from the tunnel. "Get her to safety, Charlie."

"Alicia . . ." Amity started.

"*Later*. Boys, get her clear of that. Him, too." Alicia glanced at her and held her gaze. "Please? Too many targets here, and they"—she nodded at Rebekkah and Byron—"need to get gone through the gate."

Then a hand reached out as the mouth of the tunnel cleared of whatever glow was there. Rebekkah reached out and grabbed the man's hand to free him from the tunnel. As she started to pull the dead man out of the tunnel, Charles pulled Amity into his embrace.

"Byron!" Rebekkah called out. She seemed to be falling forward into the tunnel, as if it was sucking her inwards.

Byron grabbed a hold of her with both hands, dropping his pistol in the process, and they vanished as a stranger started to step out of the tunnel.

"Get *her* gone, too, Charlie!" Alicia yelled.

That was the last thing Amity saw before the world faded, and she knew that she had been transported somewhere else in a moment.

✽ 31 ✽
ALICIA BARROW

THE MAN WHO HAD PULLED REBEKKAH BARROW INTO THE tunnel stepped out, looking far more familiar than Alicia could have imagined. She'd woken up next to him more than any other person in her life or in her afterlife, and she was responsible for his death.

"*Conner?*" Alicia asked in a low voice.

"Wife." Her dead husband scooped up Byron's gun, checked the chambers, and held it loosely. Then he lifted it, sighted at her, looking down the barrel.

Without thinking, Alicia lifted her own guns and aimed.

Before she could fire, he make a *tsk*-ing sound.

"Wouldn't try that, wife." He grinned, a look that used to make her feel warm inside. "If I shoot you, you're dead. None of this temporary death nonsense. My aim is true, still, and the bullets I fire mean you don't wake up here in Charlie's world."

She raised a hand to tell her boys to stand down. Conner was a lot of things, but she'd always been shot-for-shot with him when it came to sharp-shooting. His aim was true, even though his heart hadn't been.

"Hell, maybe that's the best plan," Conner said. "What do you say?"

"To shooting me? No." Alicia's hand itched. Her odds were about fifty-fifty as to hitting him first, and she's been itching to shoot him since they'd been alive.

"Why shouldn't I just put a bullet between those pretty eyes of yours?" Conner stepped closer, tapped the gun barrel to her forehead.

Alicia stepped to the side. It was that or shoot him. Repeatedly. And as much as she hated the thought of not-shooting him, logic was whispering that caution was essential just now.

"How are you even *here*?" she asked, keeping distance between them and her voice as casual as she could manage.

"*Undertaker*, doll. I just opened a door," he gestured behind him. "Ain't no different than when we were alive. Took longer, but I got it open. I came for you. You didn't think I was going to leave you here with that *creature*."

"Charlie's not a creature. He's—"

"Not a man." Conner's light tone fled as his temper slipped a bit more. "Whatever he is, he ain't human. He's not a *man*."

"He's Death. I know what he is." Alicia's knees felt weak, and she was fairly sure she was trembling.

"Do you?" Conner pressed. "How well do you know him, wife?"

Her husband, a man she hadn't seen since she'd caused his death, wasn't a gentle man, wasn't a kind man, but there had been years when he was *her* man. If not for her duty, she wasn't sure she'd have accepted his marriage proposal. That was the secret that she had never shared with a soul, living or dead: she wasn't mourning Conner.

Alicia had been staying behind in the land of the dead because she was happier without her husband.

"Did you miss me?" he asked.

Alicia snorted. "Not one damn bit."

She'd had no desire to spend eternity with the man she'd wed well over a hundred years ago. They were only together a decade, pulled together by duty. She'd cared for him. She'd lusted for him. She'd been sure he would keep her safe. None of that made him the one she'd have chosen for herself.

And he'd lied.

And he'd cheated.

And he'd hit her.

She didn't miss being married.

"What are you doing here?" she asked.

Conner smiled, and it was not a kind look on him. "Came to see the bastard that murdered me." Conner looked her up and down. "And the woman he tried to take from me. Maybe it's time for a new law around here. What do you think, wife?"

A chill came over Alicia. For all that she'd stood against Charlie, she wasn't interested in seeing him overthrown. She liked things the way they were; it was why part of why she stayed.

"No."

"Still loyal to him, then?" Conner prompted.

Without thinking it through, she confessed the secret she'd held most of her life and afterlife: "I was *his* first. Before I married you, I was *with* him. I didn't want to go to my wedding bed without knowing the touch of a man who actually loved me."

She heard muttered curses behind her, and she knew, later, she'd need to talk to her boys for that admission. She hoped they trusted her enough not to hate her. For now, she lowered the gun in her hand and looked at Conner.

"Go back to where you were, Conner. I'm happy here, and there's no one who wants you here."

"You're still my wife," he said, voice cold in ways that sparked memories best left forgotten. "My place is with you."

"Till death do we part," she whispered. She forced herself not to flinch as memories of his temper rose up. Bruises. Fists. That's what followed his cold voice. Alicia stared at him and declared. "That was the vow, but I'm dead. So are you, Conner."

And Conner smiled again. "And how is Charlie? Weaker lately, is he? Vulnerable perhaps?"

A horrible truth started to come over her. "*That's* why you're here? Because he's weak enough to attack?"

"Because I *made him weak.* Took too many years," Conner said, "but I'm back because I found a way to weaken him long enough to open the gate. Now that I broke through, I can hurt him, and I found my way here to do it. You're *my wife.*"

Alicia lifted her gun again and aimed at her dead husband. "I'm a widow."

"Mine."

She steadied the shaking in her hand. "No man owns me. Not you. Not him."

"Come with me," he half-asked, half-ordered. "I made mistakes, but a century without you gave me time to change. I'm a different man, a better man."

She started to turn around, flanked by her boys who stood at her sides as resolutely as before. And in seeing them, Alicia remembered who she was, who she had made herself in the centuries since her death. She glanced back and warned Conner, "Just so you know, around here? *I* am the thing that scares men. I protect the dead. I will protect Death, too. You stay out of my way, Conner, or you will discover exactly how much I've changed."

Then Alicia whispered a prayer that her great-granddaughter and Byron were safe in Claysville—and Charlie was safe somewhere with the new girl.

"It doesn't have to be like this," Conner said.

"Go away," Alicia said, but she didn't look back.

After a moment of quiet, Frankie Lee told her, "He left. Walked toward the 1930s."

Charlie's preferred era.

Alicia Barrow hadn't felt afraid often the last two centuries and change. She did her bit here and there to keep Charlie on his toes, and she enjoyed a good bottle of booze and a long nap more than any grown ass woman probably ought to do. Given a minute to ponder her afterlife, Alicia would probably say that it was a far better thing than being alive had been.

In this particular moment, however, she felt like she was a scared girl facing down the first of the Hungry Dead she'd met. Over in the living world, dead folk could be downright terrifying. They bit and snarled, slavered, and vanished. Their minds were wholly unpredictable in their ethereal forms, but they were an inevitable threat.

Today that felt like Conner: unpredictable, threatening, and vanishing.

"Boss?" Frankie Lee asked.

She shot her gaze his way. Her voice wasn't ready for extra use, and she wasn't sure what she'd do if her indiscretions with Charlie cost her the support of the men who'd had her back in troubles these last long years.

"We need to tell Mr. D," Frankie Lee added. "Johnny and Milt can go over, or we can all guard you over. We"—he gestured to the dozen or so men that surrounded her—"think maybe leaving you alone until we get a handle on this whisker-nutted jackal's plans isn't really a good idea."

"Whisker-nutted?" she echoed.

"Ma'am." His lips quirked in a smile. "Pretty, smart, terrifying lady like you might not know the signs, but that man there clearly has whisker-nuts."

Alicia allowed a smile. "And dare I ask?"

Johnny, a fellow who was better with a blade that anyone reasonable ought to be, nodded. "Like acorns from old squirrels. Nothing useful in them, you see. Probably has to talk himself through even taking a decent piss."

"You do realize he was my husband." Alicia felt her stress fade a bit as they walked.

Johnny spat before looking her in the eye. "That could explain why you're so ornery, boss. Can't imagine a whisker-nutted jackal would do right by you. Well, I'd imagine just about any man would be better than that. Women have needs."

"Oh really?" She saw the crux of what he was saying, but she waited.

"Makes sense to bed the old bastard," Johnny finished. "You two always spark like a good barn fire in the dry season. Makes sense he was able to tend those needs."

The expressions on the other men were equally friendly.

Milt nodded. "And it's one more thing we can threaten him over, I figure. Been a while since I could play angry big brother."

Cletus tried to keep a straight-face as he added, "Might be that we want to ask if he's planning on making an honest woman of you."

"You are a widow," Milt added.

Alicia open and closed her mouth. There were a lot of things she thought she could expect of them, but this teasing wasn't it.

Frankie Lee said, "We're at your side in this life or any that come after, 'licia. Who you bed down with is *your* business, not ours. We might mock your taste a bit, but you're still a helluva shot and a fair boss."

"Come on," she said, rather than engaging in some sort of feelings-talking that some of them tried to trick her into. "No one gets left alone until we figure out what damage whisker-nuts can do here."

"Dibs on best man," Cletus added.

She rolled her eyes. "Ladies have women stand for them usually."

"Not seeing any of us wearing a dress, boss," Frankie Lee teased. "But then again, wasn't expecting you to get hitched either."

Alicia snorted. "Me either. Once was more than enough. I don't think I'm exactly the marrying kind."

For a moment Frankie Lee looked more relieved than even Alicia felt, but all he said was "Glad to hear it."

Whatever there was with Charlie, whatever there had been with Conner, and whatever sparks she felt now and again, Alicia had learned back in the 1800s that marriage meant rules—and she simply didn't see the need to listen to anyone's rules but her own.

32
AMITY BLUE

"WHAT JUST HAPPENED?" AMITY ASKED, LOOKING AROUND AT what appeared to be a bar, but not the one she'd visited with Charles before. Her stomach felt sick, and her whole body ached. It was like the onset of something awful—or what she imagined "the flu" felt like. She'd read about it, but Claysville residents didn't get sick.

"I've relocated us to my preferred hideaway." Charles gestured around the nearly empty space. It was akin to stepping onto a set for a historical film; it didn't look quite real.

He continued, "No one will interrupt us here, and Miss Barrow—well, the Misses Barrow—will deal with the problem children for a while."

"So, they're just your private army or something? Risk them, and . . . what will you be doing?" Amity tried to keep her voice steady, but she felt like she was going to puke. The sensation of squeezing in the space between time and place was nauseating.

Charles motioned to a bartender who had appeared as if summoned into existence. The man had the majority of out-of-time suit, not dissimilar from what Charles had been wearing earlier. The man was lacking a suitcoat, but he had the vest, shirt, cravat. A watch chain caught her eye, glinting gold that didn't seem to be an accessory for a bartender.

As she studied him and tried to convince her body to relax, Charles ordered them drinks and leaned against the bar. "Drink this. It'll help. Live people don't usually travel the way of the dead."

Amity realized that Charles looked exhausted. "And the dead don't carry passengers?"

He nodded curtly.

As they watched the bartender pour, Amity thought about the dead guy, Michael, outside of her home and outside Gallagher's. He'd turned into mist and vanished when shot. "So that's how the dead move? Mist?"

"Mist. Smoke. Fog. Mortals explain it in varying terms, but the dead have no form. They may convince themselves that they do when they are *here* or well-nourished over there, but . . ." Charles gave a half-shrug before sliding her a highball glass with a generous pour in it. "You aren't dead, dear one, so that was . . . challenging. I wasn't entirely sure I could manage it. I've long thought it might work, but had no excuse to try. You appear to still be alive, so it worked."

Amity laughed, and then saw his expression. Charles was not smiling.

"There was a chance it would *kill* me?"

He nodded once. "But here we are, safe now. I will be keeping you safe, Amity Blue. Every last body here will step in front of you to protect you, if necessary. That is my will, and so it is. And over there, among the living, Rebekkah will return to town, and Byron will froth and foam like a rabid thing, protecting her."

He downed his drink, and she noticed that his hand shook. "And the stranger at the g—"

"Alicia will need to speak to him before I can," Charles said, sounding irritated at his own words. "They have unfinished business."

"So, you know who he is?"

"You will find that there aren't many things about those who are born in *that* town that I don't know sooner or later," Charles said, clearly trying to sound more relaxed than he was. "And I do know my Graveminders. Both the deceased and the living Miss Barrow have their own matters to address, so tell me, what would *you* like to do tonight?"

Amity paused. She was the next Graveminder, drinking a beer that didn't exist anywhere else, and hanging out with Death—who was watching her for an answer. All this talk of death, people with guns, dead guys at her home, it all made her want to do something to feel alive.

"Dance with me," she ordered.

"With pleasure." He led her to the empty dance floor in the empty bar and at a gesture a familiar song begin.

"Mr. D? Charles? Charles?" Amity leaned in closer to him. "Is any of it really your name? Or . . ."

"Wearing the same name forever gets tedious, so right now, it is. Don't you ever want to change your . . . *everything*?" He trailed his fingertips over her cheek. "Discover something new? Do something you've never done?"

Amity made her living by flirting. She'd thought it made her immune to the easy charisma of most anyone. She'd been wrong. Her voice was breathy as she asked, "Is there anything new when you've been around as long as you have?"

"You're new." He grinned, looking younger and more dangerous in that moment.

She laughed, but she didn't move out of reach. "Yeah, right. How many Graveminders have there been?"

"Twelve." He slid his hand into her hair. "You're not a Graveminder yet, though. You're a beautiful woman who chose to linger in the land of the dead. No one else has ever done that, Amity Blue. You're definitely *unique*."

"Oh."

"How many women do you know who've danced with Death himself?" he tempted, voice deep and rich like the most exquisite chocolate. "Ah, you're intrigued already, aren't you? Shall I tell what I want? The things I expect to make happen after this night? We can both enjoy something truly new, and wouldn't that be just *delicious?*"

Amity wasn't fool enough to believe that she could trust him, but she wasn't going to refuse a bit of fun either. There would be time enough to deal with the downsides of whatever her role was to be now that she was the next Graveminder. And as much as she thought he intended her to believe he meant sexual innuendo, she wasn't sure there was anything new to that when you were as old as Death.

"What could possibly be new to you?" she asked.

"Why, living, my dear. Living would be positively original," he answered with a low laugh. "Care to join me?"

He pulled her close, and Amity snaked her arms around him so she could cup the back of his head.

His laughter was a hot breath against her neck. "No formal waltzing then?"

She grabbed one of his hands and guided it to her hip.

"If we're dancing, dance like you mean it," she ordered, and then she slithered her body against his and lost herself in the music. "Dance like we're *living*."

"As you wish."

33
REBEKKAH BARROW

REBEKKAH WAS SHAKEN AS THEY CROSSED THROUGH THE TUNNEL home. The man who had been trying to reach out to her during the tunnel crossing was gone. For the first time, he wasn't reaching for her in the tunnel. Rebekkah was certain that was him who had stepped out of the tunnel and into the land of the dead, but that didn't explain why he'd been able to open the passage.

"Hold on," Byron repeated over and over as he hurried them toward Claysville.

When they stepped into the funeral home, she grabbed Byron. "What was that? Who? Why?"

"Do you mean the dead guy who stepped out of the tunnel or it sucking you in?" Byron held her for a moment, and then released her and moved her away from the mouth of the opening as he shut the passageway. He glared at it, as if expecting to be followed, even as it was sealed now.

Then he looked at her and opened his arms. "All I could think was that you were going to be lost to me."

"I was scared," she admitted. "But you grabbed me."

"I will never let anyone or anything hurt you while I am alive," he swore. "And not just because of the Undertaker and Graveminder rules, Bek. I love you."

Rebekkah nodded. "You too."

Byron grinned. He said it a dozen or more times for every once she managed. She felt it, and honestly, she'd loved Byron Montgomery for most of her life, but the words were hard. There was this fear, absurd maybe, that by saying it, she was risking someone or something stealing him away. Maylene. Jimmy. Ella Mae. People she loved kept dying.

She drew him down so their lips were all but touching, and then she whispered, "I love you."

Byron closed the distance and kissed her with a fervor that was a reminder that they never knew how long they had. No one did, but her job—retrieving the dead—and his role in defending her meant they had a risk level atypical of a traditional life in Claysville.

Everyone else was safer because they risked dying.

Every kiss they shared could be the last one.

Rebekkah held tightly to Byron, leg around him and hands clutching the back of his shirt

When he released her, Byron took her hand in his. "We're safe."

"Michael? The dead guy? He's still out there." Rebekkah motioned toward the town. "And Amity is trapped, and—"

"I will go back for Amity tomorrow, but Bek, unless it's to take this Michael person over, you are staying right here."

And uncharacteristically, Rebekkah didn't feel like arguing. She wasn't ready to deal with the way she felt about taking Amity to the land of the dead—or the burst of fear she'd felt as they left her there. Until that moment, Rebekkah was sure that leaving Amity there was the right choice. Finding out that the world was so different from what she'd known for her whole life had to be a shock to Amity. It had been for Rebekkah, but for her, at least, she'd known that her grandmother frequented funerals, whispering special words and pouring drinks onto the soil. The significance of those acts was a surprise; Rebekkah had thought them superstitions. Still, she'd had some clue—and she'd had Byron.

She couldn't imagine surviving the world she'd discovered without him at her side to lean on. She'd fought against it for almost her whole life, but being with Byron was as essential as air or food.

"She'll be okay," he said, drawing her attention away from the phone she'd just lifted. "I don't like Charles, but we both know he'll keep her safe."

"It's not that," Rebekkah admitted. "It's just going through this alone. Colton—"

"Will figure it out, or she'll find someone else," Byron reminded her. He was always the calm to her worrying. "Graveminders have Undertakers, and she'll have a partner to help her through this."

Rebekkah kissed him and whispered, "I love you. You're a good man, and if I was Amity, I'd hate me for stealing you from her."

"You can't steal what's already yours, and I've been yours since we were in high school. It just took you about a decade to admit it." Byron pulled her in and kissed her.

These post-land of the dead kisses were a habit they'd fallen into on accident after one of their trips between worlds. She always felt chilled when she came back to the land of the living. Colors dimmed, and the world became duller. Only Byron was vivid to her in this world here, and he repeatedly assured her that he certainly didn't mind taking a few moment to kiss her senseless.

His phone chimed. Then, hers buzzed. The blinking of his phone and hers made their moment pass too quickly. Whatever they missed in Claysville wasn't good.

"I want to stop at the files and see if there's anything on Michael," she told him when they pulled apart. "Then, we'll start tracking him. I don't *feel* him, though. That's worrying."

She didn't feel anything, no tug leading her to the dead man. "Maybe Charles was wrong."

"Or lying," Byron suggested mildly.

The thought wasn't entirely impossible. Charles wasn't forthcoming on the best of days.

Rebekkah started scrolling through her messages, as Byron did the same: Chris. Colton. Liz. Colton again. Daniel. Elaine. Colton again. The list of names was as worrying as the content. They all said some version of "Call ASAP" or "Awakened."

Byron started up the stairs to talk to Elaine, and Rebekkah called her cousin.

"Rebekkah?" Liz asked.

"Where was the attack?" she asked, not really ready to deal with Liz Barrow. She wasn't responsible for her mother's crimes, but Rebekkah still had a bundle of rage in her belly. And it was mixed up with a lot of guilt. Rebekkah watched her Aunt Cissy die, allowed it in fact. She could tell herself she had no other choice, but the truth was that she hadn't looked for one.

"McCormick's Pub, out on Cherry Horse Lane." Liz sounded calm, if a bit brusque.

"Headed there now," Rebekkah said. "We just got back from . . . that place."

No one in the Barrow family ever really spoke overtly of the land of the dead. A part of Rebekkah thought that there was a guilt at being chosen—ad a guilt at not being chosen. Liz and her now-deceased sister had known for their whole lives, so maybe it was easier for them. Rebekkah hadn't known until this year, and her knowing came with an awareness that Cecilia murdered for it and both Teresa and Ella Mae died for it. Maylene, of course, was killed by the dead, so Rebekkah suspected that being the Graveminder was a definite curs.

"Be careful," Liz said, but the words sounded like an order.

"I picked Amity," Rebekkah assured her. "Even if I die, it won't be your problem."

At that, Liz sighed and said in a hard voice, "I said 'be careful' because you are all that's left of my family, Rebekkah. Not 'be careful' because I'm a selfish bitch like my mother." Then she took a deep audible breath and said, "Please let us know when you've contained the danger."

And she hung up before Rebekkah could reply. Rebekkah looked at her phone and felt the stirrings of hope that she and Liz could find peace. They'd never been close, but maybe they could be in time.

Phone tucked away, Rebekkah went upstairs to find Byron looked as tense as she felt. The bag he had, with injections for stunning the dead and assorted other things, was slung over one shoulder and the strap of a rifle over the other.

"Talked to Liz," she told him.

"Colton took the body bus," he answered. "I asked Elaine to call in Allan, our temp mortician. She shouldn't have had to wait, you know? I can't not do what I need as your"—he lowered his voice—"Undertaker for that part of our obligations, but Mrs. McCormick shouldn't be laying there dead and alone. With Dad gone, I should've hired, but I thought could handle both as easily as he did. . ."

Rebekkah squeezed his hand. Whatever else there was to say, it wasn't here. If he was asking for hiring, she wasn't arguing. The dead for the whole town were handled here at his family funeral home. There was no other funeral home, so it was all their responsibility.

"I hate to have someone move *here*," he added as they stepped outside. "Claysville's no place to come to if you can avoid it."

"I know." Rebekkah climbed into the truck, a gift from a dead girl. After Daisha had killed her parents, there were no other heirs, and when she was sound of mind—a state that, admittedly, resulted from murder and taking a bite of Byron's dad—she had enough guilt to fill a few lifetimes. The beat-up ugly truck, still primer gray, was one of the ways Daisha had tried to make amends. It didn't undo anything, but the teen girl hadn't asked to be made a killer. She'd been a victim, murdered and then raised from her death by Cecilia Barrow.

"Do you ever miss her?" Rebekkah asked a few minutes into the drive.

"Who?"

"Daisha."

He gave her a hard look. “No. She killed people, including Maylene.”

“She didn’t mean to,” Rebekkah protested. “They never do.”

“Bek?” Byron’s voice had that tone that said he didn’t like what he was about to say. “Your eyes are turning.”

And Rebekkah nodded. She felt it, that tug in her belly that meant that there was a dead person nearby, someone was in need of her attention. She could see a trail that shifted like smoke in the air in front of them. “We’re headed the right direction. Faster, please.”

Byron sped up, bumping over a rutted country road toward the Hungry Dead.

34
COLTON MCINNEY

Colton was pulling in back at McCormick's Pub when he heard the scream. It was followed by a shot. A second shot. And another scream. Colton ran toward where the tech, Suzie, was seated when he left.

She was there, shaking. Her rifle was in hand, and her eyes were wide in terror.

He drew his own weapon, although he still wasn't sure how reliable bullets were on dead things. "Talk to me, Suzie."

"Something came up behind me." She looked hell, missing a chunk of shirt and shoulder. "But the only thing behind me was a corpse, Deputy Colton. Dead ladies don't bite folks. Everyone knows that." She laughed awkwardly.

"Must've been someone hiding in there that we missed." Suzie lowered her gun and put a hand to bloodied shoulder. "I don't know what they used."

"Could be." Colton looked around. Finding no one and nothing, he called the office. "Something attacked Suzie out here at McCormick's pub. I need the EMTs."

Once he hung up, he called Byron, hoping he was back from wherever and hoping that Amity was with them, too. He didn't like the idea of there being a second walking dead person out there and her unaware. As Montgomery's phone rang, Colton decided he'd make a few more calls.

"Montgomery," Byron answered.

"McCormick's. You and Rebekkah need to get here." Colton paused, feeling awkwardly like he ought to call Amity himself, but also like faster warnings were better. He added, "Tell Amity that it's another one of *them*."

Byron was silent for too long, and then said, "Amity's safe. She's not here but—"

"Then I'll call her at the bar or home," Colton snapped. "Just because she has a bag of salt—"

"She's not in our world," Byron clarified. "She stayed there."

Colton felt a sharp pain, a level of loss that he was almost embarrassed by. They hadn't known each other long, but he'd felt more for her than made sense. "She *died*?"

"No! She'll be back. . . probably." Byron's voice grew muffled, obviously speaking to someone else, and then he said, "We're about ten minutes out."

And he hung up. Colton glared at the phone. He had a helluva a lot more questions, and being hung up on wasn't amusing at all.

But Suzie's words drew his attention back to her. "Maybe the cat was silent, and I just thought it was a lady, you know?"

He nodded. "Makes sense."

The hell it did . . .

By the time the EMTs arrived, Montgomery and Rebekkah Barrow were there. They didn't speak to him.

Montgomery watched over her as she walked around the lot with her eyes turned silver and her feet gliding over the ground as if she was something other than human. Colton stayed beside Suzie, who was now wholly convinced a mountain lion ate the corpse and then attacked her while she was trying to guard the body of a dead woman. In fact, that was what she was currently reporting to the EMTs as they took charge of her. It was a fantastic story, and Colton was shaken by how easily they all accepted it.

Now that she was under the EMTs' care, Colton decided to check out the room where the puma supposedly ate the corpse. Despite knowing what he'd find, Colton had an unexpected bubble of hope as he stepped inside—not that there would be a badly mauled corpse but that there would be something, someone, a *body* there waiting.

The room looked like it had when he'd been there earlier: dingy. It was showing signs of age and patchwork efforts to hide the threadbare conditions. The words scrawled in lipstick were still there to read. The only change was the missing body.

"No signs of predation," Montgomery said from behind him.

Colton turned. "How do you deal with it?"

Montgomery shrugged. "You just do."

Rebekkah came in, eyes no longer human. How anyone could see her and think this was normal was beyond him.

"Michael and Jenni," she murmured. "I can see both traces."

"She died yesterday. Maybe the day before." Colton shook his head. "Amity said it takes more than a few weeks to wake."

Montgomery nodded, but his gaze was fixed on Rebekkah. To some degree, it always had been. Anyone in Claysville had seen that. This was more, though. He watched her like she was his mission in life, not just like a man in love.

Rebekkah wandered out of the room, a hound on the trail of prey, calling, "B, I can feel her. East. I need to go East. Help?"

Montgomery grabbed her, stopping her from running even as her legs were churning.

"Grab the door?" He grunted at the effort of stopping a flailing woman, and in the process, he looked like he was abducting her.

Colton followed and opened the truck door.

"East," she ordered.

And then they were gone, leaving him with no more answers than he'd had and a lot more worries. About Amity. About staying in Claysville. About what it meant if he did—or didn't.

35

AMITY BLUE

AMITY WAS OUT OF BREATH AND MORE RELAXED THAN SHE'D BEEN in forever, but then they stepped outside. He draped a suit jacket over her shoulders like it was a shawl, and despite her proclamations that she *still* didn't want to be treated like a lady of the past, she felt a warm rush of affection for his gentlemanly gesture.

"You weren't wearing a jacket," she pointed out.

"Someone delivered it, assuming I'd forgotten it at the house." He grinned. "I'm not sure the shock of a half-dressed Death will be easily erased."

"You really wear suits all the time?"

He shrugged, and she realized that even in his attempt to be casual, Charles looked like he belong in some elegant old world. Being clad in basic trousers and a plain shirt didn't change that.

They were in a city where horse-drawn carriages shared the road with 1960s automobiles and gunfighters chatted with gangsters. She tried not to stare in awe like some awkward country mouse, but as she stood in the midst of a city that was truly unlike anywhere else, she felt like she about to slip into shock. Inside the club, it had seemed exciting, but all of the sudden, she was overwhelmed by the wrongness of it all.

She had never even been outside the town limits at home. There were some that could leave Claysville. They always returned home, but they *left*. Others never managed to cross that line. Before she was the Graveminder-in-Waiting, she hadn't questioned the oddity of that. She'd seen television programs and movies, read books and magazines; she knew people didn't *literally* get trapped in a dead-end town. It was a metaphor.

In Claysville, however, it was literal. She'd been trapped in the same few miles her whole life, as had so many other people. Now, she was in what seemed like a boundless peculiar world. She couldn't move her feet.

"Walk with me, Amity Blue," Charles invited gently.

Mutely, she acquiesced. She took one step and then another. Soon, she was walking along the street with Charles, her hand tucked in the fold of his arm. At first, the city seemed endless, but after only a few blocks they were in a pristine, deserted park.

"Oh!"

In front of them was a fountain bubbling up from the ground. Moss-covered rocks large enough to use as seats clustered to the edge of it. The water trickled away in a stream. It was crystal clear and gurgled invitingly.

She kicked her shoes off and stepped into a stream that clearly should not appear a few city blocks from a club. Charles watched her with the sort of intense fascination that she'd craved for most of her life. That didn't mean she was going to accept his attention blindly. She hadn't missed the way he'd changed his entire look when she'd arrived in his world—or the revealing shock in both Rebekkah and Byron's reactions to both his clothes and the club they'd visited.

She stood, barefoot in the water, and looked at him. "Is any of it real? Are you?"

He didn't pretend to misunderstand. "I didn't draw your eye when you arrived, so I adjusted." He gave a slight barely there shrug. "You're pleased with the change."

"And this?" She kicked water in his direction.

"I redecorated a bit." He quirked his lips in a slight smile. "The chaos of the area seemed jarring to you, and I want you to be happy."

"Why?"

"Because each Graveminder matters to me intensely."

"Why?" She knew her blunt approach was off-putting to a lot of people, but somehow she thought that it was precisely right with Charles.

In a heartbeat, he was in the stream beside her, soaked to his knees. "Years ago, a few centuries actually, there was a woman. She found a way to cross from the land of the living to the land of the dead. Abigail was her name." His lips curled in a sad smile. "I fell in love. She was the first Graveminder. She didn't love me. I thought she might."

"So, you love all of the Graveminders?" Amity asked softly, her heart aching a little at the realization.

"I am *fascinated* with all of you," he corrected. "The role is carried by women with the traits Abigail had, and I loved those traits, so to some degree, I suppose my love is a part of that. I am half-in-love with each of you."

The words he spoke explained why Byron had lingered with her, too. She was like enough to the one he wanted that she was a fine substitute for Rebekkah. She was tired of being second choice.

"No," she said, turning her back to Charles. "We are not interchangeable. I'm not them. I'm a fucking *person*."

She started to walk away, not sure where she'd go but damn sure it wasn't here.

"I've never changed my world or my attire for anyone," he said. "Not since *her*."

Amity stopped, but she didn't turn around. The water swirled around their feet, and she tried to concentrate on it rather than the ache inside her. She was sick of not being in control of her life, of being a stand-in or second best.

"Do you find that you're drawn to the same type of man, Amity? Do you feel your body and heart react to men with traits in common?" His voice grew slightly louder. "Do you have some ideal that you can't quite define, but you hold every man up to it hoping the pieces fit?"

She swallowed, thinking of Colton.

Death was standing against her, his chest to her back. "I've met thousands of people in the afterlife. I've met a dozen Graveminders. I haven't changed for any of them. With you, Amity, I am about to *live*."

She looked back at him, true fear blossoming for the first time since coming here. "What does that mean?"

"When you have eternity, you have a lot of time to plan, my dear." He smiled, and Amity repressed a shiver. Then he added, "Once I was nothing, merely gas and flecks of potential in the universe. Then I was *made*. I became Mr. D, death ruling over this land of ghostly beings."

"They seem pretty real," she interjected.

"They do, don't they?" Charles preened as if she'd praised him. "And what makes them real is their dreams, their passions, their desperate grappling for meaning in their lives even after death."

"I guess . . ."

"*I deserve that*, too." Charles smiled the sort of smile that made terror creep over her, and then added, "And soon, I'll have it."

36

BYRON MONTGOMERY

BYRON HAD NONE OF THE HANG-UPS ABOUT WOMEN BEING IN charge that most of his friends had as a kid or a man. Maybe it was just because he was always meant to be tied to a Graveminder, but as a kid, he'd gone from following, leading, or being beside Ella and Bek. As an adult, he'd been chasing Bek for years of what felt like some sort of naked tag. They'd connect, and she'd vanish. Now, though, he had everything, and each time they had to deal with the Hungry Dead, he felt a terror he'd not known possible—and a resolve to defend the life, the woman, the joy he had.

Rebekkah did what she did for the dead, and for the town, but Byron did what he did for Rebekkah. It was fairly straight-forward. That didn't necessarily mean it was easy.

"I see her," Rebekkah whispered.

Byron skidded off the road as Rebekkah opened the door. He had learned that in pursuit of the dead, she was as illogical as a drunk with impulse control issues. The truck door was open and Rebekkah was already calling out to a woman with a bloody face.

"Jenni?" Rebekkah reached a hand out.

The dead lady paused.

"You were looking for me." Rebekkah walked closer, but by now, Byron had a gun in one hand and a loaded syringe in the other. *She* might trust the corpses, but he had increasingly become a "bullets first" kind of person.

It honestly complicated life that they found her so soon. He had no desire to take Rebekkah back to the land of the dead. Whatever had happened, whoever that was in the tunnel, Byron wanted to keep Rebekkah safe from it. Maybe he could convince her to keep this one in holding until they found Michael.

One trip. Two corpses. That was Byron's goal.

In front of them, the dead woman was so disoriented that she accepted Rebekkah's hand and accompanied her to the truck as meekly as a child. She shouldn't even be awake yet. The dead took a year to wake. That was the law, the magical law not some political nonsense.

"Can we contain her? Just until we find the other one and—"

"Byron!" Rebekkah looked at him with such fury that her eyes seemed to spark with little arcs of silver lightning.

"Things are off, Bek," he reminded her. "That business at the tunnel was weird, and she"—he pointed at the now-silent dead woman in blood-stained clothes—"ought to be dead still. If she's awake, she ought to be asking for food, drink, trying to gnaw on me."

Jenni, the dead woman, glanced at Byron. "You want me to bite you? There's a fee. I always charge for things I do with men, even Michael. He owes me. He did things that . . ." She scowled and looked at Rebekkah. "Am I dead?"

"I'll take you home," Rebekkah started.

Then, the woman began to scream. She dropped to the ground, tugging Rebekkah with her. She tried to crab-walk as if she were under attack now.

And she stared at Byron the whole time.

"Please! No! Michael! No no no no," she sobbed. Jenni tried to jerk free of Rebekkah's hand, but Rebekkah held on.

"Byron!" Rebekkah was holding the dead lady as if she was a tree, and Rebekkah was a koala on that tree. "Needle."

As he tried to get close enough to inject Jenni, Byron tried to avoid Jenni's kicks—and the one free hand she was using like claws to swipe at him. Luckily, she wasn't snapping her teeth.

"I'm sorry," Jenni yelled. "Please, don't hurt me. I won't tell anyone, Michael, please . . ."

Byron jabbed the needle into her upper arm and depressed the plunger. In moments, she was motionless, floating several inches off the ground. Rebekkah was breathing hard. She flopped on her back briefly.

"Something's broken," she announced.

"Your back? Leg? Don't move and—"

"With the curse," Rebekkah clarified, pushing to her feet without releasing the dead woman's hand. "Jenni ought to be motionless. She's *traumatized*."

"Kind of caught that, Bek."

Jenni didn't act like any other dead person he'd met. They were often fairly predictable. Not Jenni. Screaming? Panic attacks? That was not the reaction the Graveminder elicited.

In truth, Jenni should be still dead, and they ought to be able to bury and tend her, so she stayed dead. Since she was awake, a year early, Jenni ought to either be trying to bite or trying to get to the land of the dead. She shouldn't be having what appeared to be a flashback to her murder.

Rebekkah started steering the dead woman toward the truck. The act was akin to moving a body on a gurney, except this body was alert enough that she obeyed Rebekkah when told, "Sit in the truck."

It gave Byron the creeps—as did looking over to see the love of his life holding a dead lady's hand as they drove toward the funeral home.

Rebekkah didn't ever notice the blood, but he did. Jenni McCormick was a murder victim, but she'd also attacked the tech at the crime scene. The blood on her chin was not from being a victim. Her dress, face, and arms were blood-soaked.

It was all over Rebekkah, too. "Can we take her just to the mouth of the tunnel?"

"On our side? She'd be trap—"

"No," Rebekkah said. "To that side. Take her and come right back? I know you'd rather wait, but I feel an urgency in my stomach, as if I must hurry. I don't know why, but . . ."

"We'll take her now." As much as he didn't want to deal with whatever fucked up business was going on in the land of the dead, Byron was ready to see Jenni McCormick delivered to the afterlife—and hope that all that was left was capturing the Hungry Dead who had murdered Jenni.

He wasn't going to ponder why Jenni woke the day she died. He couldn't. It had to be a fluke because any other answer was terrifying.

37

AMITY BLUE

Amity wasn't sure what to think of Charles. On one hand, she was having the most fun she'd had in a long time. On the other, he was Death. If he were a regular guy, she'd be trying to decide if she was going to ask him in to her apartment—which reminded her that she wasn't sure where she was staying or anything else.

"Is there a hotel or something?" She felt in her pocket for her wallet. "I don't imagine credit cards work here, do they? I have a little cash, but I don't know how long Bek will be gone."

The reality of the situation started to settle on her.

"My home is large enough for you to stay as long as you want." Charles took both of her hands in his and studied her as if he were seeking answers in her eyes. "Unless I've offended you . . ."

"I don't really *know* you," she began.

"Then we'll correct that," he offered smoothly. "Perhaps, we can become fast friends, Ms. Blue. Tell me what you need in order to feel comfortable in my home."

"I'm not sure."

They walked a little further in silence, and Amity fought back the urge to go home to Colton. He night not make sense, but he wasn't some sort of star dust made into a man's shape or *whatever* Charles was.

He was handsome, alluring, and a part of Amity wondered if what drew her was simply the result of being born in a town cursed by death magic. A more hidden part wondered if it was her grief over losing her sister, her ex-lover, and friends. Was she longing for the man or what he represented?

A voice pulled her out of her thoughts. "I didn't know you had it in you, Charlie. Looking almost . . .*human*."

Alicia, the red-haired woman with a gun holster still slung around her hips, leaned against a tree at the bottom of the stairs to Charles' house. With exaggeratedly slow movements, she pushed away from the tree and walked toward them.

"To what do I owe the stress of your visit?" he asked.

The guards Amity had seen earlier still stood on either side of the door, but their attention was on Alicia. Two more strangers waited in the shadows. The one of the left looked like he was a contemporary of the gunslinger; the other looked like he belonged at the sort of clubs she once dreamed of visiting.

Charles turned his back to the woman and smiled at Amity. "I need to deal with this. Why don't you go inside?"

Amity was also far too curious for her own good.

The guards watched the pretty, red-haired gunslinger, who moved like someone who was more comfortable in a fight than anywhere else. And Alicia stared at Amity in blatant curiosity.

"Are you okay?" Amity asked, feeling instantly stupid. The woman was *dead*, armed, and had just faced the threat that Charles swept Amity away from. She obviously wasn't "okay."

"Alicia is the head of our little crime syndicate," he started.

"Who is she, Charlie?" The woman walked over to stand beside Amity. She narrowed her eyes, and then her gaze snapped to Charles. "Why is she here?"

Charles sighed. "Amity, meet Alicia. Alicia, this is Amity. She's Rebekkah's eventual replacement."

"Are you *sure*?" Alicia's hand dropped to the holster.

"Charles?" Amity prompted. His earlier remarks about her being able to die here came rushing back to her.

The nervousness in her voice obviously didn't escape Charles. He stepped in front of Amity. "Can you think of any other reason a living woman would be here?" He batted the woman's hand away from her gun. "Stop that. You'll frighten her, and then she'll think that you're some sort of base thug."

Alicia didn't smile, even though Charles' voice was teasing. Instead, she sounded frightened when she said, "She *sees* me, Charlie. Stop prancing around trying to impress her and think for a moment. She *sees* me. The Graveminders can't ever see me. We have rules, and that is an unbreakable rule."

No one spoke for a moment, and then Charles simply turned his back to Alicia and caught Amity's hand in his. He resumed ascending the stairs, and she went with him. He paused at the top and glanced over his shoulder. "Come on. We'll discuss whatever you need once we are safely inside."

And then he led Amity inside his house, moving at a remarkable speed.

Amity didn't understand the significance of her having seen Alicia, nor did she miss the flash of worry on his face or the way the guards stepped in front of the door as soon as they were inside.

38
CHARLES

CHARLES HAD FELT IT, THE RETURN OF THE MAN WHO'D BEEN battering the gates to this land for as long as he'd been expelled from it. He slipped through long enough to shoot Charles a few days ago, and Charles had shoved him out. This time, he was here to stay.

Conner.

He felt the change as the former Undertaker slid into their world.

My world.

Things began to set themselves right, and the energy that Charles had redirected to stop Conner from entering was back to the world and its upkeep, to his own strength. He hadn't realized how much it had taken out of him.

When Alicia came inside, he realized it was time to face the proverbial music. He'd spent so very long planning his exit that having it happen was almost anticlimactic. *Almost.*

"Ward?" Charles motioned for his trusted man-servant to leave as Alicia entered. "Would you see to whatever needs Ms. Blue has?"

Turning to Amity before she could object, he smiled and said, "I need to speak to Alicia for five minutes in private, and then perhaps, we can all reconvene."

Amity looked hurt, and he made note to amend that decrease in her trust. He took her hand. "The gentleman who was at the gate was Alicia's husband, my dear. I would like not to break *her* trust by speaking of him without her consent."

Mollified, Amity nodded.

Whatever fears or questions Ward had, all he did was meet Charles' eyes before departing with Amity in tow.

When the study door clicked closed, Charles relaxed infinitesimally. He was alone with Alicia, who had obviously already seen and spoken to Conner. She walked directly over to the whiskey, poured a glass and tossed it back before refilling the glass again.

Charles simply watched. She was the one who had rescued him, but she had no idea. She probably would be far from pleased, but she *was* his proverbial knight in modern armor. She was his hero, and soon, he was going to rejoice at the rescue she'd unwittingly enabled.

As soon as the door closed, she came over to him. "Conner is here."

"Yes." Charles stood and went to her. "I've tried to keep the door sealed against him. He hurt what is mine."

"Yours?" Alicia made a sound of derision. "He used that word, too. I'm *mine.* Not yours. Not his."

"He hurt you. I love you, and he injured you." Charles figured she deserved the words, and maybe it would ease her rage. "He hurt someone I treasure."

Instead of her usual reaction, Alicia sighed. "Many men did such things. Times were different."

It took more strength than Charles had thought he could have not to reach out. All he said was, "I could not have him near you, Alicia. I couldn't protect you in *that* world. I saw bruises on you. Often. There was nothing I could do, and you wouldn't speak of it."

"I thought you didn't know, that you believed I mourned him." Alicia refused to look away.

"You *did* mourn him," Charles corrected her. "At first you did.

Sometimes . . . you remembered the good parts. Mortals do that in grief."

She laughed, not like she was amused but in that way of laughter to prevent tears. "I have terrible luck with men. My taste is . . ." She gestured at him.

Charles stepped closer and took her hands in his. "I am not a man, Alicia. I am dust and function."

"You are far more than that, Charles." She looked up at him. "You have *become* a man."

He swallowed against the rush of emotion that welled up in him. If he were to blink into nothingness, this moment would make it all worthwhile. Death did not fall in love. It did not long for family or home. Death was without feelings. He *knew* that. A part of him that would never be a man—that part that was some infinite nothingness without form—remembered being nothing more than function shaped of dust. He was created one day, given purpose, and no one expected him to love—or be loved in return.

How could anyone?

But then Alicia kissed him as tenderly as she had when she was young and alive, and he forgot the many things that Death did not do.

"Why?" he asked.

Alicia walked away and poured two more drinks. "He can kill people here. He could kill *you.* That's my fault. I wondered if you . . . if I . . . was it worth it?"

"For me? Always."

Alicia smiled. "Death is a romantic. Who knew?"

Charles smothered a laugh. "Every Graveminder has likely guessed. Only you have loved me, though. In all these years."

"I seduced a handsome man. That's all." Alicia shrugged.

"That's not how I remember it, but if it results in your kisses, I will agree to your stance. It has been far too long since I was graced with such things."

"You still killed me," she pointed out, as if she had to remind herself that she felt no love these days.

"No," he corrected for the who-knew-how-many times, "there is a contract. You broke it. I could not control your death. I am not omnipotent, my dear."

"Fine." She leaned against him, and he knew that Alicia felt fear. She'd been bold as a Graveminder, bold in the land of the dead, but Conner was the *one man* who had harmed her. He was, however, also the only dead Undertaker who had tried to enter this world.

In doing so, he had set into motion changes that Charles was going to cherish. He had finished the process of setting Death free—and releasing the dead in Claysville in the process. All of them would wake. Everyone who died would rise.

That detail was regrettable.

Charles stood in peace with Alicia for longer than he expected to ever hold her again before she asked, "So now that he's here. . ."

"He is more than the rest. Different," Charles explained carefully. "He *can* kill people here. Wound me."

"He can . . ." She glared at him. "He's the one who shot you!"

Briefly, Charles nodded. "I pushed him back out, but he has grown stronger."

"Can he *kill* you?" Alicia sounded genuinely concerned, as if she hadn't been shooting him regularly.

He smiled and assured her, "No. I am eternal in one form or another."

"What, exactly, does that mean, Charlie?" Alicia was glaring, reminding him of a younger version of her, a living version. She'd shot him the very first time when she was still alive. Honestly, no one had yet shot him as often as she did.

Carefully, he told Alicia, "I wanted to keep him out. It weakened me, and there were complications, but Conner cannot kill me . . . or you."

"Can you . . ." Alicia shook her head, stepped away, and swore to herself. "Never mind."

"Are you asking me to murder your husband, Miss Barrow?" Charles gave her a faux shocked expression.

"Can *I* kill him then?" she asked.

"Unfortunately, no." Charles sent a summons to Ward. "Conner is now like me, an embodiment of Death. We cannot kill the other, and due to the nature of the contract no Undertaker can murder a Graveminder."

He tried not to think about the times when that clause had saved Alicia's life, but he saw her drawn expression, and he knew she, too, thought about it.

"So, we're stuck with him? And he can kill my men?"

Charles nodded. "No matter what he is now, though, I believe that you are still safe from him."

"What about Rebekkah?" Alicia asked.

"I'm not sure. She is, however, arriving, but I'd like her to stay in her world until we know," Charles announced.

"You *believe* I'm safe? You aren't sure if Rebekkah is?" Alicia had her gun in hand but not yet aimed at him.

He started, "I have a plan—"

"No." She aimed at him and ordered, "Send him back. Put things to rights. *Now.*"

Charles sighed. "Would you be so kind as to collect Rebekkah while I see to Ms. Blue?"

"I'm not done here." A look of jealousy, which Charles cherished, passed over Alicia's face.

"My dear—"

"What *is* Amity, Charlie? If I can see her she's not the Graveminder, and you *know* that."

He stood, looking at the door as it opened to reveal the appearance of the first of her kind. There stood Amity Blue, and she'd very obviously heard the question.

Charles looked between the two women, and then with a wide smile, he announced, "Amity Blue was *intended* to be the next Graveminder. She accepted, and had Connor not broken the terms, had he not lost his position as Undertaker, she would have been exactly that."

"But. . .?"

Charles poured three glasses and handed them around. Proudly, he continued, "But I added a loophole or three in the original contract."

Alicia snorted.

"You, my dear, are able to stay here because of it," he pointed out. "No other Graveminder did. That you did was possible because you hold a spark of love for *me* in your heart that is greater than what you feel for your Undertaker."

"Fine, but I *also* love leftover bathtub gin more than I love you, Charlie. Don't get too excited by the fact that you outrank that whisker-nutted jackal."

"As you say." Charles quirked a smile at her. He'd feared that Alicia's sass would be lost when faced with Connor's presence. He ought to have known better.

He smiled and turned to Amity. "And you, Amity Blue, wanted to be the Undertaker, not the Graveminder, to cross back and forth at will, to be the gun that defends the face of Death in that world."

Amity shrugged. "So?"

"When Conner returned, the rules changed. My loopholes became manifest as it were." Charles looked at two of the three people who were making centuries-old plans come into fruition. "Should I need to travel to the world of the living, Amity Blue can escort me, and until the dead that are all poised to wake *there* are contained, Alicia Barrow, you will rule in my stead, while I fill the role you once did. I will, as Abigail once suggested, have a taste of what it's like to be cursed."

"Rebekkah surely has—"

"Conner's return allows the dead to wake, including me." Charles explained. "All of them. On the day they die."

"So, you get to be *alive*?" Alicia clarified. "You risk me? Rebekkah? Everyone here so *you* can be alive?"

"I must, my dear. All those who die will wake until a new contract is formed. Until the window has passed, Rebekkah will need my help." Charles smiled at the two women. Really, they were taking it all quite well. Hopefully Rebekkah would, too.

Charles was fairly sure he could not die, but he could *live*. That was the real loophole in the contract from several centuries ago. By having an Undertaker cross the tunnel to *this* land of the dead, the rules of a long-ago contract had been broken. Now, the dead could live. It would create complications in the land of the living, of course, but Charles would offer his aid in Claysville.

"I shall go to Claysville and live there," Charles pronounced, gloating just a smidge that he had managed to make his dream come true.

Then, Alicia pulled out her gun and shot him. Three times. "You'll endanger all of us for this?"

She stepped closer. Two more shots. Charles swayed and slumped to the floor.

"I have fucking terrible taste in men." Alicia pronounced, standing over him now.

"Alicia, my dear—"

"Any more secrets you want to share?" Alicia prompted.

Charles gave her a look that he probably ought not with a witness present. "I am not in hurry to do so. I've held this secret for centuries. Your Undertaker read enough of the fine print to know he could come here—and he wouldn't have if he didn't know why you stayed. What peace could he have knowing you were here with me?"

"You're a bastard." Alicia grabbed the bottle and took a long drink. "So, all of this is because . . ."

"You love me?" Charles finished, pushing to a seated position despite the pain. "No, my dear. That's only part of it." He swallowed before continuing; being riddled with bullets truly did hurt. "It is also because I loved Abigail enough to want to visit that world, because I loved you enough to convince you to my bed, because Amity wants to be powerful, because Connor hates me, because . . . I want to be alive."

Amity stared at them, but she said nothing.

Alicia, however, clutched the bottle and walked out. "I'm going to fetch Byron and Rebekkah. Try not to start any more shit I'll need to deal with while you're over there playing human in the land of the living."

Charles watched her go with a sort of overwhelming pride. "That went rather well."

Amity stared at him.

"She'll forgive me sooner or later," Charles announced. "I may have to die to get her to do so, but. . . it could've gone much worse."

Ward came in with a new suit. "Sir."

And Amity looked at them both with the sort of stunned silence that he soon hoped to experience among the living. Really, there were so many parts to life that he could experience. Soon.

39

REBEKKAH BARROW

As they entered the land of the dead, it looked different. The color was dimmed. Typically, the land of the dead was richer, more vibrant than anywhere Rebekkah had ever visited in the living world. Tastes were stronger, and sights were crisper. Aside from Byron, much of the world of the living was dim. He alone was as intoxicating as the mismatched eras and people of the dead.

Today, though, something was wrong, and she had no idea what it was. She stumbled to a halt. "Byron?"

He was there, gun raised, scanning for something.

At their side was one of the Hungry Dead, a woman who ought to be on a morgue table or in the ground, but had somehow woken. They'd brought her home, and although Rebekkah hoped for answers, she wasn't sure that one accidentally woken murder victim was going to have them.

"Someone will come," Byron muttered, but he didn't sound certain.

"Miss Barrow? You're Maylene's girl?" Jenni McCormick asked, blinking as if she was back to herself.

"I'm her granddaughter."

"I was sorry to hear of her passing," Jenni continued, casual as if they'd met at a store. "We didn't travel in the same groups, but . . ." She looked around, suddenly seeming to process the oddity of her death and new location. "Huh. I suppose this is Hell? I'm guessing I won't see her here then. Your grandmother was a good—"

"Not Hell, Jenni," Rebekkah corrected. "This is simply an afterlife."

Jenni nodded. "Makes sense. I guess Miss Maylene went on to Heaven, though. Do you suppose I came here because I wasn't a Christian or a Jew or—"

"I have no idea," Rebekkah admitted. "I'm just the ferryman. There's a curse on our town. Sometimes the dead wake, and I bring them here so they don't hurt anyone."

"Bek. . ." Byron gestured with his gun.

And Rebekkah saw someone she was fairly sure *she* shouldn't see. She stared at the woman who was typically invisible. Her retinue was familiar, but the rules of the curse meant Rebekkah couldn't see former Graveminders.

Of course, the rules also meant Jenni ought to be dead in a grave for another year before there was a chance that she'd wake.

"Hello? You're not St. Whoever," Jenni said.

"Alicia?" Rebekkah stared at the woman.

"That's her," Byron said.

Rebekkah had seen drawings of her, but it couldn't be *her*. "Are you . . . *Alicia*?"

"Can you see me, now?" the red-haired, cowboy-hat wearing woman asked. She had gun holster hung around her hips and what looked like an ivory-handled pistol in hand. "Course you can. That old bastard broke all the damned rules."

Jenni was being led off by several men and a woman. She waved over her shoulder, and then she was no longer Rebekkah's concern. Whatever "lives" the dead lived, they weren't Rebekkah's knowledge or business. Some, her own friends and relations, Rebekkah couldn't even see.

She *shouldn't* see Alicia. It was a safeguard, a way to keep the past from aiding the present. For all that the religious leader in Claysville spun it, and the council denied it, the thing that meant the dead rose in Claysville was a *curse*.

"The world has almost no color." Rebekkah folded her arms and looked around the dusty street. It was as if she'd entered a lightly tinted black-and-white film. This was how the Undertaker saw it, not her.

Alicia's guards moved so they were guarding Rebekkah and Alicia. By now, they were familiar faces, and more than a few nodded their heads or smiled at her. Alicia's right-hand man, Frankie spoke quietly to Byron.

"I don't know how long this will last, so listen up: Don't trust the old bastard, Rebekkah. Don't trust the council either." Alicia took one of Rebekkah's hands in hers. "You can trust Byron. You got lucky. Not all Undertakers are like him. Mine was a right bastard, and—"

"Is that who he was?" Rebekkah asked. "Your husband? I've seen pictures, but . . . why?"

"Some loophole of Charlie's." Alicia shook her head. "I have so many things I want to tell you. Maybe if this lasts . . ." She shook her head. "Right *now*, though, Conner is here. He came back, so Charlie is now able to come to your world. It's no good, none of it."

"Charlie . . ."

"What?" Byron asked.

"You heard me, Montgomery." She handed the ivory-handled gun to Rebekkah. "This will kill them long enough to get them here. No one else can use it. You shoot them, bring them here, and back you go. Until this is sorted out, you stay over there."

Then one of her men, Frankie, handed over a bag he had slung on his back. "Bullets for the dead."

"Why do I need so many?"

"Because, they'll all wake now. All of them," Alicia said. "Until this loophole of his is patched, everyone will wake. Faster than we need. Faster than the town can handle. My gun will let you put them down."

Rebekkah stared at Alicia, trying to process what that meant. If Alicia was right, people in Claysville would all wake as Hungry Dead with no way to stop them, no tethering them to the grave with food, drink, and words. She felt a growing wave of horror. "What am I to do?"

"Patrol. Put them down. Ship them through," Alicia added. "Go on, then. Back over there. You can do this, Rebekkah. Byron will protect you, and you will bring them over here."

She started to walk, moving at a clip fast enough to make clear that the trouble here was also far from resolved.

Byron took Rebekkah's hand and the stepped back into the tunnel. The whispering voices seemed ominous now, and the cold that usually permeated Rebekkah's skin didn't wait until the returned to Claysville. She felt like her very bones ached with a chill that wouldn't ever end. The land of the dead had felt like a beautiful place, albeit with a few threats, until now.

She tightened her grip on Byron's hand, acutely aware that her other hand held a gun. It was a beautiful pistol, but this wasn't simply a historical artifact. Her long-dead relative, who was a great-aunt or cousin or something, had used it in the afterlife—perhaps in her *life*, as well. She's passed it on to Rebekkah.

As they stepped into the funeral home, Byron pulled her into his embrace.

They stood there quietly for a moment, and then, they began to plan.

"Call Colton. Tell him we'll need shotguns. As many as he has," Rebekkah started. Then, she grabbed her phone and rang the mayor's office. "Liz? We have a problem. Do not leave the office."

40
COLTON MCINNEY

COLTON HAD A SMALL HOUSE, ONE HE'D INHERITED FROM ONE OF the various McInneys. The family properties sort of cycled among relatives. As he was new and had neither wife nor child, he had a little two bedroom that was in good shape, other than some carpet choices that had suffered from age and remarkably bad taste. He wasn't expecting to have anyone beating on his door at eight o'clock at night. It wasn't late, but he didn't have many people in his life close enough to pound on his door.

"Hold your kittens," he muttered, feeling like an old man for being irritated. He jerked open the door to see Daniel Greeley standing there.

"Code Red, Colton." Greeley stepped inside. He glanced at the salt line at the door and nodded approvingly. "Gear up."

"What the hell are you talking about?"

Greeley raised his phone. "I have Colton. Alive. Uninjured."

Greeley listened for a moment, and then put the phone on speaker. Mayor Liz's voice came through the phone. "By the authority of the Council and due to the temporary laws listed under Statute

88.7 subpoint c, I am appointing you, Colton McInney, as acting sheriff." She paused. "We good, Dan?"

"Yes, ma'am."

"I've sent a car and messages to collect all the council members," she said, sounding weary. "We'll be locked in at the bunker tonight while we discuss the next steps."

"Bunker?" Colton echoed.

"We'll stop by to speak to Chris and Ev," Dan said. "You want me to try again to talk to them?"

Liz sighed. "Colton, we are about to be overrun by dead folks. If you can talk some sense into your cousin, do it. Failing that, talk to Ev. We need all able-bodied citizens rounded up and armed—or convinced to stay in their houses with salted sills and thresholds for the time. We'll call it a toxin leak or virus or . . . fuck, the council will figure that out. Just talk to Chris and Ev. we could use the extra manpower."

The phone blinked off as Liz disconnected.

"Can anyone other than the Graveminder actually stop the dead?" Colton asked.

"Not permanently." Daniel shook his head. "Rebekkah is here, though. They just got back, and the Barrow girl called the mayor. That's how we knew."

Something about Greeley calling Rebekkah a "girl" bugged Colton. An instinctive need to defend her flared. Colton shoved his feet into his boots. It was weird. He had no emotional tie to her, but in that instant, he wanted to tell Greeley to mind himself.

He resisted and asked, "Amity?"

"Not so far," Greeley said. "Shotguns?"

Colton stared at him for a moment. "What?"

"How many shotguns do you have?" Greeley asked.

"Three."

"Grab them." Greeley handed him what looked like a grocery sack. "Salt shot. It scatters the dead. Not anything more than relocating them, but they can't be feeding on citizens. Until the Barrow girl—"

"Graveminder," Colton snapped. "Give her respect. She's not some *girl*."

"Until the *Graveminder* contains them, that's the best we can do." Greeley followed Colton as he went to the gun safe.

As Colton pulled each gun out, Greeley loaded it with salt shells and put it aside. He held a handful out and shoved a few more into his bulging pockets.

"We make them up every year. Loading parties at the bunker," Greeley said. "You learn to prepare for the worst around here."

"How do we know where to go?" Colton asked.

"Mayor's office keeps a tight census, list of decedents each year." Greeley shrugged. "Undertaker updates us. Same with the sheriff."

"Because?"

"So we know who may not stay dead, Colton." Greeley shook his head. "Graveminder is just one person. We keep close count on all births and deaths. No births allowed unless we have a death. No deaths go unnoticed if possible."

Colton nodded. Life in Claysville was a little more complicated, and he wasn't sure he was making a mistake by agreeing to stay. If not for Amity, he likely wouldn't. But this is where he was, and people were about to get murdered by the Hungry Dead.

By the time they arrived at his cousin's place, it hit Colton that Chris had no idea that he'd just lost his job. There were two trucks pulling up to his door, and his wife was in there, and his kids were running around. Their yells were audible even outside the house.

"I need a minute with Chris," he said when he climbed out of his truck. "If he's willing to join the council, he can keep the job—"

"Dead people rising." Greeley scowled, slamming his door. "We need to make this quick. No time for sensitivity. All the dead will rise within hours of their death, and anyone who's died recently will rise, and those of us born here can't leave. It's a 'worst case' situation, and I'm not sure we're ready for it."

"Exponential biters." Colton tried not to think how quickly things could go terribly wrong as he knocked on the door.

When Chris opened the door, he looked like he knew more than a little. "Mayor Liz called," he said in lieu of a greeting. He motioned Colton inside with a wave to the heap by the door. "Bag of shells, a few guns, and I called everyone to the station."

Evelyn came up behind Chris. She slid her arms around him and said, "If you need the manpower—"

"Damn it, woman, I already told you." Chris covered her hand with his. "Those hellions probably scare away whatever *mountain lion* came around, but they're my hellions. I'll be right here."

"Salt the sills and doorway." Colton met Ev's gaze. "Keep sure they can't draw in the salt or crack the line."

"Not our first year living here," she said, smiling sadly. "You sure you want to stay in Claysville?"

"Yes, ma'am." He had no misunderstanding that they knew more than they likely admitted.

"We kept enough shells to. . ." Chris winced.

"Anyone or anything tries to get in, you shoot," Colton stressed. "Hell, if it's *me*, you still shoot."

"Don't you worry," Ev said. "We've stood shifts before to keep them all safe."

Chris nodded. "Damn woman's scary." Then he paused, winced, and added, "Tell Mayor Liz or Montgomery or Bek that they need to let folks know."

Greeley snorted. "As if we haven't tried." He grabbed one of the bags. "Stay safe, Chris."

Chris held out a hat, *his* hat, to Colton. "Sheriff."

"I don't want your job," Colton admitted.

"Me neither." Chris grinned and shook the hat.

With a sigh, Colton took it. "You want to be a deputy, then?"

"Hell, no." Chris pulled Ev forward so they were side-by-side. "I'm retired. Ev's got a list of honey-do tasks as long as one of those hellions of mine. I'll be plenty busy."

"Stay in the house, and keep them inside," Colton ordered. "Not even the garage. You hear me?"

Chris grinned and glanced at his wife. "Oh the horror! Trapped together . . ."

Colton shook his head, motioned to the door, and left. He'd done what he could. Now, he just had to help protect the town from the Hungry Dead.

41

REBEKKAH BARROW

NO PART OF BEING THE GRAVEMINDER WAS EASY, BUT IT WASN'T usually this difficult. Her entire body felt like it was being tugged in conflicting directions. Each waking dead called out to her, pulling her to them. Anyone not dead and not tethered to the soil for a full year could wake, and new dead would wake.

That's why Michael woke.

It wasn't that he was hidden for ages. He was recently dead.

The rules of the contract are gone.

"So many dead," she whispered.

"The religious leaders are setting up shelters," Byron said, disconnecting from a call.

Rebekkah was sure that she likely had heard that through the speakers. Listening was another matter. Her focus was on the sensations assailing her.

"Bonnie," she said. "Bonnie will wake. I don't want Amity to see her like that. Or Maylene. I can't—"

"One at a time, Bek." Byron reached out and squeezed her hand. "Mayor Liz sent the entire council to the cemeteries. Busses at each.

You just need to put them on the bus, and then we escort them home."

Rebekkah nodded. "Family first. I can't do this if I have to worry about—"

"I'd feel the same way if Dad was buried," Byron agreed.

They were silent until they reached the first cemetery. Several bodies had already risen, and one was, in fact, Bonnie Jean Blue.

"Bonnie. . ." Rebekkah winced. "Before Amity gets here—"

"If she comes," Byron said. "Who knows if he'll keep her there?"

Rebekkah couldn't think about that. She approached Bonnie and held out her hand. A brief moment of clarity seemed to flicker in Bonnie's expression, and then she lunged.

"Rebekkah!" Rabbi Wolfe called.

"Watch out!" Mayor Liz yelled.

A quick glance showed Rebekkah the unexpected sight of the young rabbi and the young mayor back-to-back with shotguns. Salt shells scattered several people into mist, as the Hungry Dead rose up.

Byron jabbed Bonnie Jean with a syringe, and then he continued to do so with three other risen corpses.

Rebekkah ran from one to the next, leading two at a time to the bus. Once inside, the opening at the door was re-sealed with salt by a young man she didn't recognize.

"Deputized council member," he said, eyes wide but voice steady.

Rebekkah nodded and looked around. Four more bodies were ready to put on the bus. The shotgun blasts and cries of warning interrupted the otherwise silent night as Rebekkah continued loading the bus.

SHE COULDN'T SAY HOW LONG IT TOOK, ONLY THAT WHEN THE dead stopped walking, she looked at the rabbi and the mayor in gratitude.

"What happened to a bunker?" she asked.

Mayor Liz shrugged. "I got restless."

"And the rest?"

"I left Xavier and Penelope there." Liz propped her gun against her leg and shook her arms out, one at a time. She gave Rebekkah a wry grin and said, "Not used to that much shooting, but I didn't think Father Ness would do well at it. He struggles a bit with"—she gestured at the bus—"all of this, and I'm a fair shot."

"Thank you," Rebekkah said.

"I called Daniel to send a tow," the rabbi interjected. "No one can go inside and drive with the . . . no one can do that safely." He glanced at Rebekkah. "They'll be parked at the funeral home, Miss Barrow."

Rebekkah nodded.

"So you left Father Ness and the . . . what's the term for Penelope?" Byron asked the mayor.

"Xavier is conditionally named mayor if I die," Mayor Liz explained. "I trust him to handle negotiations if we need to deal with Mr. D."

"And Penelope?" Byron prompted.

Mayor Liz gave him the sort of hard look that reminded anyone there that she was a Barrow. "I trust *her* to deal with both the priest and the devil."

"Charles isn't a d—"

"We'll guard this cemetery," Mayor Liz interrupted. Then, gently, she added, "Go find our grandmother. Please. Once we know how many we have waking, we need to find a way to talk to the 'old bastard.' We need a new contract, Rebekkah. This one was broken somehow, and without a contract . . ."

The Barrow cousins shared a look, and then Byron and Rebekkah were off.

42
AMITY BLUE

CHARLES STEPPED OUT OF THE TUNNEL INTO THE FUNERAL HOME. He should look out of place. Depression-era attire and arrogance didn't quite mesh with the sterile basement of a small-town funeral home. And perhaps it was foolish to think, but Amity expected him to be disconcerted or . . . something. Instead, he looked around as if he looked down on the peasants from atop a fortress tower.

"Are you . . . okay?" Amity asked carefully.

"Oh, my dear, yes," he said, looking thoroughly enchanted as he gazed at faded file cabinets, extra embalming fluid, and an old metal desk. "I am, indeed, okay as you say. I am fabulous, in fact."

He walked over to the door.

"It's locked," she started.

But at Charles' touch, it opened. "Would you show me around?"

And Amity shivered a little as Death offered her his arm. "It's just a little town, nothing like . . ."

"It's vibrant, and I've longed to walk here since before there were automobiles," he confessed.

The walked upstairs where Elaine—the manager, receptionist, and general assistant at Montgomery Family Funeral Home--startled at seeing them.

"Our . . . guest," Amity said. "He's early and—"

"How long will you be here?" Elaine prompted, pursing her lips and narrowing her eyes at Charles.

Charles nodded. "Six months. Byron told you, Elaine. Remember?"

She smiled then. "That's right, Mr . . ."

"Dee," he tipped his hat to her. "I'm Byron's cousin, Charles Dee."

Amity was braced for arguments, ready to jump in, but then Elaine laughed. "Of course! I swear I used to be so good at details."

"You still are," Amity interjected, earning a smile.

"Miss Elaine, did he leave the key by any chance? I'll be coming in and out of here sometimes, and I do hate to have to disturb the Barrow household."

Elaine frowned. "I'll have to grab one of the spares. Miss Barrow gave it to me after she had the locks remade."

Once Elaine had gone to find the housekey, Amity met Charles' gaze. "What are you doing?"

"Getting a housekey."

"Not that," Amity said, watching for Elaine. "Be careful with her brain. She's *alive*. Whatever you're doing—"

"I reset reality for every resident of this town, Miss Blue." Charles leaned in so he was practically touching her ear. "I slip into every mind, sort through it, and at the end, I erase the things I cannot have them recall. For centuries."

Amity gaped at him.

"Every mind, every dream, every desire, every fear," Charles continued. "I know every resident of Claysville, living and buried and risen. I've sat there, reading and erasing, but I can't *change* anything practical. I can't help them. I can't break bread with them. Until now."

The sheer enormity of what he was revealing had her at a loss for words.

"The only ones I cannot read are my Graveminders and their Undertakers—or their heirs," he continued.

"So, my mind . . .?"

"Locked tightly for years," Charles answered. He reached out and cupped her face. "You, Amity Blue, I'll have to get to know in the original ways."

"Original?"

"Why with charm, perseverance, and seduction," he whispered in her ear.

"Here you go, Mr. Dee." Elaine came back into the room, cutting off any attempt at a reply. She gave him a key ring with two keys. Then she pointed at one and the other and said, "Barrow house. Here."

"You are as much of a treasure as my cousin said," Charles told her. He lifted her hand and kissed the air over her knuckles.

Then with a shake of her head and laugh, Elaine walked away.

Amity stepped into the streets of the town she'd known her whole life. Nothing seemed quite the same with Death at her side. His suit, which seemed quite fitting in the land of the dead, had been replaced with more practical attire for her over there, but here? Here he looked like he'd stepped out of the past.

They'd gone not even a block when they ran into Colton.

"Amity!" He gathered her into his arms, and then stepped back to study her. "Are you injured? Are you—"

"I'm fine," she interrupted. "I had to go *there*, but I'm back because something changed, and the dead"—she lowered her voice —"they're all going to be waking."

"I know." Colton tried to pull her away from Charles, who snagged her hand before she'd taken a second step.

"Won't you introduce us, love?" Charles asked, and whatever kindness she'd grown used to had vanished.

"Colton, this is—"

"Death," Colton said. "I heard enough about you from Byron."

Charles snorted. "That boy has terrible manners. No sense of fun." He sighed in affected emotion. "So, does that mean that you are the presumed Undertaker?"

"Hand me the paper, old man. I'll sign." Colton glared.

Charles ignored him and stage-whispered, "Why, I think he *likes* you, love."

Amity looked between them, and a guilty flicker of pleasure washed over her as she realized that she held the interest of both an immortal entity and the man who drew her with something akin to magnetic force. Sadly, though, whatever wicked thoughts either man could conjure were put on hold as a woman started screaming.

"Elaine!" Amity turned back to the building she'd just vacated.

Inside a woman was stalking Elaine, who was brandishing an umbrella. "Stop that! Go back to the embalming room. Go! Shoo!"

"Did she shoo a zombie?" Colton asked.

"Not a zombie," Charles called cheerly as he marched up to the dead woman and took her hand in his.

The woman went limp in his touch, flopping to the ground like the corpse she was.

"Mr. Dee?" Elaine murmured. "That is not what we do with the deceased, sir. You can't drag them around like stage props."

"Stage . . ."

"I saw the strings, sir." Elaine pointed at Charles. "That sort of prank will not do. This is a respectable establishment, and—"

"It was a regrettable choice," Charles agreed. He released the corpse's hand—and it launched at Elaine.

The manager of Montgomery Family Funeral Home tripped backing up as the dead woman tried to bite her.

"Grab her!" Amity shoved Charles, forgetting who and what he was in the moment.

At his touch, the woman stilled. She turned her gaze to him and then, as if in slow motion, she snapped her teeth at him.

"Now, now, there will be none of that." Charles caught her hand, and she dropped again.

"Grab her feet," Amity told Colton.

Elaine was on the floor glaring at them. "Now, you see here—"

"The hearse broke down, Miss Elaine," Amity interrupted. "*Tell* her, Charles."

With a solemn nod, Charles repeated the lie. Then, he held onto the dead woman's hand as Colton carried the body out of the building and to the car. Once inside, Charles released her hand, and she lunged at Colton.

"You need to ride in the back." Colton pointed. "Hold on to her."

Mutely, Death slid into the backseat, where he looked around in amusement at the bars dividing the back and front seat.

"Where are we going?" Amity asked.

"Jail." Colton opened her door. "Montgomery and Rebekkah have been rounding up biters."

"They turn to mist," Amity started.

"Not with salt rings," Colton said, his voice colder than anything she'd heard from him.

After a glance at Charles, Amity whispered, "You could leave, you know? Take that time to think."

Colton stared at her like she'd just suggested they have kids. Actually, he might have taken that better. "I will sign or whatever. I had enough time to think." His gaze drifted to the rear-view mirror. "I am where I ought to be: at your side."

"For now," Charles said mildly.

And Amity had no idea if he knew something or was just a shit-stirrer. Whatever else he was, Charles wasn't to be trusted. She knew that much. He was far from unappealing—powerful, handsome, charming, and seductive. That had always been her type.

Colton had a lot of those traits, too, but he was also right there beside her. He was also honest with her. That was appealing on its own. Combined with strength and attitude? It was incredible.

"I knew before you were gone a day," Colton was saying. He glanced at her, and once she met his eyes, he swore, "I'm in, Amity Blue. However, *whenever* you want me. I'm yours."

43
MICHAEL

MICHAEL FELT CLEARER OF MIND THAN HE HAD EVEN IN HIS LIFE—and he well aware that he was, in fact, dead now. He had slid into clarity when his body took shape this time. A part of him wondered why he was walking around now that he was dead. Another part realized that such things simply *happened* here. Claysville was where the dead walked.

Maybe his death-existence would be more interesting than his life.

But then he found himself being jerked forward, as if by a hook under his sternum. Someone or something was calling him. He found himself reforming at the jail of all places. He was, admittedly, a murderer now.

"Does it count if I was dead when I committed the crime?" he asked a woman with a shotgun.

"Another one, boss," she yelled, levelling the gun at him. "Smarter than the rest of the infected."

Michael preened. No one called him smart, not since middle school, unless they wanted something. He paused then. "Infected?"

"There's been a chemical leak. Some weird brain-eating thing, so it's making people think they're dead." The woman with the gun looked familiar, but he was fairly sure he hadn't bitten her.

"Do I know you?" he asked.

"Suzie," she supplied, offering him a warm smile. "You seem a lot more coherent than the others." She wiggled the gun barrel a bit. "But if you try to bite me, I'm going to empty both barrels at you."

"Did I bite you before?"

"Boss!" Suzie yelled again. "Any time now."

Then a man in a smart suit came out of the jail with the not-really-Graveminder and the man who shot him the other night.

"Who are you?" Suzie asked.

Michael started growling. He wasn't a fan of people who shot him.

"Michael," the not-Graveminder said. "We were looking for you." She smiled. "Why don't you come inside? I can get you something to eat and drink."

His mouth felt parched as she spoke. His throat became drier than deserts. She was right. He *needed* a drink. He nodded, took a step forward, and then he noticed the man in the suit again. He was glowing.

"Like the Graveminder," Michael whispered, stalking closer to the man.

Suzie's gun raised, tracking Michael, but that didn't matter. Nothing really did now.

"Hello, Michael." The man extended his hand. "Come with me."

And Michael took it.

44
REBEKKAH BARROW

REBEKKAH WALKED UP IN TIME TO SEE CHARLES GRAB THE DEAD man's outstretched hand. Michael dropped to the ground in a slump, like a balloon gone limp and dragging on the ground.

"Hello, Rebekkah," Charles said.

"You need to go home." Rebekkah crossed her arms and glared. "Do you have any idea what it's like? How many people are waking up because of you?"

"If you don't want my help . . ." Charles released Michael's hand.

The dead man jumped up. "What the fuck?" He glared at them, looking like a petulant child. "What just happened?"

"Hush." Charles didn't spare him a glance.

Rebekkah sighed. She walked up to Michael, grabbed his wrist and walked away. Her grandmother Bonnie Jean, and a man called Joseph were all resting in the back of the truck. It had pained her, but Rebekkah injected each of them.

She called out: "I'll be back for the next batch, unless you want to bring them to the funeral home . . . or escort them over *there* yourself."

Rebekkah didn't look back, or speak more than she had to do.

The need to be sure her grandmother was escorted over seemed to overpower the rest. Byron opened the tunnel, and in short order, Rebekkah and Byron took the four of them over first.

She stepped out of the tunnel, and for a moment, Rebekkah clutched Maylene's hand.

"I'm sorry I didn't tell you sooner," she said, hugging Rebekkah. "I was so afraid you'd hate me."

"Never!" Rebekkah blinked away tears. "I love you. I could *never* hate you!"

Her grandmother held onto her, and then she glanced at Byron. "I'm glad you're at her side. Your father and I knew you'd be the one to protect my girls."

He nodded. "I loved Ella when I was a boy, and I love Bek. I swear to you I'm going to keep her safe."

Maylene kept an arm around Rebekkah, but she lifted her free hand to Byron's face. "Well, of course you are. I suspect that would be true even without the curse." Then she looked back at Rebekkah. "You need to let go of me, lovie."

Rebekkah sobbed. "I don't want to. I just . . ."

"Hush, there." Maylene kissed her forehead, and then her cheeks. "I'm so proud of you, Rebekkah. You try to mend a fence with Lizzie, though? You hear me? That girl lost her sister, just like you lost Ella Mae. She needs family—and you do, too."

All Rebekkah could do was nod.

"Well, there you are, Cousin Alicia," Maylene said, lifting her gaze to the red-haired gunslinger who came to greet them. "I've been looking forward to meeting you since William told me you were around here."

"Cousin." Alicia dipped her head and touched the brim of her hat. Then she told Rebekkah and Byron, "I've got them. Don't worry."

Rebekkah hugged Maylene one more time. "I was the luckiest girl in the world to be your granddaughter. I love you."

"I was just as lucky, lovie. We all were. Now, go handle the troubles over in town." Maylene stepped out of Rebekkah's arms—and vanished.

Rebekkah choked back a sob. "We'll be back with more. Are you . . . okay here?"

Alicia nodded and turned to the empty space beside her. "You're right about her."

Then she was gone, too. She vanished, and Rebekkah presumed Alicia's men had led away Maylene along with Bonnie Jean, Joseph, and Michael.

It was just Byron at her side.

"Come on," Rebekkah said, pulling her gaze away from the space beside Alicia where Maylene Barrow undoubtedly were.

She had at least twelve more bodies to bring over tonight.

45
LIZ BARROW

"So, what do I call you?" Liz looked at the man, the creature, who had cursed her town and her family. He sat across from her, in the mayoral office as if it was nothing odd. It was, however, unprecedented for Death to come to town. To the best of her knowledge, no one since the contract was formed had met with him other than the Graveminder and the Undertaker.

"Charles will do," he said. "And you, if memory serves, are Elizabeth. Daughter of Cecilia. Granddaughter of May—"

"Thanks, but I already know my family history, Charles." She leaned back in her chair. "You may call me 'Mayor Liz.'"

Charles nodded. If not for her family legacy, she would've expected Death to be cadaverous or even skeletal. She knew better, but it was still odd to see him sitting there, sporting a fine suit and sipping whisky.

"And will the rest of your esteemed council be joining us? I was looking forward to meeting Father Ness, and Miss Penelope, and . . . " He held his hand up. "But, of course, I shall meet all of them during my visit."

"Your visit?"

Charles leaned forward, placed his glass on her desk, and asked, "What sort of man would I be if I didn't help my community?"

Liz shook her head. "No. You are not welcome here."

"So you'd let the town all die? Trapped here? Unable to eat? Because unless the dead are stopped from waking, it will happen," Charles said, his tone as conversational as if they were speaking of the weather or the cost of suits.

"They wake because you are here," Liz snapped. "Unlike my cousin or the other women in my family, I have no patience with this curse business. It's because of you, your selfishness, your—"

"Mind yourself, Mayor Liz. I am not a man without a temper." Charles lifted his glass again, holding it up in a mocking toast.

"So, what is it you want, you old bastard?" Liz asked. "That, mind you, is merely the term we're taught to call you. Great-grandmother Abby's pet name, if family lore is true."

Death laughed. "Indeed." He held up his glass again. "To Abigail, without her and Alicia, I'd be still in the land of the dead."

Liz had thought that until Rebekkah was done transporting the dead, she was going to negotiate with the devil. She was sore from dealing with the Hungry Dead, fairly certain there were more nightmares in her future, and under it all was a simmering pool of rage. But as Death—or the devil or whatever he really was—sat across from her desk, she wondered if she was being foolish.

She obviously couldn't flirt or charm him. He was, as her grandmother and countless other people had described him, handsome. Most Graveminders had seemed half-in-love with him. If Liz was interested in men, maybe she'd have been more interested in being a Graveminder. Maybe she'd be better equipped to cajole him.

Sitting there, without the burden of her mother in her life, Liz was starting to consider what she truly wanted. And as she looked at Death, she realized that it wasn't a man, even if he was a powerful, otherworldly creature.

Liz stood and poured herself a drink. Then she returned to her desk. "Look. I'm not some girl, easily swayed. I'm the person in charge of a town *you cursed.*" She held his gaze. "What is it you want for us to negotiate a new contract?"

He smiled, slow and cunning. "I'll give you six months to negotiate terms. Half a year."

"I want the dead to stay dead during that time," Liz insisted.

"Done," Charles agreed easily.

"So we'll meet as often as needed to negotiate new terms," Liz said.

"I'm amenable to that," Charles said, still seeming agreeable.

"We can have Rebekkah bring the files back and forth or—"

"Why not simply call?" Charles held up a mobile phone.

For a moment, Liz startled. "We can *call* the land of the dead? How does that—"

Her words were lost under his laughter.

"No, *Mayor Liz*, I am a citizen of your fair town during the six months of our negotiation. You can simply bump into me at the grocer or . . . the pub. I've been looking forward to this for centuries."

Liz stared at him in new horror.

"To life in a town cursed by death," he said cheerily, lifting his glass to her. "The dead will not rise during our negotiations. On that you have my solemn vow, but the cost of such a vow is my presence."

He stood then, humming cheerily, and walked to the door.

"I must run, Mayor Liz. I'm sure I need groceries, and I feel positively energized to have this all sorted out." Death grinned.

Liz shook herself out of her stunned silence. "Wait! It's not sorted out. This is—"

"*Temporarily* sorted out," Charles said. "A détente as it were."

And then he was gone, off into her town.

In the next few moments, Liz was summoning everyone she could, telling each one: "We need to meet. Legal experts. Religious. Until we have a new contract, Death is here."

EPILOGUE

AMITY WAS STANDING OUTSIDE, AND WHEN CHARLES JOINED HER, all she could say was, "Now what?"

"Oh, it's quite simple," Charles said. "Over there, I am Death. Beholden to no one. Here? I am tied to you."

"And where does that leave me? Or Colton?"

"Ladies' choice," he murmured chivalrously. "I am *here* for six months."

"You could go back—"

"I'm alive, Miss Blue. For the very first time, I am *alive.*" Charles sounded positively gleeful. "And until the new contract is in place, the dead will not rise—as long as I am in Claysville."

"I'm not living with you or . . . things," Amity stressed.

He tucked her hand in the fold of his arm. "You'll choose me or reject me. I'm as trapped as Conner once was, as all the Undertakers are, smitten with you when we are in this world." He looked down at her. "You see before you a *man*, hopeless, begging for your attention. I am powerless."

His lips curved as he added the last, and Amity knew damn well that Death was far from powerless. He called this a *curse*, but to her, it looked like Death simply had taken a holiday among the living—and she was stuck as his tour guide.

What could possibly go wrong?

The End

GUNS FOR THE DEAD: A GRAVEMINDER PREQUEL STORY

AT THE SOUND OF BOOTS ON THE PLANK WALKWAY OUTSIDE HER shop, Alicia closed the cash box and lifted the sawed-off shotgun from a modified under-counter rack. She'd hoped that the boys would be back by now, but they weren't daft enough to be walking in the front door of General Supplies without calling out.

She swung the shotgun up as the door opened.

The owner of the boots stopped just inside the shop. He was new enough that she didn't recognize him. To his credit, though, he didn't flinch at the sight of her particular brand of customer service. His gaze slipped briefly over the shop with curiosity. The interior of the frontier town General Goods store seemed a little out of time to new arrivals. Over there, more than a century had passed. She thought about updating the look, but the comforting familiarity of the dry goods shop outweighed her discomfort over revealing her age. *Screw 'em.* With its tins and barrels, glass cases and the wood floorboards, it was home, but clearly not what *his* home looked like.

The newcomer put his arms out to the sides, demonstrating that he was either trustworthy or idiotic. "Ma'am."

She took in his frayed jeans, faded black tee-shirt, combat boots, and a relatively new revolver in a belt holster. Most of those items were commonplace here now; she'd even acquired shirts and boots much like his in recent years. The holster he wore could be purchased in a dozen spots around the city, but post-1880 weapons came from one shop only—hers. She pursed her lips. Since she didn't recognize him, he'd either taken it from a customer or bought it at significant upsale.

"Boyd sent me," he said.

"And?" She didn't lower her weapon. There was something decidedly awkward about aiming a shotgun one-armed for any time at all, but a businesswoman didn't greet strangers unarmed. She stepped back and—using her free hand for leverage—hopped up on the counter.

The newcomer raised his brows, but his posture remained unchanged. "He said to tell you that 'the old bastard started trouble' and that 'he'll be out for a day.'"

"Huh." Alicia lowered the shotgun so it was aimed at the floor in front of her. "And where is Boyd that you're delivering this message?"

"Got shot."

She tensed. "By?"

"See, that's the thing—"

"No," she interrupted. She slid off the counter and stepped forward. "Simple question, Shug. Shot by whom?"

"Me, but there were circumst—" The rest of his words were lost under the shotgun blast.

She threw herself to the side as she fired, hoping to dodge a return shot that didn't come. When she realized that he hadn't even reached for his piece, Alicia rolled to her feet.

Definitely a newcomer.

She stood and looked down at him. His blood was leaking all over her floorboards. *And that's why we don't have carpet.* She sighed. Sometimes, she had misplaced urges for finery that had no place in the shop. *Maybe if it was a dark carpet.* She walked around the counter, but not close enough that he could pull her to the ground. Injured or not, he had a size advantage.

He looked up at her. "Least it was a slug, not scattershot."

"You want to see what's in the second barrel?" She extended her arm and took aim, but didn't fire. "Why'd you shoot Boyd?"

"Had to," the man said.

"Why?" She motioned with the gun.

The bleeder on her floor had his hands pressed over his leg wound. If he was still alive, he'd be in a sorry state, but being dead tended to change things in unpredictable ways. From the way he pressed his hands down, he was even newer than she thought: getting used to living in the land of the dead took a little time.

"I came looking for him to ask about you, and things took a turn," he said slowly.

Alicia sighed. "I think you're going to need to start at the beginning . . . *after*"—she looked pointedly at his belt—"you slide that over here."

"If I didn't reach for it when you shot me, I'm not going to *now*." He muttered, but he still pulled the pistol out of the holster and held it out toward her butt first.

FRANCIS LEE LEMONS STARED AT THE WOMAN WHO, ACCORDING TO everyone he'd met since he died, ran the guns for the land of the dead.

And shot me.

He wanted a job. Straight-up, plain and simple, he wanted to work for her. He'd never been on what one might call the "right" side of the law, and he didn't see any need to change that now that he was in this odd afterlife. Getting along over here was a mite more brutal than in the living world, but he figured that a familiarity with a less-than-upstanding lifestyle would be an asset.

"Ma'am?"

Alicia glanced at him, but she didn't say anything.

"Would it offend you overmuch if I either took off my shirt to staunch this or asked for a bandage of some sort?" he asked as respectfully as he could.

"You got any funds?"

"No, ma'am."

"Job?"

"Not yet." He looked directly at her. "I'm in the middle of what I hope to be a promising interview though."

She snorted. "You're bleeding on my floorboards. That's promising?" She walked over to a basket of rags that sat alongside the front counter and pulled out an obviously stained one. She tossed it to him. "It's not the cleanest, but we don't get infections over here."

"Yes, ma'am." He tied it around his thigh, arranging it so as to cover both the entrance and exit wounds.

"Alicia," she said.

He looked up, mid-knot.

"If you know enough to apply for a job, you already know my name." She walked over and slid a bolt on the door, and then proceeded to do the same at the shutters that covered the inside of the windows.

"Alicia?"

She glanced back.

"I'm Frank. Well, Francis Lee Lemons, but—"

"I don't care who you are yet, shug." She leaned against one of the large wooden cask in the corner. "Talk."

So Frank told her: "I took the revolver off a man in a game of darts. Too stupid to realize he could even be hustled at darts and . . . I'm mostly honest, but it seemed a wise plan to be armed around here, you know?"

Alicia nodded.

"Found out who supplied it, started asking about you, and ended up at a weird bar with Boyd."

"What bar?" she prompted.

"Mr D's." He paused, but she didn't say anything, so he kept going, "Boyd was explaining that you were particular about who you took on. Lots of dead folks want a position on your team and not just anyone could meet up to make his case." Nervously, Frank looked at Alicia, but her expression was unreadable, so he added the damning part, "But we were talking, and then Boyd suddenly says, 'Shoot me.' I didn't think I heard right. He repeated it again. 'Shoot me right here.' He pointed right at his forehead. '*Now*, then go find Alicia.' He told me to tell you what I did when I walked in."

Quietly, Alicia asked, "What did you do?"

Frank had a fleeting wish that he'd kept his gun then, but he answered her in a steady voice, "Exactly what he said."

"Why?"

"Instinct?" Frank shrugged. "I don't know, really. He seemed sober, sane as anyone else here, and . . . I know he's your right-hand man, and I want this job, and I didn't know what else to do, so I did what he said I should."

"Good enough." Alicia reached behind a tin on one of the shelves next to her and grabbed a revolver. She tossed it at him. "Let's go."

He caught it and checked the chamber. "You in the habit of throwing loaded guns?"

"You expected to do me any good with an *un*loaded piece?" Alicia cocked her head.

Frank glanced at his leg before answering. "If I had to, but not right this minute."

"Call it part of the interview." Alicia held up a hand and started ticking things off on her fingers. "Assuming you're telling the truth, I know you listened to Boyd, and you reacted well to stress. That's two. Since you got here, you're not bitching over that scrape." She gestured at his bloody thigh. "Now, you caught and flipped the gun in your hand like you're comfortable."

She held her hand out to him and helped him to his feet. "Tells me you have potential."

Frank swallowed against the sting of putting weight on his leg. He knew he was dead now, but he wasn't sure what happened when the dead were shot.

Can I die more?

He looked at his blood on their clasped hands. Obviously, the dead bled.

He asked, "Did I kill Boyd?"

"Boyd's been dead almost a century." She pulled her hand free of his and wiped it on another rag she grabbed out of the basket. "Not real sure on that whole reincarnation thing."

She tossed the rag to Frank.

Frank stared at her for several moments before saying, "*Here*. Did I kill him here?"

Alicia reached up and patted his cheek. "Sweetie, only one man around here can kill the dead."

"Who's that?"

"The man who we're going to see: the old bastard, Mr D." She tucked his revolver in her own holster, slung her shotgun over her shoulder, and walked to the door.

AS THEY WALKED THROUGH THE CITY, ALICIA SLOWED HER PACE A little for him. Getting shot wasn't fatal here, but it still hurt like a bitch. *Frankie Lee.* She hadn't heard that anyone was asking about her, but he'd found Boyd, knew she was the one that ran the black market, and managed to get a meeting with Boyd. That meant that Frankie Lee was stealthy. She glanced at him. His lips were pursed, and he was limping a bit, but all things considered, he was holding up fairly well for having a hole in his thigh.

"How long you been dead?"

Frankie Lee frowned. "I don't know. Week or two, I guess."

"Well, here's your newcomer welcome information, Frankie Lee."

"Frank," he interjected.

Alicia ignored him. "The grand pain in everyone's ass around here is Charles. The old bastard and I have a regular conflict." She reached into one of her trouser pockets and pulled out a couple pills. "Take these."

Frankie Lee obediently swallowed them. He didn't ask what they were, and she didn't tell him. He'd figure it out soon enough when his leg stopped hurting.

As they walked through the ever-shifting city, a few people glanced their way. They were in one of the sections that remained steadfastly not modern. It was a bit cleaner than the way her experience of live-world equivalent was, but it was comforting all the same. Alicia had adjusted to the appearance of new sections in the city, blocks that belonged to eras that happened after she was already dead, but she felt ill at ease around flappers or—worse still—those cookie baking always-smiling women.

Not as sweet as they act, either, else they'd have moved past here.

Mr. Waverly tipped his hat to her. One of the Tadlock sisters tilted her ridiculous parasol so she couldn't see them.

"Millicent!" Alicia called out to her, and predictably, the woman had a sudden urge to dart into a milliner's shop. She was from Alicia's own era and clung to the notion that ladies shouldn't acknowledge ruffians. It didn't stop her from buying the derringer she no doubt had in her handbag.

Alicia and Frankie Lee crossed a street separating the 1800s and early 1900s shops, and one of the young news-hounds came scurrying into their path. "Who shot you, mister? Are you going to go settle up with them, Alicia?"

"Nope."

"Is *he*?" the boy pestered.

"Don't know. Are you, Frankie Lee?" She glanced at him.

He frowned at her. "No, and no one calls me that."

"It's that or Francis." She smiled. "Your choice."

After a pause, he nodded. "Not Francis."

"Frankie Lee isn't going to settle up with the one that shot him. That's all you get for now." She shooed the newshound out of the street. Once the boy was gone, she resumed her version of a newcomers' talk, "Charles thinks my organization is crude. He's a despot. Dictator, really. No free trade, no modernizing the city. If he had his way, women would all be relegated to arm candy or other foolishness. He builds what he wants when he wants, makes the laws he wants, and we're just to be content with whatever he creates."

"And you?"

"I'm not content." She scowled at one of the more modern dead men soliciting a couple of the silly flapper girls who liked to linger near the century line. One of Charles' people stepped in, so she kept going. Grudgingly she told Frankie Lee, "Charles maintains some parts of the city well, but he's stuck on the idea of empires. I don't agree."

"So it's political differences?" Frankie Lee's tone did little to hide his surprise.

Alicia laughed. "Not entirely. I'm here. I'm staying here, and I'm not his subject . . . I didn't fare well when I was under his authority."

Memories of her life, of a time when she trusted Charles, flooded her. A long time ago, she lived for Charles. Here, well, she might still exist because of him—except now it was to thwart him, not to help him.

"I have a financial interest in my politics." She walked a little faster, and thanks to her medicinal aid, Frankie Lee kept pace. "Guns in the land of the dead are the main source of my livelihood. The more modern, the better. Because of a loophole, there's a man and a woman from the living world who can come over here. I got myself in the habit of bartering with the undertaker, so he buys my help with the things he brings in. The old bastard can't stop the undertaker from supplying my prototypes, and once I get models of new gear, I can replicate some of it."

"Which I'm guessing he dislikes."

"Got it in one." Alicia didn't like taking on new people very often. Her business required a particular skill set that lots of folks *thought* they had, but there was a significant difference between wearing badass as a costume and being the real deal. Any man—or woman—could throw on the right clothes, whichever era they preferred, and posture. No amount of leather or sharp suits equaled true grit.

"Frankie?"

"Yes 'm." He kept a rolling pace now, but his attention was on the side streets, rather than on her. Whether she'd ordered it or not, he was standing guard.

"What did you do when you were alive?" She held up a hand, signaling him to wait for the 12:12 train. The conductor took pleasure at running silent in hopes of plowing over newcomers.

Frankie Lee shrugged. "I did work for hire last few years. Grew up around guns. No explosives skills or anything fancy, but I'm a quick study. I do alright in close situations, decent trigger man if you need it, seemed to fare well enough at observation."

"They pay well for that topside these days?"

"Sometimes, if you're good enough. I was good enough most of the time, but"—Frankie Lee gave her a wry smile—"not the last time."

Alicia closed her eyes against the gust of air as the train passed in front of them. It used be the 12:00 train, but the conductor moved it up one minute each month. As far as calendars went, she'd heard of worse. It certainly proved incentive to keep track of the month.

"How'd you end up qualified?" she asked.

"My Mama enlisted out of high school, and she got sore over the things she wasn't allowed to do. So she taught me and my sisters all that she *did* learn, and then we all four learned what she wasn't taught." Frankie Lee's up-until-then calm faltered. He was good at what she needed, but he wasn't unnecessarily cold—which was an asset in her book. A cold-hearted employee was a different sort of problem than one that was all sass and no ass. The right sort of associate was neither too cocky nor too cruel.

"Your Mama sounds like a smart woman." Alicia stepped into the street, and Frankie Lee followed.

"She was, but my sisters'll look out for her well enough. She's not big time, but she has connections enough that she does alright for herself."

Alicia figured the sideways scowls that more than a few of the upstanding citizens sent her way were clue enough—well, that, and the fact that he was limping because she'd shot him—but she figured it was only proper to fill him in. "You *do* get that I'm not exactly on the right side of the law here?"

"No disrespect, Alicia, but I doubt you could be any less law-abiding than my Mama was, and I don't think the law here is necessarily one I'm after following." He motioned toward a glass door with MR. D's TIP-TOP TAVERN painted on it. "This is where we were."

Alicia grabbed the brass bar that served as a door handle and yanked the door open before he could open it for her. "Let's see how well you follow orders, Frankie Lee."

FRANK WALKED INTO THE SHADOWED INTERIOR OF THE TAVERN twice in almost as many hours. He already knew that it was a wide-open club: exposed pipes ran the length of the ceiling, no alcoves to hide in. Round tables with varying numbers of high-backed chairs were spread throughout the room, far enough apart at places that a private conversation was possible. The biggest risk was the curtained doorway beside the bar. It would allow cover to sight down on any of the customers with either a rifle or a handgun, depending on who minded whatever space was on the far side of that curtain.

Without asking, he knew that Alicia was well aware of the same threat. She'd paused, swept the room, seeking someone or maybe just assessing threats. Then, she swung her shotgun from where she'd carried it over her shoulder and held it barrel-down as they walked into the room.

"Don't say anything unless I tell you to," she murmured.

Frank nodded.

At the dead middle of the room, Alicia stopped, pumped her

shotgun, and aimed it at the baby grand piano on the stage in front of them.

All around them, people stood and walked out. No one ran. No one said anything. They merely stood, pushed in their chairs, and headed toward the exit.

Once the room was cleared of everyone but the bartender, Alicia winked at Frank and then shot a pipe that was just to the left of the stage. Steam hissed from it.

"I'd like to talk," she called.

The barmaid caught Frank's gaze and widened her eyes imploringly. He didn't think she was in any real danger though. Alicia seemed to be concentrating on the piano: she shot a second pipe. This time, water sluiced from the fragmented pipe. It didn't pour down on the piano, but it was very close. Something shorted, sparked, and smoked off to the side of the stage.

A man came from behind the curtained doorway. He carried himself with the easy confidence of someone who's always been obeyed—and had the power and money to keep it that way. He wore an old-fashioned dark gray suit broken up by the scarlet of his tie and his pocket square.

"We have telephones here, Alicia. Telegraphs, too." He shook his head and then turned his attention to Frank. "Francis, I see you've met my dear Alicia. Is she helping you get your sea legs?"

Frank didn't reply.

"Aaaah, already on her payroll." The man tsk-ed. "With your mother's influence, one would expect as much, I suppose. As I doubt Alicia will introduce us"—he touched his fingertips to his chest lightly—"I am Charles."

How does he know about my family?

Alicia dropped her shotgun on the table, looked over her shoulder at Frank, and said, "Go on up to the bar and grab me a drink."

He raised his brows at her, but kept his mouth shut.

She nodded and turned back to Charles. "Leave Frankie Lee out of it."

Frank walked over to the polished wooden bar. By the time he got there, the barmaid already had two highball glasses and a wine glass out. She filled two glasses with bourbon and the third with some sort of wine. "The wine is for the boss."

He looked at her.

"My boss," she corrected.

And he carried the three drinks back over to the table. As he approached, Alicia poked Charles in the chest. "You can't bully Boyd. He's *mine*."

"At what point did you gain any authority in *my* domain? You live in my city because I allow it." Charles nodded absently to Frank and took a seat.

Alicia grabbed one of the glasses from Frank and upended it. Her shotgun lay like a line bisecting the table. "Make me leave then."

Charles remained silent. He sipped his drink and stared at Alicia, who now stood with her hands on her hips. Not knowing what else to do, Frank handed his drink to Alicia and stood to the side so she could draw without interference, and he could still be there if she needed help. Something older than logic told him that Charles, for all of his polish, wasn't the sort of man who'd go down easy in a fight.

Even as he thought it, Charles smiled at him. "You'll do just fine around here, Francis."

Alicia tensed.

And Frank said the only thing he could think of in the moment, "My name is Frankie Lee, sir."

ALICIA GRINNED. FRANKIE LEE WAS GOING TO WORK OUT JUST fine.

"I don't want semi-automatic weapons on my street, Alicia." Charles motioned at the seat across from him. "I overlook a lot, but there are limits. I explained that to Boyd last week. On this, I *will* crush you."

She sat and motioned for Frankie Lee to do the same. She tried the same argument that usually worked, "I don't see why these—"

"No. Not this time. I play by the rules. That means, here and there, you'll outmaneuver me. On this, it's not going to be any time soon. I overlook revolvers, but that's where we are staying. The damage, the loss of life . . . I can't explain it." Charles looked genuinely sad, but she knew well enough that the old bastard was able to fake emotions. "You have been out of that world for years, Alicia."

"Dead. Because you had me killed," she corrected.

Beside her, Frankie Lee tensed, but he stayed silent.

"True." Charles sipped his wine. "I'll negotiate, or I'll start killing your boys. Permanent death so as they'll be removed from the city."

Alicia paused. "And me?"

Charles leaned back in his seat. "I won't kill you. You know that."

"Again. Say it, at least. You won't kill me *again*."

"I won't kill you *again*, but"—Charles gestured at Frankie Lee —"I'll kill him, Boyd, Milt, each and every one you employ."

Charles made a come-hither gesture.

One of her information runners, Lewis, was brought in.

"You *all* exist because I allow it; you can die because I prefer it. No semi-automatic weapons, Alicia. You will agree to stop pushing this matter," Charles said softly. "Or he dies."

She started, "I'm not going to give in because of a threat."

Charles fixed his gaze on her and snapped his fingers. Lewis crumpled. "There are always unbreakable rules. Right now, this is one of them, and you, of all people, know that I will do what I must to enforce the unbreakable rules."

Alicia looked at Lewis. *Where do they go if they die in the land of the dead?* She'd asked that question often enough, but Charles never answered. "No automatic weapons for how long?"

"You have no room to barter," Charles said.

She suppressed a shiver at the threat in his voice. "Just checking the rules."

"Thirty years. We can renegotiate then."

"Thirty years," Alicia agreed. "*But* you owe me a replacement or undo what you did to Lewis."

For a moment, Charles was silent. Then he nodded and said, "I can't undo his death, but as a gesture of good faith, I'll allow you to take one of the staff to replace your employee."

Alicia kept her expression bland, but she felt the wave of sorrow that she'd been resisting. Charles had finally answered her: some deaths apparently were even fatal enough that they were out of his reach. She'd known there were other dead cities, and hoped that those who didn't reanimate here went to another world, a world where they were happier. She knew such worlds existed: her own loved ones had gone on to them. She'd hoped, though, that the dead folk who were re-killed *here* went on to other dead worlds, but if that were the case, Charles could have un-done Lewis's death.

Lewis is dead.

Thinking about the metaphysics of living in the land of the dead made her head hurt, so she didn't. *Lewis is dead because I pushed Charles too far*. The same trait that had made her good at opposing Charles, both before and after her death, got Lewis killed. Silently, Alicia walked over to the bar and accepted the drink the barmaid held out as she approached.

Behind her, Charles said, "Shall I invite my staff here or would you deign to visit my home?"

Without looking back at him, she said, "Here."

AN HOUR LATER, FRANKIE LEE WATCHED AS SEVERAL DOZEN PEOPLE tromped into the room. Beside him, Alicia sat with her boots propped on the table as one of them—the only one Charles said was 'off limits'—told Alicia their names and roles. Charles had cooks, maids, barmaids, singers, a personal tailor, and God knew how many other employees.

Frankie Lee tuned most of it out after the first fifteen minutes.

Finally, Alicia pointed toward a young woman. "I'll take her."

Charles frowned. "There are others—"

"No. Her." Alicia folded her arms over her chest.

"She's not suited for your sort of work, Alicia. Perhaps, Steven. He's handy with some sort of martial art, or Elizabeth . . . she's an accomplished companion." Charles gestured toward a pretty redhead.

"No."

"Why?" Charles asked.

The smile Alicia offered was as frightening as her glare. "I'm a good judge of character. You softened at the sight of her."

Charles frowned at Alicia. "What kind of job do you have for a *singer?*"

"I'm sure I'll find a good use for her." Alicia's boots thunked to the floor as she stood. "I expect her and Boyd delivered to the inn."

Frank felt a twinge of worry for the girl, as, apparently, did Charles. However, Charles merely inclined his head slightly and then walked out.

Once Charles and his people had all left, Alicia glanced at Frankie Lee. "Let's go."

"What *will* you do with her?" he asked.

Alicia leaned as close as she could get without her lips touching his and whispered, "Don't ask questions I don't feel like answering."

He hadn't ever been intimidated by much, but he knew when to have a healthy respect for a predator. Alicia was definitely on the predator list, and maybe her attitude *should* intimidate him. She'd shot him when he walked in her door, shot up the tavern, and in general, seemed pretty quick on the trigger.. Frank could hear his mother's voice in his memories, *Don't poke a rattler, Francis. No matter how contrary you're feeling. Good sense keeps a person alive.* He grinned. He was already dead now, and by the way Alicia had reacted to Lewis' death, Frank was pretty sure that the permanent sort of death was rare.

"I suspect you're aiming to intimidate me. I probably should step back, but"—Frank stood up, invading her space as he did so—"I've grown up with hardass women. Tell me what you have in mind for the girl, *please?*"

"Charles likes her. He won't strike her easily, and I've been thinking about ways to spruce up the inn. He's a pushover for music, so she must be good. We cater to a . . . *rougher* crowd, so it's a high-risk spot. I can't lure his favorites away, but this time . . ." Alicia shrugged. "She can work at my inn, and she'll be safe because Charles is fond of her and aside from the people who work for me, no one crosses him. "

"Smart." Frank smiled at her, and they walked toward the door. "I think I'll like working for you."

"Who says you're hired?"

Frank opened the door. "All the same, I might as well walk back that way."

Alicia laughed, and together they crossed the weird city in comfortable silence. Once the General Store was in view, she linked her arm with his. "You did good work."

"Thank you, Alicia."

She stopped in the street. "I guess you ought to go home."

"Home?"

Alicia gestured at the inn across the street. An unknown man stood at the door watching them. "Milt will give you a key to whichever room's yours. It's not fancy, but it's ours."

"Ours," Frank repeated.

"I do try to take care of what's mine, Frankie Lee."

"I'm sorry about Lewis."

She nodded. "You might get truly killed working for me. I'll need to be telling the rest of the boys later, but before you decide—"

"Decided when we were there." Frank shrugged. "I like having a family. Yours feels like home to me."

"Thank you." Alicia smiled then and added, "Guess your interview was promising after all."

Frank chuckled. "Yes, ma'am."

He had a healing gunshot wound in his thigh, a job, and a home.

All told, Frankie Lee figured that it was the best day he'd had since he died. Being dead wasn't anything like the preacher said it would be, but considering the life Frankie Lee had led, that wasn't such a bad thing. He nodded his head at his boss and headed off to find his room.

"Frankie Lee?"

He paused and looked at her.

"Is it as bad as all that over there?" she asked haltingly. "It's been a while since I was alive."

Frankie Lee thought about the bullets that had ended his own life. *A bullet is a bullet*. The difference was how many of them tore into him that day. He shrugged. "I won't be eager for those thirty years to end."

"Oh." Alicia faltered, but it lasted only a moment, before she said, "Maybe it'd be good for you to tell me what's new over there in the living world; I can't take care of everyone if I'm out of touch."

And Frankie Lee saw the side of his boss that proved he had done right by trusting his guts: Alicia was good people. He kept his smile subdued and nodded. "You're the boss."

"I am," Alicia agreed before going back into the General Store.

For a minute, Frankie Lee stood there, looking at the strange pioneer era building, and then out over the city where a towering castle loomed. Eras clashed and co-existed. *Nothing at* all *like the preacher said*. It wasn't the life he'd known or the afterlife he'd expected, but he couldn't wipe the grin off his face. Some things were constant: finding a place where a person belonged, a job that made a man feel good about himself, and a boss he could respect--those were the keys to a happy life. *Or a happy afterlife, in this case.*

CHANGING GUARDS: A GRAVEMINDER PREQUEL STORY

ALICIA MET WILLIAM MONTGOMERY AT THE MOUTH OF THE tunnel. The peculiarity of her inability to enter the tunnel was no stranger than the fact that anyone could transverse it, but it still felt odd to her. Once, more than a century ago, she'd believed the preachers with their beautiful sermons. She'd trusted them when they told her that death was the end, that a fiery pit waited for those who sinned, and that peace was an option for those who lived a good and righteous life. Then the dead woke, and she'd found out that death was not the end.

"Alicia." William stepped into her world, the land of the dead. He was the only living man who could do so right now. There'd been others, including her own husband, but they were gone. Another would replace William, as he'd replaced those before him, but for now, there was only him.

She said nothing. It pained her to hear an old man's voice coming from his lips. Years ago, he'd caused a flutter in her heart every time he entered the land of the dead. Of course, the fact that he was still alive made him more alluring than most everyone here.

He held out a bag, and she tried not to see the wrinkles on his hand. It always seemed wrong to see the Undertaker grow old when she was frozen at the same age.

"I brought a few surprises." William's expression was the same bold one that he'd worn as a young man, and Alicia knew without asking that the bag he passed over to her contained items sure to upset Charles. She didn't pressure William to cross the old bastard as she had a few decades ago when William had first become the Undertaker, but that didn't mean that the temptation had passed—only that her affection for William had grown.

A little shiver of excitement rippled over her as she peered into the bag. Inside was a thin book on homemade explosives, a bunch of wire, assorted gadgets she couldn't identify, and various packages wrapped and labeled with only numbers.

"There's a key to the numbers in the book," William said.

"Not that I don't appreciate it, but what gives?"

"Just thought I'd settle up and buy myself a little credit." He walked toward her little corner of the land of the dead with the comfort of someone who'd trod this path more times than either of them probably liked.

Alicia fell in step with him.

In the alleyways of the old wooden buildings, her boys waited and watched. Milt and Mickey were nearest, but a good half dozen more were scattered about the area, standing guard and keeping order. The streets of the land of the dead weren't always safe . . . truth be told, they were rarely safe. Any illusion of an afterlife filled with sweet cherubs and fields of flowers had been shattered long before Alicia died, but sometimes she regretted the loss of those idealized fancies. She supposed, sometimes when she was feeling a bit more hopeful, that those things might exist beyond this land. Most of the time, though, she wasn't given to hopeful musings. The fact was that this world was a strange one, and she had no way of knowing if what came next would be better or worse. Here at least she occupied a singular position: she was the only Graveminder who had not moved on after her death. Out there, presumably, her long gone husband waited, but the idea of facing him after she'd killed him was reason enough to stay where she was.

"Alicia?" William voice interrupted her reverie. "Are you well?"

She forced a smile. "Well enough."

He nodded. "Understandable." His grandfatherly face wrinkled with lines as he frowned. "Does the love for your partner change after you pass?"

There was no question as to which partner he meant. Every Undertaker had a Graveminder, a woman who could lead the Hungry Dead to this world. He lived as her partner, her guard, and often her lover. They were a pair, bound together more surely than any marriage contract. It made living a life with anyone else nearly impossible. William had done it, but only because both his wife and his Graveminder accepted the inevitable division of his heart. Alicia couldn't have done so. She'd have gleefully murdered anyone who took her Conner's attention away from her for even a moment.

"Course it does," she lied. "It's just a part of the contract, William, but even if not, your Graveminder won't ask to stay here in this world. She'll move on like all the rest."

"Except you," he amended quietly.

After years of steadfast refusal to talk about who she was and what she was, she'd given in recently. William knew what most of the Undertakers before him hadn't: she was a Graveminder, same as his beloved Maylene. She'd served Death in her life, minding the dead, keeping them in their rightful place, just as the women before her and after her. Telling him was probably why it was on her mind too much of late. Her life was long since over, and any hope she had of a peaceful afterlife was quashed by the reality of the land of the dead.

"Soon, my son . . ." William's words dwindled, and he steadfastly didn't look her way. He'd been almost fifty when his son and heir, Byron. He'd delayed for a long time on passing on his duties, not by choice, but because his Graveminder asked it of him. William would do anything for her. It was why he'd carried on his duty long after he should've passed it on to Byron.

William cleared his throat and said, "I've been talking to Maylene about telling the kids about the contract. It would be easier if I knew that you were . . . amenable to rolling my credits on to him."

"You know better," she chided him. "He has to find his way here just as you did. It's the way of it. I can't offer him any special consideration any more than I did when you were young and stumbling around here."

William nodded, and they walked the next few blocks in silence. He'd needed to ask, and she'd needed to refuse. The transition as the Undertaker prepared for death was always hard. The question of the passing on of the duties of Undertaker was raised by every generation. Some focused on the "what next" question, as if being in *this* land of the dead gave her special insight into what happened in the next plane. It didn't, and she told them as much. The other, *harder* questions were the sort she expected of William. They were also the sort she couldn't quite answer.

A warning whistle from her left made her stop and shove William to the ground.

She felt the sharp sting of the bullet a moment after she'd heard the warning from one of the boys.

"Damn it." The bullet grazed her shoulder, tearing through her jacket and bloodying her skin.

The Undertaker stood, gun in hand, eyes scanning the shadows where the shooter could hide.

Milt arrived a few moments later. He exchanged a nod with William, and then both men turned on her.

"What were you thinking?" Milt snarled. He pulled his shirt off and wadded it into a ball that he pressed to her shoulder.

"William could've been hit." She knocked Milt's hand away, but kept the shirt. Now that it was already bloodied, there was no sense in trying to use it for clothing. She'd buy him a new one and add this to the always-growing pile of rags they kept. Infection wasn't a problem once you were dead, but bullets still hurt, and blood still stained. Some things were truths regardless of the world around you.

"Thank you," William murmured as he slipped an arm around her. She didn't need his protection, any of theirs actually. Death could only truly kill her twice.

And although the old bastard had done just that over a century ago, he wasn't likely to kill her now that she was here, and no one else in the land of the dead had the power to cause a second passing. In the land of the living, everyone can kill. Bullets, animals, illnesses, the causes of death were myriad and omnipresent. In the land of the dead, there was only one person who could end a life. The rest of them had to settle with taking a person out of commission for a few days.

Still, she wasn't going to rehash it with the boys—or the Undertaker—again. They were always surly when she got shot. It was far less hassle to let them have their moment of worry.

"One of Charles' people?" Milt asked. "I didn't think there was any trouble brewing right now."

"Look into it." Alicia hoped so, as the pleasure of another quarrel with him would be welcome, but it seemed unlikely. Charles usually didn't do anything underhanded. With them, the exchange of gunfire was more a matter of habit than of maliciousness. He found it a necessary evil, a thing that helped remind her that she was under his domain, and she tended to resort to it because . . . well, because it simply made her feel better. Some women took up needlework, and some took up arms.

#

Over the next few weeks, Alicia threw herself into creating the explosives that she'd sought. It wasn't that she had any particular need for them, but they were *new*. New was a rare and valued commodity in the land of the dead. She did what she could to stave off boredom, but after so long in the land of the dead, excitement was harder to come by than she'd like. Her sole source of dangerous thrills was provoking Charles.

After what she considered sufficient experimentation, Alicia bribed a delivery boy to take an innocuous looking box to Charles' house. She timed it on a day when he was busy with a few quarrels she'd set to brewing in the Depression Era section of the city. They were often the easiest to rile. Their steadfast desire to live in houses that resembled shanties seemed tied to some sort of religious theory about Purgatory and completing penance. For the most part, those citizens weren't even people who'd lived during the Great Depression, but Charles allowed them their peculiarity—and Alicia leverage it for distractions time and again.

Milt and Boyd stood on either side of her as they waited to "field test" the explosives they'd made. They weren't scientists, and no one on their employ had made homemade explosives before now, so they weren't entire sure of the ratio. Their small-scale tests were successful, so they'd used that as the basis.

"Do you think it's big enough to even hear it?" Milt asked.

Alicia shrugged.

"Maybe there will be a vibration," Boyd suggested. "Dynamite shakes the ground. This is like dynamite, so—"

His words were abruptly cut off by a deafening *boom!* Dust and debris scattered outward as a wall crumbled. It was a much, much larger explosion than they'd planned.

"Shit, boss!" Milt muttered.

Immediately, a crowd began to gather.

"Move," she ordered Boyd and Milt. "*Now*."

She'd never done something quite this . . . extreme. Charles wouldn't hurt her, not really. She counted on that. It enabled her to poke and prod at him in a way no other resident of the land of the dead would dare. Her people weren't impervious though.

"Get moving before he gets home and sees . . ." She glanced back as the second floor of his beautiful mansion started to slope toward the ground.

"Holy fuck," someone nearby muttered.

Gazes were turning to her. There was no doubt who was responsible. No one else would be foolhardy enough to blow up Charles' new parlor. Alicia strode through the crowd, hoping that she hadn't finally gone too far.

She glanced back as that second floor section of wall came crashing down.

"Faster," she urged her people.

#

When Charles returned to his home to find flames, debris, and dust, he shook his head, but said nothing. What was there to say? Alicia, no doubt, had either been irritated by something he'd done or was in a mood again. Sometimes he thought he'd be lost when she finally moved on to join her own Undertaker. Right now, fear and guilt kept her here—in the land of the dead that he ruled. Eventually, she'd realize that she should go.

Ward, his right-hand man, muttered a curse that included the oft-uttered phrase "damn Barrow woman."

"It's unexpected," Charles said.

Ward snorted, but didn't engage in an argument. He was respectful of Charles' strange friendship with the dead Graveminder even though he had told Charles years ago that he thought it was twelve shades of stupid. Charles, for his part, respected both Ward's loyalty which resulted in his opinion of Alicia *and* his willingness to mostly keep silent on that opinion. He was a good man.

"How much shall I repair?" Charles mused. He liked to let the destruction she wrought stand, but in this case, there would have to be repairs made. He couldn't have his house collapse or allow a gaping hole in it. The repairs would give focus to some of his citizens, and the reminder that he was unpredictable served his purposes too.

He visualized the building once more intact, and with that thought, the walls were replaced. The rubble from the original walls remained—both inside and outside the building. It was a concession to both his practicality and Alicia's destruction.

"Hire some workers, Ward. That part of the house was due to be remodeled anyhow. Have them submit designs and teams, and I'll pick among them." Charles made sure his voice carried, and then he smothered the smile their excited murmurs evoked. He might not be able to relieve all of his citizens' unhappiness, but he saw no reason that being dead should have to equate to being miserable.

#

Charles was sure that he had more than enough patience to manage the Land of the Dead. He'd been doing it since before the humans had built proper cities over on the mortal side. Dealing with emotions was an altogether different situation. The peculiar nature of his domain was that every era in history existed within the reaches of the Land of the Dead. Boomtowns and modern cities vied for attention within the space of several blocks. The inhabitants of each area were all sure that the way the world had looked during each of their lives was how it *should* be.

And Charles had the unenviable job of keeping order among the lot of them.

For the past week, he'd been concentrating on the tedium of just that—instead of going to Alicia's General Store and demanding answers. She'd come when she was ready. Until then, he'd concentrate on the business of the dead, including choosing a new design for the section of his home that she'd destroyed.

"Sir?" Ward stood in the doorway of the study; the steady man was as patient as the statues that sat in the alcoves of the room.

Charles rubbed his eyes again. "Did I have an appointment?"

"Of a sort." Irritation flickered over Ward's expression so briefly that Charles wouldn't have noticed if they hadn't spent the past two centuries together. Only one person evoked such irritation in his right-hand man.

Charles rolled up the blueprints on his desk. "I gather Ms. Barrow is finally here?"

A curt nod from Ward answered the question without Ward himself having to find polite words.

"Where is she?" Charles asked.

Ward hesitated before admitting, "The west parlor. . ." He paused, cleared his throat, and amended, "The *remains* of the west parlor, sir."

Charles' smile became a laugh. "How long has she been there?"

"She did not have an appointment, sir." Ward stared directly at his boss. "She decimated the parlor, and today, she arrived wearing boots with . . . *dung* on them again. The foyer will need scrubbed, and the new rug"—Ward let out a pained sigh—"will need laundering. There is nowhere more suited for that woman than the ruins she created."

"I see." Charles stood and came around the desk. "So . . . she's been waiting a while then."

"She doesn't get *more* difficult with waiting," Ward muttered.

Charles walked toward his valet-bodyguard-friend. He clapped Ward on the shoulder. "I trust that the chairs that are *not* in the room will arrive not long after I do."

"Of course." Ward gestured for Charles to precede him down the hall. "Would you like full tea?"

"I suspect a bit of whiskey will be more useful." Charles didn't admit that the weight of the day slid from his shoulders as he left Ward behind and headed to the ruined part of the house, and Ward, likewise, didn't remark on the fact that he knew exactly how much Charles didn't admit.

Alicia might be the one dead person who always irritated Ward, but she was also the only person in the Land of the Dead who surprised Charles. If she ever decided to get over her anger and fear and move on to a better realm, Charles feared he'd be inconsolable. They weren't friends in any traditional sense, but she was valuable to him in the way he had rarely known.

#

Alicia sat in the center of a debris-strewn room. One knee was pulled up to her chest, and the other leg was extended in front of her. She didn't like sitting in the dirt, but it wouldn't make her jeans much filthier than they already were. The old bastard had left her in a chairless room for over an hour. Idly, she studied the space she'd been forced to occupy while she waited for *him* to decide he was done making her stew.

Never get tired of showing me who's really in charge, do you?

She had to admit that the punishment was fitting this time: her boys had detonated the charges that resulted in the debris around her. *It was just business.* She grinned. Charles might be the law, but she had become more than adept at provoking him—and getting results on a few key reform areas.

Alicia tensed at the sound of footsteps behind her. Without turning around, she knew the old bastard had arrived. No one else walked with that same cadence. He moved across the stone floor with music in his footfall. She wasn't sure he even noticed the song in his step. She did. After over a century of dealing with him in the land of the dead—and a few years more when she was still alive—she knew Charles better than she knew any person alive or dead.

Despite her best efforts, her spine stiffened, and her every nerve was on alert. It wasn't that she was frightened. *Much.* It was simple caution. He was the one person—*thing*—here that could end her existence. The land of the dead was his, absolutely and completely. That was why there had been no competition to setting up her business: no one crossed the old bastard.

Except me and mine.

"Alicia," he murmured. "Lovely to see you, as always, my dear."

She still didn't turn around. She wiped her hands on her jeans, but she didn't rise.

"I would've had lunch prepared if I'd known we had an appointment." Charles stood just behind her. "Perhaps you'd care for a drink since you're here."

Finally, Alicia looked over her shoulder at him. She patted the dirty floor beside her. "Have a seat, Charlie. It's quite cozy here."

"Ah, yes." He looked around. His gaze slid over the charred bits of wood and tile. He frowned as he spotted a painting that had been made unrecognizable by the blast. "I liked the room a bit more before you left that little package here."

"The explosives are a new item," she said softly, drawing his gaze back to her. "We made it ourselves, and I didn't realize how much damage it would do."

Charles didn't smile, not quite, but his expression softened. "That almost sounded like an apology, Alicia."

She shrugged. "Near to one as I'll get."

"Thank you," he murmured.

Alicia nodded. They couldn't exchange civilities as well in public, but here behind closed doors she knew she'd make more progress with Charles if she tried to be cordial. She wasn't sure if she'd ever admit that she preferred their civility to the hostility they needed to embrace if there were witnesses, but the rare quiet conversations she shared with Death these days reminded her of long gone times, back when she was alive and only visiting this realm.

"William's getting old," she said as politely as possible. "The boys and I notice it more and more each time he comes in to the General Store. He isn't as careful around town as an Undertaker needs to be." She paused, weighing the words as carefully as she ever did when the subject of the Undertaker and Graveminder came up. "It's time to replace him."

Charles frowned. His relationship with the Undertaker—as with every Undertaker before William—was contentious. They were both adversaries and allies, both dedicated to the one human woman who could move between the land of the dead and the living world. The complicated relationship didn't mean Charles disliked William or wished ill on him. Alicia understood that as she hadn't years ago when her husband, Conner, was the Undertaker.

"He'd not that old," Charles objected. "It was only a moment ago that he became—"

"It's been *decades*, Charlie," she interrupted.

His sense of time was skewed at best, and she'd realized several Undertakers back that it was up to her to help Charles notice when time had passed. Being the embodiment of Death made for a peculiar relationship with time. She'd taken it upon herself to be loyal to the calling she'd embraced when she'd been alive. She might be dead, but she *was* still a Graveminder.

She watched as Charles paced away from her. He stooped and

lifted a handful of rubble. Silently, he let the powder slip through his fingers. She knew it would take only a thought to turn the white chalky dust and bits of rubble into a wall again. He wouldn't though. Whatever she destroyed, he left broken. That, too, was on the long list of topics best not pondered. He'd done only enough repair work to keep the building intact, and now he was auditioning designers to repair and renovate his home.

While they waited in silence—her on the floor and him surveying the destruction—Charles' personal assistant, guard, and all-around pain in Alicia's ass came in with a tray. On it were glasses, an ice bucket, and decanter. Behind Ward were lackeys with chairs and a small table, as well as two men with brooms. In minutes, they'd cleared a space, arranged the furniture, and left the drinks.

Ward looked to Charles, ignoring her as if she weren't visible to him, and at Charles' nod, he departed again.

Alicia and Charles sipped their drinks in silence, a companionable peaceful habit that she knew they wouldn't admit to cherishing.

"I've not met the new Graveminder yet," Charles admitted somberly after he finished his drink. "After the way things went when I met Ella . . ." His words faded, but they weren't necessary. The unprecedented actions of the young girl who was to replace Maylene Barrow had led to this awkward situation. Ella Mae had committed suicide, determined to hasten her journey to the land of the dead, and the current Graveminder had decided to hide the truth from the girl who would replace Ella. William, by extension, had hidden that same information from the next Undertaker. Neither Byron nor Rebekkah knew of the land of the dead. It was well past time for that to change.

And Alicia was going to make sure it happened.

"William is weary," Alicia pointed out. "He's vulnerable every time he comes here. If you don't act, I will."

She didn't specify how she'd act, but Charles knew—as did William. The Undertaker and Death were both too worried over the current Graveminder. Maylene was hiding her replacement, letting the girl wander outside Claysville, utterly unaware of her duties. It was well past time for the changing of the guard, and even though Alicia's descendent was cosseting the next Graveminder, Alicia wouldn't be.

"Insist he bring the boy to meet you, or I'll force the matter," she announced.

#

Charles sat in the destroyed parlor long after Alicia had left. Alicia's ability to offer to kill William bothered him. He wanted to think that her willingness to kill was a result of having been here in the land of the dead where shooting, stabbing, strangling, or any variety of heinous acts only resulted in temporary death. He wondered sometimes, though, what she'd have been like had she not been trapped in Claysville because of the contract he'd made with her long-gone ancestor.

The only person who could kill the already dead was him, and that was an act he rarely took. He didn't want to do it now either. Minding the dead wasn't quite the same as taking their lives. He found the curious spark of the living rather intoxicating. Every Graveminder was special to him, not just because they were living but because, through them, Charles knew the world of the living. None were as special as the first Graveminder. He'd been in love with Abigail; it was why the contract was created. Love for her had made him unable to deny her anything. The result was a gap between the living and the dead, and the inhabitants of Claysville were still paying for that. There, the dead didn't always stay dead, and it was all because Charles couldn't say "no" to a living woman who looked at him fondly and sais, "Please, Charles?"

Unfortunately, that very same weakness for his Graveminders meant that he was at odds with their living partners. There was no love lost between William Montgomery and the ruler of the land of the dead. That did not mean, however, that Charles was keen to commit murder. The death of the Undertaker would cause the subsequent death of the Graveminder. The peculiar bargain Charles had made with their predecessors centuries ago meant that the mortality of the two was entwined.

Reluctantly, Charles admitted that Alicia was probably right. He sipped the remainder of Alicia's drink in silence. It was as close to actual contact with her that he ever got.

He was still sitting there when Ward returned some time later.

"I need to see Maylene and William," Charles told them. "It's time that I meet the next generation. The new Graveminder and Undertaker need to be brought back to Claysville so they can be ready to assume their duties."

Available now: ***Cold Iron Heart*!**

How far would you go to escape fate?

In this prequel to the international bestselling WICKED LOVELY series, the Faery Courts collide a century before the mortals in *Wicked Lovely* are born.

Thelma Foy, a jeweler with the Second Sight in iron-bedecked 1890s New Orleans, wasn't expecting to be caught in a faery conflict. Tam can see through the glamours faeries wear to hide themselves from mortals, but if her secret were revealed, the fey would steal her eyes, her life, or her freedom. So, Tam doesn't respond when they trail thorn-crusted fingertips through her hair at the French Market or when the Dark King sings along with her in the bayou.

But when the Dark King, Irial, rescues her, Tam must confront everything she thought she knew about faeries, men, and love.

Too soon, New Orleans is filling with faeries who are looking for her, and Irial is the only one who can keep her safe.

Unbeknownst to Tam, she is the prize in a centuries-old fight between Summer Court and Winter Court. To protect her, Irial must risk a war he can't win--or surrender the first mortal woman he's loved.

COLD IRON HEART: CH 1 TAM

VOICES ROSE AND FELL IN THE STREETS OF THE FRENCH QUARTER. A woman with hair that seemed as delicate and white as if spiders had woven it walked arm-in-arm with an elegant man with a bone topped cane. They were only humans. The inhuman ones who strolled the French Quarter were even more remarkable. Invisible to the eyes of the city's mortals, faeries slithered and danced along the edge of the city where the water moved and the iron-laced buildings ended.

"She's a pretty girl," a lion-maned man purred.

The creature beside the maned faery stared at her as if Tam was ghastly. "If you like *their* sort."

And Tam felt self-conscious, awkward and embarrassed. She wasn't ugly. Plain, perhaps, maybe even a little too fit for a woman. Her hair was too red. Her eyes were too curious. Her body not soft enough. Her hands rough from working with metal or laundry. She'd earned every muscle though, taking in wash when she needed and working her art as often as she could. Nice women were able to be fashionable. Wealthy women were able to be delicate.

And the other kind of women, those who worked over near Canal

Street selling favors, were allowed to be luscious. Maybe if money wasn't scarce, she'd have voluptuous hips and breasts, but the softness of a woman required excess money for foods that were too dear for her to buy. Her curves were there in outline, but she was neither lush nor delicate.

Thelma Foy suspected she'd be forgettable if not for her hair and her mouth, which was fuller than most and noticeable because of her habit of saying the wrong thing, the audacious or dangerous thing. Other than that, she was merely Tam, a woman who wanted to find a place in the world and maybe a bit of comfort if she could. That meant, for now, pretending she didn't hear invisible men discussing her.

"She's perfect," the *other* one said.

He was the real complication in Tam's life. Irial—a faery whose name she'd heard the others whisper as if it were a prayer—watched her with a different kind of studiousness. And despite every bit of logic she possessed, Tam watched him back. How could she not?

He was beautiful: close-cropped hair, blue-black eyes, and Creole skin. He was wearing fine trousers and a crisp shirt. Although he had no jacket, he had completed his attire with a sharp vest. Tam thought he very might be the most handsome man in the whole of New Orleans.

He also wasn't visible to any human but Tam.

With effort, she pulled her gaze away from him and opened the door of yet another jeweler's shop. She needed to focus on business, not beautiful creatures. If she didn't sell her jewelry, she'd have no food.

Inside the shop, the man, because they were always men, looked past her as if a husband or father would materialize behind her. When he saw no one, he looked Tam up and down. Proper ladies didn't wander around in shops alone.

He took in her worn and patched dress, and he saw her lack of gloves. She watched him weigh her and decide if she was an "abandoned woman," a woman who sold her affection. She wasn't, and her appearance made that clear. Her hair was controlled, pinned and forced into as modest a look as she could manage. And, most tellingly, her bosom, shoulder, arms, and legs were all modestly hidden.

She was not a woman who sold her body in Storyville. But she was also not accompanied by a man. No husband. No lover. No father. Tam was poor, unaccompanied, and instantly dismissed.

"Can I help you?"

"I hope so." She stepped further inside the shop, admiring the gleaming wood and glass display cases. They filled the space in a way that said that the wares inside were worth attention. It was not crowded. Each piece of jewelry was nestled in its own place. It was exactly the sort of space where Tam would love to see her own work. Diamonds and rubies sparkled like the stars in the clearest skies, resting on velvet displays. Lesser gems adorned other pieces.

"I have work to sell . . ." Tam pulled out the pieces she'd brought. Carefully, she untied the scarf she'd wound and tied around her jewelry. Her hands shook as she gently lowered the scarf onto that glass case, but her nerves faded a little when her pieces were spread out in front of the shop owner. She knew they were good.

"Mmmm." He was a short man with tufts of ear hair like wisps of smoke.

Tam swallowed her fear, her instant words of desperation, and said, "They're fine pieces."

It was a bit bold for a woman, but she wasn't built for simpering or false modesty. The work was equal to that in the displays. The gems weren't as precious, but the settings were equal to that of a queen's jewelry.

"Did you steal these?" The shop owner stared at her, his gaze taking in Tam's sewn and re-sewn dress and her worn boots.

"No." Her hands, calloused and stained from hours handling metals, were held at her side. The urge to defend herself vied with the hunger in her belly. She needed the sale. Calmer, she repeated, "No."

He stared at her, assessing.

Tam wore none of her own work. Doing so was—to quote her Gran—like lipstick on a pig. Sparkling jewelry stood out, and thieves saw no reason not to steal what they assumed was already stolen.

"I made them," she told the jeweler levelly, just as she had told the others who'd sent her away.

The jeweler continued to stare at her in silence. He didn't laugh outright. Instead his lips pressed together like her Aunt Ethelreda had so often done. Distasteful. Unpleasant. He held his mouth as if a lemon slice was suddenly slipped under his tongue.

Tam wasn't surprised to hear him say, "Women don't make jewelry."

That wasn't true, of course. She knew several women who did metalwork, as well as one who cut and polished stones, but their work was credited to a father, brother, husband, or in one case, a son. Behind the scenes, there were others like her.

"We *do* create art," Tam argued quietly, her voice far more level than her emotions but wavering slightly from the effort. "Look at these. Please. Just look at them."

She gestured at the pieces on the worn bit of cloth that she had wrapped them in to carry them here: A ring, perfectly formed and polished with a cairngorm set levelly; a brooch, twisted vines of silver holding a polished thistle blossom; and a locket with such polish that she could see the lights glinting in it. The locket was a particularly lovely piece. She'd painstakingly etched a rose vine around it.

"They're fine pieces." The man looked again at the cairngorm ring. "I'll buy that one from you, and if your father or brother wants to sell more wares, we can do business."

This was it, the moment of decision. Tam could either walk away or accept the lie he was willing to offer to justify his willingness to buy a piece. Neither option was appealing, but there wasn't a third choice. Women weren't in possession of a great many choices in a man's world—and even here in a city where a woman could be educated or own property, it was a man's world.

"The pieces are all for sale," Tam said, re-positioning the locket to its best angle. Each tiny thorn on the roses was impossibly there.

Selling her work was the best outcome she *ever* had when she tried to find her way into the jewelry business: the sale of a few pieces and a lie. What she wanted was an apprenticeship. What she found were closed doors and derision.

"Let me see them in better light," the jeweler said.

He swooped them into his palm and walked away. At such times, she feared that he'd simply keep them. A man could say she was lying, that she was a thief, that no woman could create jewelry such as this. There was little she could do if such a thing happened. At best she could go see the other jewelers who rejected her and ask them to acknowledge seeing her work.

Behind her, the door opened and closed.

"When you enter a shop, close the door behind you, young lady," the jeweler said without looking up.

"I thought I had." Tam glanced to the door where the dark faery now stood. The shadows in the store seemed to stretch out to caress him, as if they couldn't resist.

Irial smiled at her, and she had to struggle to pretend not to see him. If ever there were a man—a creature—striking enough to lure her away from her plans of spinsterdom, Irial was the one. Her gaze slid over the width of his shoulders as she forced herself to pretend to seek the phantom wind that had opened the door.

"Courage," Irial whispered as he walked close behind her.

Tam stiffened. Faeries ought not speak to her. They were to think that she couldn't see them.

Better a faery than a human come so close, though. Human men were anything but appealing to her. They spoke to women as if they were either daft children or dolls. They made the rules, controlled business and laws, and women had to learn to make do—or marry. It was outrageous. At least the faeries seemed to treat men and women, or the faery equivalents of them, the same.

The female ones could be as monstrous as the male ones.

Humans weren't like that. Men acted, and women reacted. Men decided, and women coped. It was absurd. Tam had hoped it would be different in New Orleans. The city was even more vibrant than Chicago. The first legal "red light" district? Who could imagine such boldness, such audacity? It made the city seem forward-thinking, so Tam had moved.

Not to work in the sin dens, but in hopes that a city where women were educated, where they owned business, would be better for a female artist, too. She'd had such dreams.

"Would you be interested in purchasing the pieces?" Tam asked in a ladylike, gentle voice, hating the need to use such a tactic. "Few women could resist their beauty."

"This one." He held up the ring and quoted a lower price than the piece was worth.

"If you doubled that, I'll give you a second piece," she gestured at the brooch.

"Double for all three."

Reluctantly, Tam nodded. She couldn't afford to refuse—or to demand more. She needed money to live. Everyone did, but a woman alone had fewer options for finding it. Selling a few pieces of her jewelry here and there meant she had enough to afford rent and food. Selling these would allow her a full four months if she was careful. Three if she bought more supplies to create more pieces and try yet again with another jeweler. Creating art wasn't reliable work, but if she sold it, she earned enough to live on for months. No other job would pay so well—at least no other job that allowed her to stay clothed.

Work in a brothel—or marrying a man—would pay better, but with men came children. Children were a whole set of demands that would end her ability to create jewelry, and worse still, they'd lead to a level of risk that she couldn't fathom. Hiding her ability to see the fey things was hard. Hiding a child's ability? That was a terrifying prospect.

As Tam waited for her money, she tried not to look at the faery who was studying her yet again. Shadows from the wall seemed to ooze toward him, as if they had a mind or heart. She understood the impulse. He was breath-taking, but some prickle on the back of her neck reminded her that faeries and humans never mix well.

"Here you go." The jeweler handed her a bag.

Again, she was left hoping he was honest. Counting the money out would be insulting, and if he'd shorted her, she couldn't expect to get money. Life was about power, and Tam had none.

If she was shorted on what he owed, there was always wash she could help one of her neighbors do. They took on a little more if she offered to help, and it let Tam make ends meet when there were no other options.

"Courage, love," the faery whispered again.

"What about an apprenticeship?" Tam asked the jeweler hurriedly before he walked away, sounding a bit desperate now.

"For a woman?" he sounded thoroughly shocked.

"I could learn and then carry the information to home. My father's not well enough to leave the house, you see. It would be as if you were teaching him, but—"

The jeweler reached over the glass display case and patted her hand. "Women are gifted in many ways, but in learning such a skill? I think not. I'll take the three pieces, and you tell your father I'll need him to come himself next time—or I'll come to him."

"I'll tell him," she said. She would speak it into the air. There wasn't any more likely way to reach him—if he was even alive.

Money in her possession, Tam stepped out of the shop, the third one this week. There would be no fourth one. She'd sold the only thing she had to use to convince a jeweler to work with her. The sale was good enough, better than nothing, but it also meant she had to begin again and hope that in a few weeks or months she'd have better luck.

Someday, her luck would change. It *had* to.

She swiped at the tears on her cheeks, not quite able to stop them from falling today but not letting them run free either. The faery glared at the shop as if he was as affronted as she was.

"Fool," Irial, who had followed her into the street, said.

Tam didn't reply—although she agreed with him.

COLD IRON HEART: CH 2 IRIAL

IRIAL WATCHED HER LEAVE. TEAR TRACKS WERE STILL FRESH ON her skin, and every impulse in him said he needed to follow, to comfort, to touch her. There were good reasons not to, but Irial rarely felt compelled to follow *reason*. That was the prerogative of the High Court. The Dark Court had the opposite motivation. Passion drove those that aligned with shadows. The Dark King would rather lose himself in pleasure and impulse than logic and restraint.

"How in the name of madness am I to keep you safe if you never are where you say you are?" Gabriel slid from his steed with a rumble that had mortals looking around to see why the ground shook.

Irial gave his closest friend, guard, and all around most-trusted faery a look that would've sent most creatures to their knees.

The muscular Hound snorted. "Don't give me that look. One of these days you're going to get stabbed or burned alive or—"

"And unless it's a regent, I'd be fine." Irial shook his head. "Most of those bold enough to stab me aren't kings or queens, are they?"

"Both Beira and Keenan would gladly stab you." Gabriel folded his arms.

"But the kingling is weak, and Beira isn't here." Irial started to walk, stepping around the passing humans. He trailed his hand over the cheek of a woman who startled as he passed. She wasn't Sighted, not like lovely Thelma, but she had an ancestor somewhere in her past who had been. Those who were sensitive to the fey were alluring enough that Irial made note of her. Sometimes a man had needs.

Of course, seducing the forbidden was even better. The Summer King's faeries were not to so much as glance his way, and the Sighted . . . oh, the Sighted mortals were a particular treat.

Irial was born to tempt, and he was not one to refuse that nature.

"What are you pouting about?" Gabriel asked in a tone that said he'd really rather not know the answer.

"No one ever says no."

"No." Gabriel grinned. "There. Now—"

"To *relations*, Gabe."

"Oh hell, no." The Hound made a face of distaste. "Scrawny thing like you . . ."

Irial laughed. He was quite certain that *scrawny* was an inaccurate word—in all ways—but to a creature that shook the ground with every step, the word was quite relative. He had no interest in his best mate, of course. Who else would stand at his side and lure him from his many moods? Or toss bodies to the side when Irial's temper led to brawls?

"She's mortal," Irial said quietly. He didn't mention that she was *the* mortal. The one human in all the world who could change the shift of power between the faery courts. If he said that, Gabriel would want to be reasonable, and that sounded positively dreary.

"Do you have a sudden aversion to mortals?" Gabriel shoved a man in a tall hat into the street, causing traffic to erupt into chaos.

Irial raised his brows.

"He was too near you."

"He couldn't *see* me, Gabe." Irial grinned though. His friend's protective impulses were endearing, even when they resulted in screams and blood—perhaps more so when they did, in truth.

They stood in the French Quarter watching the mortals who'd

nearly been trampled, women on the sidewalk clutching their parasol handles, and Irial couldn't help inhaling the madness of it all. Mortal feelings weren't sustaining as fey ones were, but he still appreciated them.

"I may want her watched," Irial said lightly.

Gabriel hesitated. "By the Hunt?"

If not for Thelma having the Sight, Irial might say yes, but the Hunt carried terror in their wake, spilling fears and nightmares where they rode. As a Sighted mortal, Thelma would either be susceptible or immune to them.

"Maybe." Irial looked in the direction she'd gone. "For now, send a few of the Scrimshaw Sisters her way."

Then before the Hound could ask questions Irial was afraid to answer, Irial ordered, "Do not follow me today. Check on the arrival of Winter and Summer."

The order spelled itself in ink on the arm of his most trusted.

"Are we expecting them?"

"Maybe." Irial lifted the cane he liked to carry of late, carved head and jeweled eyes. It looked a lot like Lady War, and Irial carried it to spite her.

"You're hiding things."

"Wise man," Irial murmured, and then he slid between the fascinating new carriages that the mortals had made. Horseless carriages. Automobiles. If not for the stink of them and the sluggish speeds, he'd own one already. Some day. The joy of eternity was that he had so many centuries to live, to learn, to fuck, and to brawl. It was good to be the Dark King.

WHEN IRIAL SET OFF IN PURSUIT OF THELMA, HE KNEW SHE'D SEE him, blessed or cursed as she was. She saw every faery in the city—but she didn't look at *them* with that pulsing in her throat. She didn't look at them and think wicked thoughts that made a tinge of pink tint her cheeks.

She watched Irial that way, though, as if he was a delicacy she wanted to sample. Such temptation was always glorious, but it was more so with Thelma. As a Sighted mortal, she was immune to the allure that Irial had for most faeries and most mortals. She had the beautiful, irresistible ability to *refuse* him. That made her a challenge. A treat. He hummed happily to himself as he went to stalk his quarry.

He wouldn't ever force a woman, but he'd dust off old skills he hadn't needed to use in a few centuries. She was forbidden in so many ways, and she was immune to the very thing that made him alluring to fey and mortal alike. The perfect quarry. The exact enticement to lure the king of temptation.

Until the Summer and Winter courts arrived in his fair city, Thelma Foy was all his, and he intended to make the most of it.

The Dark King whistled a cheery tune as he approached the edge of the Mississippi River. Thelma came here, pulled to water as if she was part-fey. She wasn't. She was simply an artist.

"Irial?"

He turned, caught off-guard in a way that would make Gabriel gnash his teeth.

His solicitor was there. Saunders. For reasons of practicality, he had been given a salve that allowed the man to see the unseen. The Dark King didn't go around passing out the Sight carelessly, but he needed the occasional human assistant. Saunders handled legal and business matters, and that meant that to protect him, Irial had given him the Sight. It was that or the poor man would end up crouched in a corner cowering from unseen attacks.

"Sire," Saunders started.

Irial smiled at the man's tentativeness. What *was* the correct term for a king when you were not of his court—or species? There weren't guidebooks for such things.

"Did you sort out the details on the house?"

"I did, sir." Saunders cleared his throat. "They were eager to sell once I offered the sum you authorized."

Irial nodded. He's made the somewhat unplanned decision to purchase the house he'd been renting in the Garden District. Even if he hadn't admitted it to anyone outright, he liked the idea of staying here for as long as they could. He still planned to exit before things were unpleasant with the Summer Court and Winter Court, but a house purchase wouldn't change that.

"A jeweler."

"Sir?"

"I want to purchase a jewelry shop." Irial pictured the moment, telling Thelma. What woman wouldn't be charmed by such a gesture? He gave Saunders the instructions and sent him to the shop in question.

A warning voice in Irial's mind suggested caution, but caution was tedious. Why waste time when mortals died so often and quickly?

"I loved *The Wicked and The Dead*! A sassy, ass-kicking heroine, a deliciously mysterious fae hero, and a wonderful mix of action and romance. Add that to Melissa's usual great world-building, and I'm already looking forward to book 2!"
—Jeaniene Frost, *NYT* Bestselling Author

AVAILABLE Now!

In near-future New Orleans, *draugar*, again-walkers, are faster and stronger than most humans, but not venomous until they are a century old. Until then, they shamble and bite. Since not everyone wants to see their relatives end up that way, Geneviève Crowe makes her living beheading the dead.

But now, her magic has gone sideways, and the only person strong enough to help her is the one man who could tempt her to think about picket fences: Eli Stonecroft, a faery who chose to be a bar-owner in New Orleans rather than live in *Elphame*.

When human businessmen start turning up as *draugar*, the queen of the again-walkers and the wealthy son of one of the victims, both hire Geneviève to figure it out. She works to keep her magic in check, the dead from crawling out of their graves, and enough money for a future that might be a lot longer than she'd like. Neither her heart nor her life are safe now that she's juggling a faery, murder, and magic.

Continue the Faery Bargains series with

Under a Winter Sky (19 November 2020)

Under a Winter Sky **includes "Blood Martinis and Mistletoe" (Faery Bargains 1.5)**

Half-dead witch Geneviève Crowe makes her living beheading the dead--and spends her free time trying not to get too attached to her business partner, Eli Stonecroft, a faery in self-imposed exile in New Orleans. With a killer at her throat and a blood martini in her hand, Gen accepts what seems like a straight-forward faery bargain, but soon realizes that if she can't figure out a way out of this faery bargain, she'll be planning a wedding after the holidays.

And also ...

The Kiss & The Killer (1 March 2021) Book 2 in the Faery Bargains series

The next installment in a new faery and fanged world written by the author of the internationally bestselling Wicked Lovely series.

For readers of Patricia Briggs, Chloe Neill, and Jeaniene Frost.

HALF WITCH, HALF KILLER, WHOLLY UNSUCCESSFUL AT EVERY FAERY Bargain so far...

Geneviève Crowe makes her living beheading or resurrecting the dead in near-future New Orleans. After entering an accidental engagement, overcoming attempted murder, and discovering a family secret, Geneviève is ready for things to settle down, but carnival season in New Orleans is not the best time of year for "normal."

When Eli Stonecroft, the faery who has claimed her heart despite her best attempts, offers her a new faery bargain--she's smart enough to say no . . . right up to the point when she has to decide between dealing with the consequence of this faery bargain or facing the killer alone.

As the *draugar* mix with the locals and tourists, and bodies start to pile up, Geneviève is enlisted by the faery king and the *draugar* queen to find the killer amidst the swirl of parades and parties of carnival season...

THE WICKED & DEAD CHAPTER 1

AUTUMN IN THE SOUTH WAS STILL BOTH HUMID AND HOT. NEW Orleans was always a wet city. Wet air. Wet drizzle. Beer soaked streets. *Other* things spilling out from behind trash bins. Sometimes, the heavy air and frequent rain was just this side of too much.

Most nights, there was nowhere else I'd rather be. We were a city risen from the ashes, over and over. Plagues, floods, monsters, New Orleans didn't stop, didn't give up, and I was proud of that. Tonight, though, I watched the fog roll out like a cheap film effect, and a good book in front of a warm fire sounded far better than work. The nonstop rain this month would wash away evidence of the things that happened in New Orleans' darkened corners, but I could prevent bloodshed. It was more or less what I did. Sometimes, I spilled a bit of blood, but if we weighed it all out, I was fairly sure I was one of the good guys.

More curves and sass than actual *guys*, but the point held. White hat. Dingy around the edges. I blame my persistent nagging guilt.

A *thump* on the other side of the wall made me pause.

Could I hurl myself over the wall into Cypress Grove Cemetery?

It wasn't the *worst* idea ever—or even this month—which said more about my life than I'd like to admit.

I listened for more sounds. *Nothing*. No scrabbling. No growling.

I needed to be on the other side of the wall where tombs were lined up like miniature houses. The tree branches I'd used last time were gone, probably trimmed by someone who saw their potential. Now, there was no graceful way to hurl myself over the ten-foot wall.

Every cemetery in the nation now had taller walls and plenty of newly-opened space for the dead. Cemeteries had become "stage one" of the verification of death process. Honestly, I guess graves were better than cold storage at the morgue. The lack of heartbeat made it impossible to know if the corpses would walk-again, and those of us who advocated for beheading all corpses were deemed callous.

I wasn't sure I was callous for wanting the dead to stay dead. I knew what they were capable of before the world at large did.

At least I was prepared. A moment or so later, I shoved a metal spike into the wall, cutting my palm in the process.

"Shit. Damn. Monkey balls."

A ripple of light flashed around me the moment my blood dripped to the soil. At least the light was magic, not the police or a tourist with a camera. While the laws were ever-changing, B&E was still illegal. And I was breaking into a cemetery where I might need to carry out a contracted beheading. *That* was illegal, too.

It simply wasn't a photo-ready moment—although with my long dyed-blue hair and nearly translucent skin, I was far too photogenic. I won't say I look like I've been drained of both blood and color, but I will admit that next to a lot of the folks in my city, I look like I've been bleached.

I fumbled with my gloves, trapping my blood inside the thick leather before I resumed shoving climbing cams into gaps in the wall. Normally, cams held the ropes that climbers use. Tonight, they'd be like tiny foot supports. If I were human, this wouldn't work out well.

I'm not.

Mostly, I'd say I am a witch, but that is the polite truth. I am more like witch-with-hard-to-explain-extras. That smidge of blood I'd spilled was enough to send out "wakey, wakey" messages to whatever corpses were listening, but the last time I'd had to bleed for them to rest again, I'd needed to shed more than a cup of blood.

I concentrated on not sending out a second magic flare and continued to insert the cams.

Rest. Stay. I felt silly thinking messages to the dead, but better silly than planning for excess bleeding.

At least this job *should* be an easy one. My task was to find out if Alice Navarro was again-walking or if she was securely in her vault. I hoped for the latter. Most people hired me to ease their dearly departed back in the "departed" category, but the Navarro family was the other sort. They missed her, and sometimes grief makes people do things that are on the wrong side of rational.

My pistol had tranquilizer rounds tonight. If Navarro was awake, I'd need to tranq her. If she wasn't, I could call it a night—unless there were other again-walkers. That's where the beheading came in. Straight-forward. Despite the cold and wet, I still hoped for the best. All things considered, I really was an optimist at heart.

At the top of the wall, I swung my leg over the stylish spikes cemented there and dropped into the wet grass. I was braced for it, but when I landed, it wasn't dew or rain that made me land on my ass.

An older man, judging by the tufts of grey hair on the bloodied body, in a security guard uniform had bled out on the ground. Something--most likely an again-walker--had gnawed on the security guard's face. Who had made the decision to have a living man with no special skills stand inside the walls of a cemetery? Now, he was dead.

I whispered a quick prayer before surveying my surroundings. Once I located the *draugr*, I could call in the location of the dead man. First, though, I had to find the face-gnawer who killed him. Since my magic was erratic, I didn't want to send a voluntary pulse out to find my prey. That would wake the truly dead, and there were plenty of them here to wake.

Several rows into the cemetery, I found Alice Navarro's undisturbed grave. No upheaval. No turned soil. Mrs. Navarro was well and truly dead. My clients had their answer—but now, I had a mystery. Which cemetery resident had killed the security guard?

A sound drew my attention. A thin hooded figure, masked like they were off to an early carnival party, stared back at me. They didn't move like they were dead. Too slow. Too human. And *draugar* weren't big on masks.

"Hey!" My voice seemed too loud. "You. What are you . . ."

The figure ran, and several other voices suddenly rang out. Young voices. Teens inside the cemetery.

"Shit cookies!" I ran after the masked person. Who in the name of all reason would be in among the graves at night? I ran through the rows of graves, looking for evidence of waking as I went.

"Bitch!"

The masked figure was climbing over the wall with a ladder, the chain sort you use in home fire-emergencies. Two teens tried to grab the person. One kid was kneeling, hand gripping his shoulder in obvious pain.

And there, several feet away, was Marie and Edward Chevalier's grave. The soil was disturbed, as if a pack of excited dogs had been digging. The person in the mask was not the dead one in the nearby grave. There *was* a recently dead *draugr*.

And kids.

I glanced back at the teens.

A masked stranger, a dead security guard, a *draugr,* and kids. This was a terrible combination.

The masked person dropped something and pulled a gun. The kids backed away quickly, and the masked person glanced at me before scrambling the rest of the way over the wall—all while awkwardly holding a gun.

"Are you okay?" I asked the kids, even as my gaze was scanning for the *draugr*.

"She stabbed Gerry," the girl said, pointing at the kid on the ground.

The tallest of the teens grabbed the thing the intruder dropped and held it up. A syringe.

"She?" I asked.

"Lady chest," the tall one explained. "When I ran into her, I felt her—"

"Got it." I nodded, glad the intruder with the needle was gone, but a quick glance at the stone by the disturbed grave told me that a fresh body had been planted there two days ago. That was the likely cause of the security guard's missing face. I read the dates on the stone: Edward was not yet dead. Marie was.

I was seeking Marie Chevalier.

"Marie?" I whispered loudly as the kids talked among themselves. The last thing I needed right now was a *draugr* arriving to gnaw on the three dumb kids. "Oh, Miss Marie? Where are you?"

Marie wouldn't answer, even if she had been a polite Southern lady. *Draugr* were like big infants for the first decade and change: they ate, yelled, and stumbled around.

"There's a real one?" the girl asked.

I glanced at the kids. I was calling out a thing that would *eat* them if they had been alone with it, and they seemed excited. Best case was a drooling open-mouthed lurch in my direction. Worst case was they all died.

"Go home," I said.

Instead they trailed behind me as I walked around, looking for Marie. I passed by the front gate—which was now standing wide open.

"Did you do that?" The lock had been removed. The pieces were on the ground. Cut through. Marie was not in the cemetery.

Shaking heads. "No, man. The ladder the bitch used was ours."

Intruder. With a needle. Possibly also the person who left the gate open? Had someone wanted Marie Chevalier released? Or was that a coincidence? Either way, a face-gnawer was loose somewhere in the city, one of the who-knows-how-many *draugar* that hid here or in the nearby suburbs or small towns.

I pushed the gates closed and called it in to the police. "Broken gate at Cypress Grove. Cut in pieces."

"Miss Crowe," the woman on dispatch replied. "Are you injured?"

"No. The *lock* was cut. Bunch of kids here." I shot them a look. "Say it wasn't them."

"I will send a car," she said. A longer than normal pause. "Why are *you* there, Miss Crowe?"

I smothered a sigh. It complicated my life that so many of the cops recognized me, that dispatch did, that the ER folks at the hospital did. It wasn't like New Orleans was *that* small.

"Do you log my number?" I asked. "Or is it my voice?"

Another sigh. Another pause. She ignored my questions. "Details?"

"I was checking on a grave here. It's intact, but the cemetery gate's busted," I explained.

"I noted that," she said mildly. "Are the kids alive?"

"Yeah. A person in a mask tried to inject one of them, and a guard inside is missing a lot of his face. No *draugr* here now, but the grave of Marie and Edward Chevalier is broken out. I'm guessing it was her that killed the guard."

The calm tone was gone. "There's a car about two blocks away. You and the children—"

"I'm good." I interrupted. "Marie's long gone, I guess. I'll be sure the kids are secure, but—"

"Miss Crowe! You don't know if she's still there or nearby. You need to be relocated to safety, too."

"Honest to Pete, you all need to worry a lot less about me," I said.

She made a noise that reminded me of my mother. Mama Lauren could fit a whole lecture in one of those "uh-huh" noises of hers. The woman on dispatch tonight came near to matching my mother.

"Someone *cut* the lock," I told dispatch. "What we need to know is why. And who. And if there are other opened cemeteries." I paused. "And who tried to inject the kid."

I looked at them. They were in a small huddle. One of them dropped and stomped the needle. I winced. That was going to make investigating a lot harder.

Not my problem, I reminded myself. I was a hired killer, not a cop, not a detective, not a nanny.

"Kid probably ought to get a tox screen and tetanus shot," I muttered.

Dispatch made an agreeing noise, and said, "Please try not to 'find' more trouble tonight, Miss Crowe."

I made no promises.

When I disconnected, I looked at the kids. "Gerry, right?"

The kid in the middle nodded. White boy. Looking almost as pale as me currently. I was guessing he was terrified.

"Let me see your arm."

He pulled his shirt off. It looked like the skin was torn.

"Do not scream," I said. My eyes shifted into larger versions of a snake's eyes. I knew what it looked like, and maybe a part of me was okay with letting them see because nobody would believe them if they did tell. They were kids, and while a lot had changed in the world, people still doubted kids when they talked.

More practically, though, as my eyes changed I could see in a way humans couldn't.

Green. Glowing like a cheap neon light. The syringe had venom. *Draugr* venom. It wasn't inside the skin. The syringe was either jammed or the kid jerked away.

"Water?"

One of the kids pulled a bottle from his bag, and I washed the wound. "Don't touch the fucking syringe." I pointed at it. "Who stomped on it? Hold your boot up."

I rinsed that, too. Venom wasn't the sort of thing anyone wanted on their skin unless they wanted acid-burn.

"Venom," I said. "That was venom in the needle. You could've died. And"—I pointed behind me—"there was a *draugr* here. Guy got his face chewed off."

They were listening, seeming to at least. I wasn't their family, though. I was a blue-haired woman with some weapons and weird eyes. The best I could do was hand them over to the police and hope they weren't stupid enough to end up in danger again tomorrow.

New Orleans had more than Marie hiding in the shadows. *Draugr* were fast, strong, and difficult to kill. If not for their need to feed on the living like mindless beasts the first few decades after resurrection, I might accept them as the next evolutionary step. But I wasn't a fan of anything—mindless or sentient—that stole blood and life.

Marie might have been an angel in life, but right now she was a killer.

In my city.

If I found the person or people who decided to release Marie—or the woman with the syringe--I'd call the police. I tried to avoid killing the living. But if I found Marie, or others like her, I wasn't calling dispatch. When it came to venomous killers, I tended to be more of a behead first, ask later kind of woman.

ABOUT THE AUTHOR

Melissa Marr is a former university literature instructor who writes fiction for adults, teens, and children. Her books have been translated into twenty-eight languages and have been bestsellers internationally (Germany, France, Sweden, Australia, et. al.) as well as domestically. She is best known for the Wicked Lovely series for teens, *Graveminder* for adults, and her debut picture book *Bunny Roo, I Love You*.

In her free time, she practices medieval swordfighting, kayaks, hikes, and raises kids in the Arizona desert.

facebook.com/MelissaMarrBooks
twitter.com/melissa_marr
goodreads.com/melissa_marr
bookbub.com/authors/melissa-marr

CPSIA information can be obtained
at www.ICGtesting.com
Printed in the USA
LVHW092013280421
685861LV00019B/846/J

9 781953 909022